# LEAPHOLES

## *Also by James Grippando*

Lying with Strangers

Got the Look

Hear No Evil

Last to Die

Beyond Suspicion

A King's Ransom

Under Cover of Darkness

Found Money

The Abduction

The Informant

The Pardon

# LEAPHOLES

## JAMES GRIPPANDO

**Defending Liberty
Pursuing Justice**

**Criminal
Justice
Section**

Cover design by ABA Publishing

10  09  08          5  4  3

Cataloging-in-Publication data is on file with the Library of Congress

Leapholes / Grippando, James
    ISBN: 1-59031-666-5

Discounts are available for books ordered in bulk. Special consideration is given to state bars, CLE programs, and other bar-related organizations. Inquire at Book Publishing, ABA Publishing, American Bar Association, 321 North Clark Street, Chicago, Illinois 60610.

www.ababooks.org

For Kaylee, Ryan, and Ainsley.
Read.


And in memory of Sam,
affectionately known as "Sammy Cu-koo,"
our beloved Golden Retriever
and this writer's faithful friend
for eleven novels in nine too-short years.

# Part I

---

# *Casting Lots*

# 1

yan Coolidge did not want to go to prison.

He'd been going to prison every Saturday for the past eleven months. Without fail, his mother would wake him, she'd put him in the car, and off they'd go. He didn't like the smell of prison, didn't like the feel of prison. He didn't like the drab beige walls, the cold concrete floors, the countless pairs of dark, soulless eyes that stared out from between iron prison bars. He didn't like anything about prison.

The thing he liked least of all was visiting his father there.

"Do we have to go, Mom?" Ryan was holding up his head with his hands, elbows on the kitchen table, a soggy raft of cornflakes floating in the bowl of milk before him.

"You should want to go."

"I don't." He dropped a piece of toast on the floor. His Golden Retriever pounced on it like a half-starved wolf. It was gone in one bite, and then Sam laid his huge head in Ryan's lap, begging for more. Sam was a smart and beautiful purebred, but his table manners had gone right out the door with Ryan's dad.

"A boy should want to see his father," said Dr. Coolidge.

"I don't."

"Your father loves you."

"Well, I don't love him."

"Never say that about your father. *Never*. Do you hear me?"

The dog sighed, as if wondering if that next piece of toast would ever drop. Ryan stroked the back of Sam's neck.

"Did you hear me?" Ryan's mother said.

Sam sighed even louder. *My sentiment exactly*, thought Ryan.

"Ryan Coolidge, answer me right now."

"Yes, I heard you," he muttered, but the cry of a baby in the next room had already stolen his mother's attention. It was his little sister, Ainsley. Dr. Coolidge popped from her seat as if she'd just sat on a tack, the way she always did when Ainsley made the slightest peep. Ryan loved Ainsley, too, but lately the world seemed to revolve around her. Poor Ainsley doesn't get to see her Daddy. Poor Mr. Coolidge doesn't get to see his new baby. If it weren't for the way Sam shadowed him everywhere, Ryan would have sworn he was the invisible boy.

"Your father is a good man. Shame on you for saying otherwise." She left him with his dog in the kitchen.

*Shame on me*, he thought. Shame, shame, shame. Being a Coolidge was all about shame. How could you not feel shame when you'd seen your father stuffed into the back seat of a police car? How could you feel anything but shame when your family name was blasted all over the television news, when kids at school shoved newspaper headlines in your face and laughed, or when you came home from school early one day and caught your mother crying? Dads could be doctors, lawyers, or plumbers. Some dads coached football, baseball, or soccer. Whatever they did, they usually came home and sat down for dinner at night. They hugged and kissed their wives and kids and said, "So, what did you do all day?" Ryan's dad used to do all those things. But not anymore. He lived his days, slept his nights, and took his meals all in the same dreadful place, a place where a question like, "So, what did you do all day?" always drew the same answer.

Nothing. Not a thing. *Nada.*

So the last thing Ryan felt like doing was visiting his father. Frankly, he didn't care if he ever saw his father again. And one thing was for sure.

He wasn't going to visit him today.

Ryan paused to listen for his mother's footsteps. Silence. She was busy with Ainsley, probably changing a diaper. He gobbled up one last slice of toast, then pushed away from the table. Sam raced toward the back door. His retriever lived for these moments, just him, Ryan, and maybe a tennis ball to fetch.

"Stay," Ryan said. Sam stopped cold and assumed his most regal pose, sitting tall with shoulders back, chest out, and ears alert. Ryan was guilty of cutting his dog far too much slack at the breakfast table, but when it came to basic commands, he had taught Sam well. With just one word, Sam would "stay" all day. Ryan gave him a bear hug, which was answered with a sloppy wet lick across the chops. It was almost like a cow's tongue, but Ryan didn't mind. Sam was the one friend whose loyalty could never be questioned.

"Goodbye, boy," he said.

Sam cocked his head, as if to ask where Ryan was going.

"Don't worry, I'll be back." He glanced toward the hallway that led to Ainsley's bedroom, and a fleeting thought crossed his mind. "But just in case, you take real good care of them, Sammy. You hear?"

Sam gave him a puzzled look, but somehow Ryan was sure he understood. Then Ryan turned and ran out the back door.

# 2

yan hopped on his bicycle and didn't stop pedaling until his thighs were on fire.

They weren't really flaming, but it was a good burn, the same tingling sensation he got when leaving the competition in the dust at the BMX races. Ryan had the coolest bike at Central Middle School, the fastest thing on two wheels that didn't come with a motor. It was silver with dark red striping. He'd paid extra for the striping, but it was worth every penny. It was his money. He'd earned it mowing lawns. Kids used to see him speeding by and say, "Cool bike, Ryan!" Parents would look at their little ones and say, "See, children, hard work does pay off. Look at Ryan Coolidge." But now that his father was in jail, people had a different take on it.

They figured the bike was stolen.

"Move along, boy," said Mrs. Hernandez.

Ryan was sitting on the curb, still breathing hard from the ride. His sandy-brown hair was in a tussle from the wind. He was wearing his favorite basketball jersey beneath his sweatshirt, and he could feel it sticking to his back with perspiration. He looked up to see old Mrs. Hernandez standing on her front porch.

"I said, move along!" she shouted, scowling.

Ryan got back on his bike and continued down the street. It seemed that someone always had an eye on him. No one trusted him. They told him to move on, get lost, beat it. They assumed he was up to no good, that he was a bad kid. It was all because of that old saying, "The apple doesn't fall far from the tree," which meant that a son (the apple) is usually a lot like his father (the tree). Ryan wanted to hop off his bike and say, "Hey, I'm not like that. I know you think the apple doesn't fall far from the tree, but the truth is, this tree was planted on a very steep hill, and when this apple hit the ground it rolled, and rolled, and kept on rolling clear into the next county. And it didn't stop rolling until you could make a pretty good argument that my father and I were no longer members of the same species, let alone related as father and son, or tree and apple, or whatever else you wanted to call us."

But he knew he'd be wasting his breath. The apple didn't fall far from the tree, and the tree was in jail. People just figured that the apple wasn't far behind. Both of them, rotten to the core.

Ryan stopped at the traffic light. A red convertible pulled up beside him. It was a perfect day to ride around town with the top down, sunny and mild, the kind of weather people craved in south Florida. Ryan was admiring the old Mustang when he suddenly recognized the high school kid in the back seat. He tried to ignore him, but the kid spotted him.

"Hey, Coolidge!" he shouted.

Ryan refused to look.

"Are you deaf, kid?"

Ryan wished he would just go away. Teddy Armstrong wasn't the coolest kid in high school, but he sure thought he was. His father was a hotshot lawyer, a hard-nosed State Attorney who had been re-elected to his post three times. Some said he might run for Congress someday. Ryan hoped he would run, and he hoped to be old enough to vote against him when the time came. Mr. Armstrong was the man who had prosecuted the criminal charges against Ryan's father.

"Coolidge, you want to race?"

The driver revved his engine. Ryan just made a face and shook his head.

"Come on," the older boy said. "It's a fair race. A six-cylinder Mustang against you on your bike. You can whoop us. Just pretend the cops are chasing you."

The teenagers in the car roared with laughter. The light hadn't turned green yet, but Ryan couldn't take it anymore. He came down on the pedals with all his weight and sped through the red light. A truck screeched to a halt in the intersection, the driver lying on his horn. But Ryan didn't care. He had to get away from his house, from Mrs. Hernandez, from Teddy Armstrong and his father. From everybody.

Ryan was gaining speed, pedaling harder, flying down the street. His mind was racing even faster. It bugged him to no end when people said he was like his father, and no one said it more often than his own mother. To make things worse, she would always follow up by saying, "And you know Ryan, your father loves you very much." That, in turn, would lead to a conversation that Ryan could have repeated in his sleep, he'd had it so many times.

"If he loves me, then why does he lie to me?"

"Your father doesn't lie to you."

"Yes, he does. Every time I go to see him, he tells me that he's innocent."

"He's not lying."

"But he's in jail."

"Just because your father's in jail doesn't mean he did anything wrong. Sometimes innocent people end up in jail. It happens."

"But he told the judge he did it. And now he wants me to believe he was innocent? Why would he have confessed if he didn't do anything wrong?"

"I'm sure he had his reasons, Ryan. We can't stop believing in him."

*Yeah, right,* thought Ryan. The prisons had to be full of innocent people who had confessed to crimes simply because they had their reasons.

*Stop lying to me, Dad!*

A car flashed in front of him. Ryan swerved, but the car swerved with him. He hit the breaks, but he was going too fast. The rear tire slid out from under him. He released the break to stop the skid, but the momentum jerked him too far in the other direction. The front tire caught a hole or a bump or maybe it was the curb. Ryan didn't see it exactly.

All he saw was the rear end of a station wagon sliding straight toward him.

Suddenly, it was as if he were flying in slow motion. He could smell the burning rubber as the tires skidded across the pavement. He could hear the screech of metal against metal, his precious bicycle slamming into the car. He could feel the seat yanked out from under him, feel his hands leaving the handle grips. At that very moment, someone should have shouted, *We have liftoff,* because that was exactly how it felt. He was soaring in mid-air, and there was absolutely no way to stop.

Until his head hit the window.

It must have been a glancing blow, or maybe he was just lucky to have been wearing a helmet. He landed on the pavement and lay still for a moment, wondering if he were dead. But he wasn't dead, he was sure of it. He was in too much pain to be dead.

"Oh, my elbow," he said, groaning.

A man came running out of the car from the driver's side. He went straight to Ryan. Ryan looked up into his face.

"You all right, kid?"

Ryan tried to focus, but it was difficult. The man had a strange face. It was remarkably flat. Or maybe Ryan just wasn't seeing straight. "What just happened?"

The man picked him up.

"Hey, put me down!" said Ryan.

The man didn't listen. He carried Ryan to his car and opened the rear hatch to his station wagon. Ryan did a double take. It was the strangest looking car Ryan had ever seen. It looked normal on the outside, but inside was a stretcher and all kinds of gadgets and medical supplies. It was like an ambulance with no lights or sirens, no markings on the outside to identify it as an emergency vehicle.

The man laid Ryan on the floor. This was starting to give him the creeps. A strange man with a flat face. A car that opened up and looked like an ambulance. Where had that car come from, anyway? It seemed to have appeared from nowhere, which was appropriate enough. That was exactly where Ryan had been headed—nowhere.

"Let me out of here!" said Ryan.

The man raised his index finger, as if to quiet him, placing it just a few inches before Ryan's nose. Then he moved it back and forth, slowly, like a windshield wiper. Ryan's eyes followed his finger, side to side, left to right, and back again.

"You should feel better now," the man said.

Ryan blinked, trying to stay focused. He wasn't sure, but he thought he saw the man smiling. Yes, there was definitely a broad grin stretching across that ugly flat face. Ryan held onto that image for only a moment, just a flash in his mind. Then he could fight no longer.

His world turned black.

# 3

R yan was flat on his back in a hospital bed, the white
fluorescent ceiling lights assaulting his eyes. Squinting,
he propped himself up on one elbow and peered across
the room. People wearing white smocks and green hospital scrubs
were moving in every direction. They were at least fifty feet away,
and Ryan quickly realized that he was in a large, common area
with lots of other beds just like his. He had a semi-private cubicle,
and the only thing between him and the patients on either side of
him was a beige plastic curtain that was suspended from the
ceiling.

"Where am I?" Ryan said to a passing nurse.

She stopped in her tracks and came to his bedside. Quite
large in stature, she reminded Ryan of the girls' field hockey
coach at school, the kind of woman who could pick up Ryan
with one arm and toss him out the window with the other. "Hey,
Rip Van Winkle's awake," she said. What do you know?"

"Rip Van Winkle?" said Ryan.

The nurse pressed a button on the headboard, and the
mechanical bed adjusted to bring Ryan into an upright, seated
position. "You've been out cold since you got here. We were
worried about you."

"I still don't know where I am," said Ryan.

"You're in the ER, honey. Emergency Room."

"How long have I been here?"

"Seventeen years."

"Yeah, right. What are you going to tell me next, Mt. Rushmore is a natural phenomenon?"

"Oooh, you're a smart one, aren't you?" She checked her watch. "I'd say you've been here about two hours."

"What happened to me?"

"I was hoping you would tell us that."

Ryan felt a pain in his elbow, and the sight of the bandage sparked his memory. "I remember riding my bicycle. A white car came out of nowhere, knocked me down. I think I skidded across the windshield and then hit the pavement. A man picked me up and took me to his car. Strange looking guy. Then I blacked out."

"Hmm. That must have been the man who brought you here."

"Is he still here?"

"No. Looks like he pulled a little hit and run."

"Well, he didn't exactly run. He brought me to the hospital."

"Thank goodness for that. But he dropped you here and disappeared. Didn't leave his name. I guess he was afraid the police might arrest him for reckless driving. He didn't give us your name, either."

"Oh, my name's Ryan."

"Ryan what?"

"Ryan—" He started to answer, then stopped. A simple question like *What is your name?* wasn't so simple for a boy like Ryan. Not that he didn't know his surname. The problem was, everyone else seemed to know it, too, ever since his father's picture had been plastered all over the front page of the newspaper. "Oh, you're Ryan *Coolidge*," they would say. Then their faces would fill with disapproval, and Ryan would know exactly what was going through their minds: *You're Ryan Coolidge, son of that jewel thief, aren't you?* Ryan suddenly remembered why he had jumped on his bicycle in the first place, and why he had been pedaling so fast. He was tired of the stigma, the embarrassment. He was tired of being a Coolidge.

He didn't want to see that look of disapproval anymore— not from anyone ever again, starting with this nurse.

"My name's Ryan . . ." He scrunched his face, as if straining his brain. "I—I don't remember my last name."

"Oh, my. That's not a good thing. Do you remember your phone number, maybe? Or where you live?"

Ryan gave her that same blank expression. "Nope, sorry. All I seem to remember is that my name is Ryan."

"No need to apologize. It's not your fault, honey."

"What do we do now?"

"I'll let the ER physician know that you're awake. She'll come and examine you. Meanwhile, you just rest. I'm sure your memory will start coming back to you in time. And just as soon as it does, you can give us your phone number so we can call your parents. They must be so worried about you."

"I'm sure my mom is," said Ryan. Then he realized he wasn't supposed to have any memory of his parents. "And my dad, too," he added quickly. "Whoever they are."

She seemed puzzled by his response, but she let it go. "How's that elbow feeling?"

"Hurts."

"I'll see if I can get you a painkiller." She gave him a gentle pat on the hand and walked away.

Ryan retreated into thought, which took some of the edge off his elbow pain. He wondered how long he could pretend not to know his own name. How long could he convince the world that he was not a Coolidge? He'd tried that charade only once before, and the results had been disastrous.

It was the day of his father's final court appearance, the worst day of his life. Many months had come and gone since then, but the memory still burned in Ryan's mind as if it had all happened yesterday. He closed his eyes, and even though he was still lying in a hospital bed, he could see the car pulling into their driveway. He could see the woman dressed in the gray business suit walking to their front door. It was all coming back to him again, playing in his mind's eye like an old movie from which there was no escape.

The doorbell rang, and Ryan knew it was the lawyer.

From the very beginning, Ryan's father had assured him that he was innocent of the charges against him. Ryan wanted to go with him to the court hearing. He needed to be there when his father looked the judge in the eye and told him that he'd done nothing wrong. For some reason, however, his parents told him to stay home. Courtrooms were open to the public, so Ryan couldn't understand what they were trying to hide from him. At three-thirty in the afternoon, his parents got in the car with the lawyer and drove to the court hearing, leaving Ryan with his grandmother. Ten minutes later, Ryan snuck out of his room and bicycled to the courthouse.

It was impossible to approach the Justice Center and not get the immediate impression that something important was going on inside. It was an imposing limestone skyscraper more than eighty years old. Visitors had to climb not one but two long tiers of gray granite steps made smooth by decades of foot traffic. The fluted columns in front were at least fifty feet tall. Heavy brass doors at the entrance were encased in marble moldings. Ryan's teacher had taken him to the courthouse on a field trip once before, so he knew that the criminal trials were on the first floor. Ryan quickly chained his bike to the rack and scampered up the steps, and he was still trying to catch his breath as he entered the building. He hurried down the long corridor and peeked into a few empty courtrooms before he found the right place. Without a sound, he slipped into the last row of public seating. No one seemed to notice. His father and the lawyer were standing before the judge, their backs toward Ryan.

The judge was seated high on the bench, rocking back and forth in his big leather chair. On the wall behind him was a brass plaque with the scales of justice. His hair was the color of ash, and he was quite possibly the oldest living person Ryan had ever seen. The judge peered over the top of his wire-rimmed glasses and asked, "Mr. Coolidge, how do you plead?"

Ryan's heart raced. He'd arrived just in time. *You tell him, Dad. You tell him that you're innocent.*

Ryan's father glanced at his lawyer, then lowered his head and said softly, "Guilty, Your Honor."

It was as if the air had suddenly been sucked from Ryan's lungs. *Guilty? What do you mean, guilty?*

The judge said, "Mr. Coolidge, do you understand that by entering a plea of guilty, you are waiving your right to a trial by jury?"

"I do, Your Honor."

"Do you enter this plea of your own free will, without any pressure or coercion from any person?"

Again Mr. Coolidge glanced at his lawyer. "Yes, Your Honor."

"Very well, then. The court will accept the plea of guilty. Does the state attorney have any recommendation as to sentencing?"

A man rose. He was wearing a pinstriped suit, and the bright ceiling lights reflected off the perfectly round bald spot on the crown of his head. He cleared his throat and said, "Yes, Judge. The government recommends that Mr. Coolidge receive a sentence of—"

"Wait!" shouted Ryan.

All heads turned, and Ryan immediately felt the weight of their collective stares. Ryan was on his feet, alone in the back row, not sure what to say. His shouting had been completely involuntary, a gut reaction brought about by absolute shock.

The judge banged his gavel. "Young man, there will be order in my courtroom. I won't tolerate outbursts from anyone, least of all spectators. Who are you?"

Ryan's mouth opened, but the words didn't come. He'd heard the judge's question—*Who are you?*—but he couldn't answer. Ryan's gaze slid across the courtroom, from the judge to the prosecutor to his father's lawyer. His mother was seated in the first row of public seating, and the pained expression on her face seemed to say, *Good gosh, Ryan, what are you doing here?* Finally, he made eye contact with his father. Ryan searched in vain for a silent explanation, some signal from his father that this was all a mistake, a terrible misunderstanding. But Ryan sensed only betrayal.

Once again, the judge's gravelly voice filled the courtroom. "Young man, I asked you a question. Who are you?"

Ryan couldn't speak. It wasn't enough to say *My name's Ryan Coolidge*. He needed to say, *My name's Ryan Coolidge, and my father is innocent.* But not even his father was willing to say that much. He'd told the judge that he was guilty, and Ryan had heard it with his own ears.

"For the last time!" the judge said. "Who *are* you?"

A bitterness rose up in Ryan's throat, and the words seemed to leap from his lips, something beyond his control. "I'm nobody!" he shouted.

Then he turned and ran from the courtroom.

# 4

or breakfast Ryan ate blueberry waffles with butter and extra maple syrup. To drink, he had a chocolate milkshake. A whole pitcher of milkshakes, and another one with whipped cream, and the pitchers were never empty, no matter how many glasses he filled.

Then he woke, and there was nothing but hunger in his belly.

He'd had no food since breakfast. Even then he'd managed only a few bites of toast and some cereal before his anger had driven him from the kitchen. That painkiller from the nurse had promptly sent him off to dreamland, and the dreams were only making him hungry.

"Man, what does it take to get something to eat around here?" He was speaking aloud but to no one in particular.

The plastic curtain slid open, and suddenly Ryan was no longer alone. A girl was in the cubicle beside him, lying in a bed just like his. With the curtain thrown back, it was suddenly as if they were sharing a room. She said, "I have a granola bar, if you want one."

Ryan looked at her curiously. She seemed nice enough, with light brown hair, a dimple when she smiled, and hazel eyes that sparkled. Girls that pretty often made him nervous, especially when they looked older than him.

"I'm Kaylee." She reached across the gap between them, offering her granola bar. "Go ahead. I have more."

"Thanks." Ryan took it and tore off almost half of it in one bite.

"You're Ryan, right? Ryan L'new?"

"L'new?" said Ryan, his mouth full of granola.

"That's what it says on that chart over there."

Ryan glanced toward the busy work station in the center of the ER. A big white board on the wall had all the patients listed, their names written in colored grease pen. The box for ER bed number twelve read: *Ryan LNU.*

Ryan thought for a moment, and then it came to him. "Oh, you think my name is pronounced L'new? That's just an abbreviation. LNU—Last Name Unknown."

"Lucky you. L'new is a pretty goofy sounding last name."

*Beats the heck out of Coolidge,* thought Ryan. "Yeah. I guess so."

"So, what's up with you? Can't remember your own name? You got amnesia or something?"

Ryan chewed off another bite of granola bar. "Something like that. I just can't remember."

"Well, maybe I can help you."

"I don't think so."

"No, really. I'm good at these kinds of things. Let's try it this way. I'll bet you like knock-knock jokes, don't you?"

*Oh, yes. And Barney and Teletubbies, too.* Ryan said, "To tell you the truth, I hate knock-knock jokes."

"Work with me on this."

"No. I mean, I really hate knock-knock jokes."

"Trust me," said Kaylee. "This just might work. Now, you start."

"All right," he said with a sigh. "Knock-knock."

"Who's there?"

"Ryan."

"Ryan *who . . .?*" She made an exaggerated gesture, as if *that* were supposed to trigger his memory.

Ryan shook his head. "It's not working."

"Hmm. This is going to be tougher than I thought. Well, to heck with your name. Maybe I can just make you laugh. I'll start this time. "Knock-knock."

"Can we do something else? I'm just not a knock-knock person."

"Knock-knock."

"Kaylee, please."

"Knock-knock."

"Come in!" he said. His tone had a certain finality to it.

Kaylee paused, not quite sure what to say. Then a smile came to her lips. "Knock-knock—Come in!" She snickered and said, "Cute. I like that."

Ryan returned the smile. "Works every time. It's the perfect knock-knock buster."

He rolled the empty granola bar wrapper into a ball and shot it into the waste basket. Two points. "So, what happened to you?"

She sighed, then glanced at her leg. "I got hit by a car."

"Really? Me too. How did your accident happen?"

"Well, I was out jogging, because my dance instructor says I need to improve my wind. Anyway, I was crossing the street when this car seemed to come out of nowhere."

"What did it look like?"

"I think it was a white station wagon."

"You've got to be kidding," said Ryan, his voice racing. "Did you see the driver?"

"Yes. But not at first. The car cut right in front of me. It didn't exactly hit me. It was more like a bump or a glancing blow. Knocked me right to the ground."

"And then—don't tell me—a guy with a flat face jumped out, right?"

"How did you know?" she said.

"Because that's what happened to me! I was riding my bike, and this white station wagon came out from nowhere. Then this strange-looking dude got out and put me in the back of the car."

"Yeah. Except that when he opened the back of the car, it didn't look like a normal car. It was more like . . . like an ambulance."

Ryan's mouth was agape. "We're talking about the exact same guy! Did he do that finger-waving thing to you?"

"Yes," she said. "Back and forth, like a windshield wiper. And then I blacked out."

"And the next thing you know . . ." Ryan paused and gave her a chance to catch up. Then they finished his sentence together: "I'm waking up in the ER."

They locked eyes but said nothing. They'd been through the same experience, the same strange accident. The fact that it had happened to someone else was comforting on one level. But in some ways, it made it even more bizarre.

"Except I'm not having any trouble remembering my last name," said Kaylee.

"Well, maybe you didn't bump your head like I did."

She glanced at the bandage on Ryan's elbow. "Yeah, sure. Head injury, huh?"

Ryan smiled nervously, sensing that perhaps she was beginning to see through his little LNU-charade. The doctor showed up just in time, before Kaylee could probe any further.

"Hello, I'm Doctor Morales. How are we doing here today, Ryan?"

"Pretty good, I think."

Dr. Morales checked Ryan's chart, speed-reading from top to bottom. She had a round, full face, and her short black hair was in tight, efficient curls. Ryan saw only concern in her dark brown eyes. No scorn, no ridicule—no clue as to who he was.

She laid the chart aside. "How's that memory coming along?"

"I thought it was getting better, but now I don't remember."

She smiled, realizing that it was a joke. "Do you know your last name yet?"

"No."

"Well, don't worry. I'm sure it will improve with time. But I want you to know that we've notified the police that you're here. As soon as your parents get worried enough to file a missing persons report with the authorities, we'll be able to link you up, okay?"

"Okay, great."

"I'll check back with you in about an hour," the doctor said as she walked away, moving on to the next patient.

Ryan's head settled back into his pillow. A missing persons report. Wonderful. Ryan hadn't figured on that. He had no plan, and running away from home was a pretty stupid idea. But he wasn't ready to go back. He didn't want to cause his mother too much heartache, but the fact was, both his parents had lied to him. They'd both assured him that the criminal charges were bogus. For the first time since his father had pleaded guilty and gone away to prison, Ryan wasn't a part of the Coolidge family. It felt good, and he wanted to keep that feeling going, at least a little bit longer.

Kaylee said, "You don't want to go home, do you, Ryan?"

"What makes you say that?"

"Instinct. Intuition. I don't know. Something tells me you like being Ryan L'new better than Ryan whatever your name is."

Ryan didn't answer. He just looked at the big white board, toward the name penned in beside bed number twelve. Ryan LNU. A little goofy, but he'd heard worse. His gaze drifted toward the EXIT sign over the ER's double doorway. They were automatic doors, and people seemed to come and go at will. His elbow still hurt a little, but his legs were fine. He could ask to use the bathroom, walk out those doors, and just keep going. His mother would find him when he was ready to be found, not when she filed that missing persons report and the police came to get him.

"Hey, Kaylee."

"What?"

"You think anyone named L'new has ever been to prison?"

"I don't know. Why do you ask?"

Ryan drew a deep breath, then let it out. "Just wondering."

# 5

**R**yan's plan was working like a charm.

The automatic doors closed behind him, and he was cruising down the hall away from the ER. The bathroom was around the corner, first door on the left, the nurse had told him. Ryan didn't really need to use it, but he stopped there anyway. His clothes were in a bag that he'd concealed under his loose hospital gown. He ducked into the bathroom and made a quick change. He used the sharp corner of the paper towel dispenser to cut off his plastic hospital ID-bracelet. Two minutes later he was back in the hallway, dressed in his street clothes, headed for the hospital's main exit. His bicycle accident had left a small tear at the knee of his blue jeans, but that only made them cooler. His sweatshirt covered the bandage on his elbow. No one gave him a second look. This was almost too easy. He even waved to the receptionist as he breezed past the radiology department.

"Hey, how you doing?" he said.

Cool. So cool. Just act like you know what you're doing, and people assume that you own the place.

He kept walking, following the directional signs that pointed to "HOSPITAL MAIN ENTRANCE." The corridors were long, cold, and brightly lit, and of course that sterile hospital smell was everywhere. Ryan reeled in the urge to sprint for the exit. Absolutely no running, he told himself. So long as he walked at a normal pace, no one would ask questions. He couldn't help but smile, however, as he turned the final corner and spotted the hospital's main lobby, dead ahead. It was just beyond the final set of sliding glass doors. He was a mere twenty feet away, fewer than ten steps to freedom. This was going to be fun. He could be Ryan L'new as long as he wanted.

And then an alarm sounded.

It was a shrill, pulsating alarm, so loud that it drowned out every other sound in the hospital. Ryan stopped dead in his tracks. The security guard sprang from his chair. He was an imposing figure with rock-hard biceps that bulged from his tight shirt sleeves. He was standing between Ryan and the hospital's main entrance, and he looked at Ryan suspiciously. Ryan wasn't sure who had sounded the alarm. His plan had been working perfectly, but obviously someone had figured out what he was up to. Or maybe someone had discovered that he was a Coolidge. Yes, that had to be it. They were afraid he had stolen something and was trying to sneak out of the hospital.

Ryan took a long look at the security guard, and the big man returned the glare. Whatever was going on, Ryan didn't want to have to explain himself to the Incredible Hulk. He turned and ran in the opposite direction.

The guard may have yelled at him, but Ryan heard only the blaring alarm as he raced down the hallway. Doctors and nurses suddenly emerged from behind closed doors. In a matter of moments, the corridors were flooded with people. They were standing around, looking at one another in confusion, trying to make themselves heard over the screaming alarm. Ryan never broke stride. He wove through the crowded hallway, arms and legs pumping. With so many people in his way, it was like running through an obstacle course. He didn't know where he was headed. It only seemed logical, however, that the hospital would have another exit, probably at the other end of the hall. He had no intention of stopping until he found it, but he nearly screeched to a halt as he rounded one last corner.

Thick, black smoke was pouring from the cafeteria.

"Fire!" a nurse screamed.

Suddenly, it all came clear. The hospital was on fire! The alarm hadn't been for him after all—unless they thought Ryan had started it.

*Oh, great,* thought Ryan. *They think I snuck out of the ER and started the building on fire! They* do *know I'm a Coolidge!*

A human stampede emerged from the cafeteria. Scores of people flew past Ryan, their clothing covered with soot. Many were coughing and trying to catch their breath. Others screamed and ran as fast as they could. Ryan had no time to get out of the way, and they trampled him in their hysteria. A man stepped on his leg. A woman stepped on his hand. Ryan tried to get up, but he was immediately knocked back to the floor. His head smacked against the tile, and it hurt almost as much as when that car had hit him and he'd flown into the windshield. He was dizzy, and the smoke was making it even harder for him to get his bearings. Ryan was on his knees, his body pressed against the wall, as the crowd whisked past him. Finally, every last one of them was gone, and he was able to climb to his feet and focus. As he rose, he could see the flames poking through the open door to the cafeteria. Smoke was creeping down the hallway like a ghostly gray snake. Ryan cleared his lungs with a deep cough, then turned and ran. The crowd was well ahead of him. He knew where the exit was, but if he didn't outrun the smoke, he might never find it. Suddenly, the alarm blared even louder, and water was squirting from the ceiling.

*Sprinklers!* Ryan was sprinting around a corner at full speed just as the water hit him. He slipped on the wet tile, his feet went out from under him, and he slammed into the wall like a NASCAR crash. Water from the sprinklers continued to rain down on him, but it wasn't nearly enough to extinguish the raging fire. Smoke was pouring from the cafeteria. He picked himself up, but before he could take a step, someone raced past him and knocked him to the floor again.

"Sorry, Ryan!"

He recognized the voice. It was Kaylee's.

"Come on, Ryan! There's a fire!" She was running toward the cafeteria, leading four other ER patients straight toward disaster.

"Stop, you're running the wrong way!" He was shouting, but she didn't hear him.

Ryan knew the way to safety, and he was only minutes away from saving himself. But if someone didn't catch up with Kaylee, she and the others could be trapped by the flames. Ryan couldn't let that happen. On impulse, he turned and ran after them, but it was like running through a rainstorm—blindfolded. The sprinklers continued to soak him. The smoke was thick and black. He could barely breathe, and with the alarm blaring, he could scarcely think. In a matter of seconds, he completely lost sight of his new friend.

"Kaylee, where *are* you?" he called into the darkness.

# 6

A hand emerged through heavy smoke, snatched Ryan by the collar, and yanked him into a side hallway. Ryan found himself running alongside a complete stranger. Oddly, a cool breeze was flowing toward them, as if the air conditioning were running full blast. It was blowing the cloud of smoke away from them, back toward the main corridor. No smoke meant no sprinklers. The floors were dry, the air was breathable, and the fire alarm was audible only in the distance.

"I'm over here," said Kaylee.

She was standing in an alcove where the hallway jogged to the right. Ryan didn't recognize the four other people in her group. Two of them were wearing hospital gowns. One was an old man with his arm in a sling. The other, a woman, had a bandage wrapped partially around her head. The rest of it trailed behind her like a fifteen-foot-long streamer. A second woman was wearing a business suit, and she looked nauseous, probably with the flu. She was carrying a plastic bucket.

Ryan said, "You don't expect to put out this fire by throwing a bucket of water on it, do you?

Her skin turned a pale shade of green, then she made a retching sound and deposited the rest of her lunch into the bucket. "It's not that kind of bucket," she said weakly.

"Sorry, my bad," said Ryan.

The fourth patient—the one who had grabbed Ryan—was a younger man. He wore jeans, a T-shirt, and a red football jacket from Central-City High School. A white name tag with green lettering was sewn onto the front of his jacket. It read, "Coach Jenkins." He had a patch over one eye, as if someone had forgotten to say *Hey, Coach, catch!* before tossing him the football.

Ryan dried his face with the sleeve of his sweatshirt. The emergency sprinklers had yet to activate in this stretch of hallway, but everyone was already soaked from the run through the main corridor.

Kaylee said, "Why were you calling my name, Ryan?"

"You were going the wrong way," he said. "I had to stop you."

"You mean you came back to get me?"

"Well, yeah. All of you."

"You were trying to save me?" she said. " That's so sweet."

Coach Jenkins groaned. "Okay, okay, Romeo and Juliet. Balcony scene's over. If we don't get moving pretty quick, we'll all be toast."

"I know the way out," said Ryan. "We have to go back past the ER, toward the hospital's main entrance."

The woman with the flu stood up straight, though it seemed to take all her strength just to talk. "That might have been a great plan about five minutes ago. But not now."

Ryan glanced back toward the main hallway. The smoke was thicker than ever.

"We'll go the other way," said the coach.

"But it could be blocked off," said Ryan. "Then we'll be trapped."

The coach shook his head. "Can't you feel that fresh air blowing toward us? It's coming from straight ahead. I'm no firefighter, but if I want to get out of a burning building, I know enough to head toward the fresh air, not toward the smoke. Come on, everyone. Follow me."

The coach had a firm manner of speaking. He obviously was accustomed to giving out orders, and Ryan didn't want to waste time arguing. "Okay, lead on."

"What's your name, kid?"

"Ryan." He left off the last name.

"L'new," added Kaylee. "His name's Ryan L'new."

"I'm Coach Jenkins. This here is Mr. Bronson, Ms. Rodriguez, and Mrs. Levine."

The names washed over Ryan, and he seemed to remember them only as Sling Man, Flu Lady, and Head Case, respectively.

The coach said, "You bring up the rear, Ryan. Make sure no one falls behind."

The coach went first, followed by Sling Man and Head Case. Kaylee was next, then the Flu Lady, and finally Ryan. They were walking at a brisk pace, but the coach kept them in single file. He was determined not to let them scatter in a panic. Still, Ryan had the feeling they were headed in the wrong direction.

"Coach, check that out," said Ryan.

The sign on the wall read, AUTHORIZED PERSONNEL ONLY.

"That doesn't apply when there's a fire," said the coach. "Just keep going."

The pace quickened. Sling Man and Head Case—the old man and woman—were breathing heavily. Flu Lady was sweating more than any of them, probably from fever. The coach kept them moving, repeatedly shouting words of encouragement like *Almost there*, or *Just a little bit farther, gang!* They walked for several minutes, and Ryan had yet to see a single door or window—nothing that even resembled a way out of the building. The walls were painted cinder blocks, solid, like a tunnel. The floor had a slight slope to it, like a downward ramp.

Another sign on the wall read, "RESTRICTED AREA. DO NOT ENTER."

Ryan said, "This doesn't feel like the right way."

"Zip it," said the coach. "Don't you feel that breeze getting stronger against your face? The wind doesn't blow like that in a normal hallway. There's obviously an open door or window just ahead of us. It's pulling in fresh air. We can get out this way."

"But I don't think—"

Ryan was in mid-sentence when the ceiling behind them came crashing to the floor. The tangle of metal, wood, and wires landed with a thundering crash. Smoke was pouring through the gaping hole. Then came a burst of heat and flames from the floor above them.

"Run for it!" shouted Kaylee.

Behind them the hallway was choked with smoke and debris. Scorching hot flames were the only source of light. They had to move forward, and the coach led the charge. The breeze in their faces strengthened, which kept the smoke from catching up with them. Ryan hoped the coach was right. Just ahead, there had to be a window or an opening to the outdoors that would account for the flow of fresh air. But Ryan could see only the end of the hallway—a solid brick wall.

"An elevator!" said Kaylee. The door was wide open, and she was about to jump inside.

"Don't get on it!" Ryan cried, but he was almost too late. At the last moment, the coach grabbed her and pulled her back to safety.

"You don't ride the elevators in a fire," the coach said sternly. "Especially when the elevator is missing."

Kaylee stepped to the edge and peered into the opening. Although the door was open, no elevator car was waiting. She was staring down a dark, open shaft. "Yikes," she said. "It must be at least ten stories to the bottom."

"You mean it goes down?" said Sling Man. "How can that be down? We're on the first floor."

"It must be an underground facility," said Coach.

"With its own ventilation system," said Ryan. "That's where our breeze is coming from. Fresh air is being sucked up the elevator shaft, out this open door, and down the hallway."

"That means there's no open window at the end of this hallway," said Head Case.

"No door to the outside," said Flu Lady.

"No way out," said Kaylee.

Another section of the ceiling collapsed behind them. Flames roared into the hallway from above. The sprinklers should have activated, but ruptured water pipes were dangling from a huge hole in the ceiling. Water spilled uselessly to the floor, not a drop of it reaching the sprinkler heads. The raging fire continued to spread, and it was creating more smoke than the breeze from the elevator shaft could disperse. Ryan's eyes were watering.

"Everybody get down!" said Ryan. He remembered from his fire drills that smoke rises, so it was safest on the floor. They all hit the deck.

"We have to get out of here!" said Kaylee.

"There must be a stairwell," said Ryan. "There are always emergency stairs near an elevator."

"And they're right over here!" shouted Coach. He ran to the door, but the handle wouldn't turn. "What kind of place locks the emergency stairwell?"

"*This* kind of place," said Ryan as he pointed to another sign on the wall. Though barely visible in the smoke, it read:

DANGER: NO ADMITTANCE. LEVEL ONE CLEARANCE ONLY.

The coach's expression soured. "All that restricted area nonsense goes out the window when there's a fire. Out of my way." He backed up, then ran toward the door at full speed, putting his shoulder into it. On impact, he cried out in pain, but the door didn't budge.

"That's not going to work," said Kaylee.

The coach grimaced. "No kidding, Einstein."

"I have an idea," said Ryan. "All I need is a rope."

"I got an idea, too," said Coach. "All I need is a fire truck."

"I can find a rope," said Kaylee. She went to Head Case—the old woman who had that fifteen-foot streamer of extra bandage trailing behind her. "You don't need that, do you?"

"No. They were bandaging my head when the alarm went off. I was still attached to the roll when I ran out of the ER."

"Good." Kaylee tore off the extra bandage, then ripped it into thirds, long ways, from end to end. She was left with three skinny bandage strips, and she started braiding them together. "Ryan, you start at the other end, and do exactly what I'm doing."

Quickly, they twisted the three lengths together until they had a rope. Kaylee knotted both ends, and Ryan gave it a tug. It was much stronger than a single bandage strip. "This should work," he said. "Now, Coach, you're going to take this rope and lower me down the elevator shaft to the floor below us. Hopefully, the door to the stairwell will be unlocked down there. If it is, I'll run up and unlock this one from the other side."

"That's way too dangerous," said Kaylee.

"Do you have a better idea?" said Coach.

The old lady coughed from the thickening smoke. "Whatever you're going to do, make it quick!"

Kaylee said, "Why can't someone else go?"

"I weigh less than anyone here," said Ryan. "I should be the one who goes."

The others were like a chorus: *That's right. Yes, yes. Definitely, Ryan should go.*

Kaylee seemed a bit put off by their lack of concern for Ryan's safety, but his mind was made up. "It's just one floor," he said. "It's not like I'm going bungee jumping."

Ryan felt his way through the smoke to the open elevator door and lowered the makeshift rope down the shaft. It was just long enough to reach to the floor below. The coach tied one end around his wrist and braced himself against the wall for leverage. Ryan took the other end in both hands.

"Ready?" asked the coach.

"Ready," said Ryan.

Feet first, Ryan slid past the half-opened elevator door. It was breezy inside the shaft, and darker than he'd expected. Dangling at the end of his rope, swaying side to side, he finally grabbed a cable to steady himself. But he could find nothing to stand on. He was hanging in midair, the rope in one hand, the greasy elevator cable in the other.

"Okay, lower me!" said Ryan.

The coach let out too much rope, too quickly. Ryan plunged several feet and nearly lost his grip. "Slower!" shouted Ryan.

Coach reeled back, and Ryan inched his way down the shaft.

"I'm there!" shouted Ryan.

Coach stopped feeding him rope. Inside the dark shaft, Ryan was suspended before the closed elevator door that served the floor below. It was a typical elevator door that slid from left to right. A vertical strip of light at the far edge told him that lights were burning in the hallway, just on the other side of the door. Ryan quickly formed a plan. It was like the rock climbing wall at a carnival. All he had to do was rappel. He put his feet on the panel and braced his back against the wall. Then he pushed. Slowly, the door started to slide open.

"How's it going, Ryan?" the coach shouted.

"It's going!" he said through clenched teeth.

"I can't hold on too much longer. You're heavier than you think!"

Ryan glanced at the gaping hole below him. It was ten stories, maybe more, straight down. That couldn't be a pleasant way to die. "Just hang on, Coach!"

Ryan pushed one last time with all his leg strength. The door slid open. Ryan swung on the rope like Tarzan on a vine. Then he let go. For a moment, it seemed as if he were flying in slow motion. He could smell the smoke above him. Beyond the opening, he saw the clean, tile floor stretching out before him. Mostly, however, he saw the dark, seemingly bottomless shaft below. He was falling, not flying. He had nowhere near enough liftoff to soar all the way to safety. He was going down the shaft.

"Ryan!" the coach shouted.

Ryan was dropping fast, but the rope was beyond his reach. Thankfully, the elevator door was still open. Somehow, he managed to reach up and grab the very edge of the floor. Ryan was hanging by his fingertips at the threshold. He stayed there just long enough to regain his strength. His elbow was a throbbing reminder of his bicycle accident, but he worked through the pain. His Phys-Ed teacher would have been proud. It was the fastest pull-up in the history of the universe. Ryan shot through the opening and rolled onto the tile floor.

He looked back through the open doorway. All he could say was, "Whoa."

He quickly got his bearings. This floor, one-story below his friends, appeared to have been untouched by the fire. It was definitely the safest way out. He spotted the emergency stairwell near the elevator. He ran to it and turned the door handle. It opened.

"Yesssss!" he said aloud.

He sprinted up the stairwell, gobbling up two and three steps at a time. In no time, he reached the door to the higher floor. He turned the deadbolt and pushed the door open.

Smoke immediately hit him in the face. The fire had reached a new level of intensity. He coughed and said, "Come on, everyone! This is the only way out!"

They came in a rush—Coach, Sling Man, Head Case, and Flu Lady, who was still toting her bucket. "Where's Kaylee?" said Ryan, holding the door.

"Right here." She emerged through the smoke, then gave him a wink and said, "Nice of you to worry."

It made him blush. "I wasn't—oh, never mind. Follow me."

Ryan led them down the stairwell. The smoke followed them. When he reached the bottom, he tugged on the door handle. It wouldn't turn. "It's locked!" said Ryan.

"It must have locked automatically from the other side," said Coach.

The stairwell was sucking in smoke like a chimney. They rushed down another flight of stairs and found another door. "This one's locked, too!" said Kaylee.

"Stand aside," said Coach.

The door was made of metal, but it had glass on the top half. The coach stepped back, then leaped and delivered a martial-arts kick. The glass shattered and fell to the floor. An alarm sounded, but they didn't care. Coach reached through the opening and unlocked the door. It opened, and the six hurried inside.

"We made it!" said Kaylee.

"Stop right there!" a stranger shouted.

Ryan spotted a man at the end of the hallway. He was dressed in what looked to be a spacesuit. The alarm suddenly stopped. Two other men in identical strange suits ran to the broken door. They quickly sealed the opening with heavy tape and thick plastic sheeting.

"Sorry about the door," said Ryan. "We're just trying to get to safety."

"It isn't safe here," the man said. His voice had a mechanical sound. He was speaking through a microphone in the glass helmet that encased his head.

"Please," said Kaylee, "this is the only way out."

The man's tone turned even harsher. "You have no idea how much danger you're in."

"Where are we?" asked Coach.

Ryan's gaze drifted toward the broken glass on the floor. He hadn't noticed earlier, but now he saw the red-painted lettering. The glass was shattered, so it was a bit like a jigsaw puzzle. The jagged shards were just large enough for him to piece together the warning.

It read: INFECTIOUS DISEASE CONTROL CENTER: QUARANTINED.

At that moment, Ryan realized that these men weren't wearing spacesuits. These were hazmat suits. They wore them as protection from contagious diseases.

"Oh, boy," was all Ryan could say.

"You can say that again," the man said through his hazmat helmet.

# 7

yan and his five new friends were seated at a table in a brightly lit conference room. It was easily the cleanest place Ryan had ever seen, so spick-and-span that it could have made a dentist's office look like the inside of his friend "Sweaty" Colletti's gym locker—and *that* was a very dirty place indeed. The floor and walls were a glossy white, not a speck of dust anywhere. The table and chairs were highly-polished chrome. There were no pictures on the walls, no potted plants in the corners, and no clutter of any kind on the table. There were no windows, of course, and two men in yellow hazmat suits stood guard at the only door.

Ryan saw no easy way out.

The door opened, and another man entered the room. He also wore a hazmat suit, but his was bright orange. The men in yellow showed him a level of respect; he was obviously their leader. He positioned himself at the head of the long rectangular table. He remained standing, looking down on his uninvited guests. "My name is Dr. Watkins," he said through the speaker in his helmet. "It is my duty to inform you that no one will leave this room until I say so."

"We can't stay here," said Ryan. "This building is going up in flames. We'll all die."

"The fire can't reach us here," Dr. Watkins said. "This is an insulated, self-contained, underground bunker. You six are the first ever to breach our security. Congratulations."

"We weren't trying to breach anything," said Ryan.

"I understand that. Unfortunately, the fire caused our security system to malfunction. Had it not been for that, you never would have found your way down the wrong hallway."

"I guess that's why I didn't see any windows," said Ryan.

"Exactly. But you're here now, so I can tell you this much about your misfortune. This underground facility was built with the cooperation of the international medical community. Its location—indeed, its very existence—is top secret. We are not evil scientists trying to take over the world. We are men and women from around the world who have come together to create a research center to fight a disease called BODS."

"BODS?" said Ryan. "Never heard of it."

"It is extremely rare at this point. There are only eight documented cases in the United States. But it's very deadly. And it's highly contagious, if it is not contained immediately. That's why the infected patients are treated here, where they are quarantined."

"Why is your work a secret?" asked the coach.

"If word were to get out that the most deadly disease ever known to mankind could be spread from one person to another simply by breathing the air, a worldwide panic would ensue."

"What exactly is BODS?" asked Ryan.

"The letters stand for Blood Oxygen Depletion Syndrome. Healthy red blood cells normally carry oxygen throughout the body. In patients who are infected with the BODS virus, the blood's ability to transmit oxygen is severely impaired. Eventually, the blood is completely unable to carry oxygen."

"What happens then?"

"You die. Plain and simple. Without oxygen, your tissues and organs shut down. It's as if your whole body suffocates."

The Flu Lady cringed. "It sounds awful."

"It is," said Dr. Watkins.

"How do you catch this BODS?" asked Coach.

"As I mentioned, it's airborne."

"Meaning what?"

"Meaning that every one of you was infected the minute you walked in here and took your first breath. The virus enters through the lungs, then invades the bloodstream through the pulmonary system."

"So . . . we're all going to die?" said Kaylee.

Dr. Watkins gave them a somber look. His answer seemed to echo through the mouthpiece in his helmet. "That's entirely possible."

The coach popped from his chair, slapping the table in anger. "This can't be. There has to be a way to stop this. I mean, we've only been here a few minutes."

"Sit down, sir."

The coach stopped, then returned to his seat. Dr. Watkins continued. "There is one bit of hope. This is a research facility, so naturally we have been working on a vaccine for BODS."

"You can give us a shot?" said Flu Lady.

"Let me explain, please. The vaccine is in an early stage of development. We do know that it is also effective as an antidote, so long as it is administered no later than half an hour after the patient is exposed to the virus."

Coach checked his watch. "We've only been here ten minutes. Bring on the vaccine!"

Dr. Watkins pressed a button on the wall, which activated a loudspeaker. "Mr. Yoo, if you please," he said, his voice carrying over the P.A. system.

The door opened and an Asian man entered the room. He was wearing a traditional white lab coat. No hazmat suit, no protective gear of any kind. He looked like an ordinary doctor in a typical hospital.

Dr. Watkins said, "This is Dr. Yoo from Tokyo. He was one of the first volunteers to test the vaccine. As you can see, it works. He's completely healthy. Dr. Yoo, will you do the honors, please?"

Dr. Yoo bowed politely and walked toward a wall safe at the other end of the room. He dialed the combination, turned the handle, and opened the safe. With great care, he removed a small metal box and placed it on the chrome table.

Dr. Watkins said, "Inside this box you will find glass vials. Each vial contains enough vaccine for one person. You must drink it completely. If you don't, I'm quite sure you will be dead before sundown."

His words seemed to hang in the air: *Dead before sundown.*

Dr. Watkins opened the box. All six of his guests leaned forward and peered inside. There were two rows of glass vials. They were standing upright in a soft, foam base. Each vial contained a yellow liquid.

"That's the vaccine?" asked Kaylee.

"Yes," said Dr. Watkins.

"But there are only five vials," said Ryan, "and there are six of us."

They each counted to themselves. An uneasy silence fell over the group.

"Is there another dose in that locker?" asked Ryan.

Dr. Watkins shook his head. "That's the bad news. Like I said, the vaccine is in a very early stage of development. The chief ingredient, as it turns out, is a protein found only in the stingers of bees. Do you have any idea how many bee stingers we have to collect just to make one dose? Millions, I assure you. This is all we've been able to develop so far."

The old woman's voice shook. "But . . . but you said that each vial has only enough for one person."

"What does this mean?" asked the Sling Man.

They looked at one another. It was as if they knew the answer but were afraid to say it.

Finally, the coach spoke up. "It means one of us is going to be dead by sundown."

# 8

"Is it a painful death?" asked Coach.

"I won't lie. It isn't pleasant." Dr. Watkins closed the lid on the box and placed it in the center of the table. "It's a terrible decision to make. But we have to decide."

"The doctor's right," said Coach. "If we don't drink the vaccine soon, none of us will survive. But let's be fair about this. First, does anyone volunteer to be left out?"

No one made a sound.

"I didn't think so," said Coach. "Which means that we have to choose someone."

"How?" said Ryan.

"We should vote," said Kaylee.

"Good idea," said the Sling Man. "I vote to leave you out."

Kaylee looked at him in disbelief. "Why me?"

The Sling Man said, "Because you told us that you knew the way out of the Emergency Room. We all followed you, and we ended up going down the wrong hall. It's your fault we're in this mess."

"Wait just a minute," said Kaylee. "It was Coach who took the lead once we got in the hallway."

"That's right," said the Flu Lady. "This is all Coach's fault. He should be left out."

"This is so wrong," said Ryan. "We can't vote on who should live and who should die."

"The boy's right," said Coach. He took a seat, then rested his elbow on the table and flexed his bicep. "Let's arm wrestle for it. The strong will survive. The weakest will die. It's only natural."

Kaylee glared and said, "How about the stupidest? That's natural, too."

"Who you calling stupid, missy?"

"Stop!" said Dr. Watkins. His tone gave them all a jolt. It was the kind of voice you'd expect from someone who was in charge, but it was even more forceful coming through the amplifier in his helmet. "You're not going to vote. You're not going to arm wrestle. You're not going to decide who's stupid and who's smart."

"Then how do we decide?" asked Kaylee.

"God should decide," said the oldest woman.

The doctor smiled ruefully. "With all due respect, ma'am. Unless God hurries up, you're all going to die. So let me suggest the next best thing. You should cast lots."

They exchanged nervous glances, as if waiting for someone to come up with a better suggestion. No one said a word.

"That's the answer then," said Coach. "We'll leave it to chance. Or to providence."

"I'll be right back," said the doctor. The man in the hazmat suit opened the door and allowed the doctor to exit the room. The others were silent while he was away, except for the Flu Lady. "Could I have something to drink, please? This is making me sick."

The guard stepped out and quickly returned with a cup of water. Flu Lady tried to drink, but her hand was shaking, and she could only manage a sip or two. They were all nervous, and waiting on Dr. Watkins was hardly putting them at ease. Finally, the door opened, and the doctor returned. He was carrying a dinner tray. The first thought that popped into Ryan's mind was that this was someone's last meal, like they did for prisoners before their execution. But this was even stranger than that. On the tray were six small piles of pure white sugar. The piles were of equal size, and each looked exactly like the next one.

"What is this for?" asked Coach.

"This is how we're going to choose lots," the doctor said. "I raided the kitchen. It may seem odd that we have food in a quarantined area, but we do have to feed our BODS patients and people like Dr. Yoo, who have already been vaccinated. In any event, five of these piles contain only sugar. In the sixth, I've buried a bottle cap. Whoever chooses the bottle cap loses. Do we all understand?"

They nodded their understanding.

"Ma'am, why don't you start?" he said to Head Case.

The old woman stared at the six piles. She reached toward the far end, then retracted her hand quickly, as if burned by a flame. She reached toward the middle, then pulled back again. Finally, she went to the nearest pile and raked her fingers through it.

Nothing but sugar.

"Praise be," she said with relief.

There were five piles left. Kaylee was seated beside the old woman. "Young lady," the doctor said. "Your turn."

Kaylee withdrew. "No, I don't want to choose. Let the others go first. I'll take whatever pile is left."

"Fine. If that be your choice. Sir, it's your turn."

The Sling Man moved closer to the five remaining piles. Without a moment's hesitation, he chose the fifth pile from the left. It was pure sugar. "How *sweet* it is!" he shouted, raising two fists in the air.

The Flu Lady was next, and she chose sugar. Just three piles remained. One of them concealed a bottle cap.

The doctor's voice tightened. "Ryan, it's your turn."

Ryan shook his head. "No. I feel the same as Kaylee. I don't like this game."

"Well, one of you is going to have to choose."

"I'll choose," said Kaylee. "But I'm choosing for Coach Jenkins."

"What?"

"I can't bring myself to choose for myself. So the pile I choose will be the coach's fate. Can you accept that, sir?"

The coach swallowed hard. The suggestion seemed to have taken him by surprise, but he was eager to get this over with. "I accept," he said. "Choose one for me."

The girl stared at the three remaining piles of sugar. Her eyes opened wider, but she was otherwise still. Not a muscle moved. She didn't even blink. Ryan wondered if she was even breathing. Finally, her arm stretched forward. Her fingers shook as they approached the pile. She placed her hand over the middle one, then raked it clean off the board with her fingers.

There was only sugar.

The coach let out a nervous chuckle of relief. Then he looked at Ryan and said, "I guess it's down to you two."

Ryan stared at the two remaining piles. He looked at the four players who would live, and then he looked at Kaylee. The four looked smug. Kaylee looked terrified. He realized that he, too, must have looked frightened. Who wouldn't have been scared? He had his whole life ahead of him. Whether he would live or die came down to this: two piles on a tray. One was pure sugar, the other was hiding a bottle cap. One was life; the other, death. It all seemed so unfair.

"Come on, Ryan," said Dr. Watkins. "Choose."

His heart was thumping in his chest. He swallowed the lump in his throat and picked the one on the right.

"That one," he said.

"Sift through it," said the doctor. "It's your lot."

He drew a deep breath, then dragged his fingers through the pile.

All eyes turned toward Kaylee. She was stunned, silent. The doctor tilted up one end of the tray. Slowly, the last-remaining pile of sugar dissolved, and the bottle cap rolled onto the table. It landed in front of Kaylee.

The doctor looked at her and said, "I'm sorry, young lady."

Her body began to tremble, and then she let out a scream. "No, not me!"

"It's what we agreed," said Coach.

"No, it's not fair! It's not fair at all."

"It is as fair as we can be."

"Why should it be me? Why should I die? I'm just fourteen!"

*Fourteen,* thought Ryan. She was actually younger than he had guessed. Ryan could hardly stand to listen. It could have been him. It had come down to just two piles of sugar. He could have chosen the wrong one. He'd chosen the right one, but it didn't feel right.

*For this, I deserve to live?*

Ryan said, "There has to be another way."

"There is no other way," said Coach.

Kaylee screamed even louder. Then she sprang like a cat toward the box of glass vials on the table. The men in the hazmat suits grabbed her.

"Take her away!" Dr. Watkins ordered.

The men tried to restrain her, but Kaylee was kicking and screaming at the top of her lungs. She refused to go without a fight. The guards wrestled her to the floor, but she kicked one man in the shins. He cried out in pain, and Kaylee wiggled free. The doctor jumped into the fracas and tried to subdue her, but Kaylee was twisting in every direction. The coach pounced on her and slapped her across the face.

"Please!" she cried. "Somebody help me!"

Ryan had no time to think, but his instincts took over. He grabbed the box of vials and jumped atop the table.

"He's got the vaccine!" the coach shouted.

"Stop right there!" said Ryan. "Or I'll smash the vials against the wall."

The others stopped dead in their tracks.

The doctor said, "Put the box down gently, boy. There's no need for this. You're one of the winners."

"A winner?" he said, scoffing. "Is that what you think this is? Some kind of game?"

"It's the best we can do," said Coach.

Ryan shook his head, disgusted by such a lame response. "No, it's not the *best* we can do. We're in this together. We'll all make it out of this mess. Or none of us will."

The coach glared. "You're talking nonsense. Give us the box."

Ryan took a half-step backward. He nearly stepped on the Flu Lady's cup of water—and suddenly he had an idea. He grabbed the cup and pitched the water onto the floor. Then he reached inside the box of vials.

"What are you doing?" the coach asked nervously.

"Just stay back, or all five of these vaccines will be sprayed across the wall." Ryan kept one eye on the lookout, and one eye on the cup. He opened one vial and poured some of the vaccine into the empty cup.

"Don't be a fool," said the doctor.

Ryan said, "We have five vaccines. If each of us takes a little less, we can make six."

"We'll all die!" said the Sling Man.

"Or maybe we'll all live," said Ryan.

The guard took a step toward him, but Ryan raised the box over his head once again, threatening to smash the vials to bits. The guard backed away. Ryan opened the remaining vials. "Don't do it!" the doctor shouted.

Ryan ignored him. One after the other, he emptied a small amount of liquid from each vial and poured it into the cup. When he finished, he had six vaccines. The others looked on, angry and astonished. To Ryan, however, it felt completely right. He looked at the coach and said, "Bring Kaylee here. She should drink first."

Nobody moved. Ryan and the coach were locked in a stare-down, but the others were watching the cup, the concoction that contained some of the vaccine from each of the five vials. Ryan smelled something strange. He, too, glanced down at the cup.

"It's bubbling," said the guard.

"It's about to boil," said the other.

It *was* boiling. As it boiled, the yellow liquid inside began to expand. The cup was half full, then two-thirds full. The sixth share that Ryan had created was boiling and growing right before their eyes.

Then they heard a noise. It was a deep rumbling that sounded like a distant earthquake. It was coming from inside the cup.

"What is that?" asked Kaylee.

"I don't know," said Ryan.

The cup started to rattle. The boiling yellow liquid was bubbling over the sides like a science project gone bad.

"I think it's going to explode!" said Coach.

The rumbling grew louder. The rattling spread to the table. The legs were tapping on the floor. Then the floor, itself, began to shake. At first, it was a vibration beneath their feet. Soon, the whole room was in motion. Ryan could barely stay on his feet.

"Run for it!" the doctor shouted.

One of the guards flung the door open. Ryan tried to run, but the floor was shaking too violently. He fell to his knees and dropped the box containing their vaccine. He heard the glass vials shatter. He saw the others running. He heard himself screaming as the cup exploded and released a bright flash of light. The colors were more intense than any fireworks display he had ever seen.

And then there was only darkness.

# 9

*T*he bright light of interrogation was shining in Ryan's eyes.

The blast in the Infectious Disease Control Center had knocked him out, cold. Apart from that, he was unhurt. He didn't know how long he had been unconscious. Even more disconcerting, he had no idea where he was.

"You are in a tremendous amount of trouble, young man." The deep voice filled the room, but Ryan's interrogator was a dark silhouette in the shadows, standing behind a bright spotlight. It was like staring into the headlights of an oncoming car in the dead of night and trying to identify the driver. Somehow, however, Ryan could feel the weight of the stranger's stare.

"Who are you?" asked Ryan.

"I'm Detective Frank Malone. And *I'll* be the one asking the questions from here on out, thank you."

Ryan couldn't look into that white light another minute. As he averted his eyes, he noticed that he was no longer wearing his jeans and sweatshirt. His basketball jersey was gone, too. Someone had removed his street clothes. He was clad in a jumpsuit. An *orange* jumpsuit—the same kind of orange jumpsuit that his father wore whenever Ryan visited him at the state penitentiary.

"Am I in prison?"

"No more questions," said the detective. "It's time for you to cough up some answers, Mr. Coolidge."

*Coolidge!* They knew his name. But how? It must have been the missing person's report that the ER physician had mentioned. His mother had probably filed it, and the police figured out that Ryan LNU was Ryan Coolidge. "Sir, I know what you must be thinking. But I'm not like my father. I didn't do anything wrong."

"We'll see about that. Right now, I'd venture to say that you're in far more trouble than your father ever got himself into."

Ryan couldn't imagine why the detective would say such a thing. Then it came to him. *They must think I started that fire.* "It wasn't me. I didn't start that hospital on fire."

"I'm not talking about that. Don't play dumb. Your friend Kaylee confirmed everything that Dr. Watkins told us."

"Kaylee?" he said aloud, and the wheels began to turn in his head. So far, he hadn't been thinking too clearly. He suddenly remembered that he had been exposed to a deadly and contagious disease. "Is Kaylee all right? She should be . . . I should be . . ."

"Dead?"

"Yes. We were all infected by that virus. BODS."

"Both you and Kaylee are fine."

Ryan sighed with relief, but his concern quickly returned. "What about the others?"

"Oh, you're worried about them, are you?" he said, his voice dripping with skepticism. "Funny, you weren't quite so concerned when you took away their vaccines."

"I wasn't trying to take anything away from anyone. There were six of us and only five vaccines. I was trying to make enough for everyone."

"No, you were trying to save Kaylee, at the expense of everyone else."

"That's not true."

"You agreed to cast lots, did you not?"

"Yes, but—"

"The five winners were supposed to get the vaccine. The loser would not."

"Yes, but it didn't have to be that way."

"But you agreed to the system," the detective said.

"The others wanted it. I never agreed. It wasn't right."

The detective chuckled. "You mean it wasn't right because you didn't like the result."

"No. It just wasn't right."

"So when Kaylee lost, you went berserk."

"I did what I had to do. That's all."

"You took the vials. You tried to stretch five vaccines into six."

"Yes."

"Which was foolish, of course. There was only enough vaccine for five. If you try to stretch it into six, none of them would be any good."

"We had to try. We couldn't just let Kaylee die."

"So you admit that you broke the agreement to cast lots?"

Ryan hesitated. It sounded bad, the way the detective said it. "Yes, sir."

"You had a better idea. Mix up the vials and blow everything up."

"I had no idea that mixing up the vaccines would cause an explosion."

The detective leaned closer, his eyes narrowing. "Like I said before, son. *You* are in a lot of trouble."

"Why?"

"You and Kaylee were the only survivors. Four people died."

The detective's words hit him like a punch in the chest. "Coach, Flu Lady, Sling Man, Head Case. All dead?" he said, his voice quaking.

"That's right. Thanks to you."

Ryan's mouth went dry. He'd never hurt anyone in his entire life, and now four people were dead. "This can't be. I didn't mean for this to turn out this way."

"It is a rather interesting result, isn't it," said the detective.

"I wouldn't call it interesting at all. It's terrible. I'm sick over this."

"Actually, you're not sick. That's what is so interesting. You see, the BODS virus had never been tested on children before. Turns out it's lethal only in adults. Dr. Watkins believes that it has something to do with lower levels of certain hormones in children."

"So Kaylee and I are safe?"

"Yes. But we know all too well that BODS is fatal to adults. Without the vaccine, none of them survived."

Ryan swallowed the lump in his throat. Each time the detective reminded him of the consequences of his actions, it became more difficult for Ryan to speak. "I'm very sorry about that," he said softly.

"You should be," said the detective. "If you had honored the agreement to cast lots, none of those four adults would have died."

"But . . . it didn't seem fair, us deciding who should live and die."

The detective held up his hand, as if he'd heard enough. "Tell it to the judge, young man."

"The judge?" said Ryan.

"Yes. You're going to stand trial."

"Trial? For what?"

"Manslaughter, of course. Like I said: *You* are in a lot of trouble."

Ryan sank into his chair, his mind awhirl. On his last visit to a courtroom he'd watched his father plead guilty to a crime. "Another Coolidge in trouble with the law," he said, almost speaking to himself. "Our neighborhood is just going to have a field day, isn't it?"

"Don't worry. This trial won't be anywhere near your hometown."

"It won't?"

"No. Like Dr. Watkins told you, everything connected to a possible BODS epidemic is top secret. Your trial will be no different. You will be tried before a special tribunal assembled by the Court of International Justice. The exact location is of no concern to you. It will be a fair trial. That's all I can guarantee you."

Ryan wasn't sure what to say, so he said the first thing that came to mind. "Can I call home, please? I want to speak to my mother."

"Call *home*?" The detective's head rolled back with laughter. "You really have no idea what you're up against, do you?"

Ryan felt an emptiness inside, a dark loneliness. "No, sir," he said quietly. "I honestly don't."

The detective switched off the intense interrogation lamp. The room was suddenly black, and Ryan's heart skipped a beat. He heard another flip of a switch, and the lights were back on. It was a softer light, however, much easier on the eyes.

"Guards!" the detective called.

The door opened, and two men entered. Both were dressed in dark green uniforms. Ryan gave them a quick once-over, searching for any markings or insignias that might tell him who these people were. He spotted nothing useful. The only thing he could say for certain was that these guys were absolutely huge. Both were well over six feet tall. Their necks were like sequoia trees, and rock-hard biceps bulged beneath their shirt sleeves. One guard was armed with a nightstick. The other carried a heavy-duty flashlight.

"Hands behind your head," said the man with the nightstick.

Ryan did as he was told. They cuffed his hands behind his back and escorted him from the interrogation room, one man on his left, the other on the right. The passageways were dark and narrow, and the guards led him down a winding, metal stairwell. At the bottom of the stairs, the lead man opened a sealed hatchway, which led to total darkness.

"In you go," the guard said.

"What's this?"

"The brig, of course."

The beam of the flashlight pointed the way. Ryan stood in the open hatchway and stared inside. Cold metal walls, a metal floor. No windows. A bunk on one side, a smelly toilet with no seat on the other. *So this is what prison is all about.* It almost didn't feel real to him.

"Move it, kid!"

The nightstick poking at his kidney—*that* was real.

Ryan stumbled into the brig, then something came to mind. "I noticed you called this the brig. I thought brigs were on ships."

"Not necessarily. But good guess, genius. You are on a ship."

"Where are we going?"

The guard snorted with laughter.

"What's so funny?" asked Ryan.

"First of all, they don't tell us. Second of all, if they did tell us, we wouldn't tell *you.*" The guard handed Ryan an extra flashlight, and Ryan switched it on.

"Use it wisely, kid. The batteries won't last forever."

The door closed, and Ryan was left alone in the cell. The dim glow of the flashlight was his only relief from total darkness. Wherever he aimed it, the sweeping beam of light sent cockroaches scurrying. They were on the floor, the walls, and even on the ceiling. Some were as big as his baby sister's foot. They disappeared behind the toilet or between cracks in the metal planks, though Ryan knew they would return as soon as the light went out. He sat on the bunk and tested the mattress. He wondered if there were roach nests in there, too. It didn't matter. He couldn't possibly sleep in that bunk anyway. The mattress was hard and lumpy, about as comfortable as a sack of corn husks. The blankets and sheets had a strong, musty odor. It reminded Ryan of the pungent smell of the bay when the tide went out. Or the smell of his socks after soccer practice.

He sat quietly for several minutes, until the sensation of movement made him start. It was a gentle sway, almost imperceptible. But no doubt about it, the ship was moving. Ryan was on his way, sailing off to some undisclosed location to stand trial before the Court of International Justice—for manslaughter!

It was hard for him to believe that any of this was happening. But then he reconsidered. Of course it was happening. He was a Coolidge.

*That's why I'm being charged.*

Somehow, Ryan had known for months that it would come to this. He knew that all the taunting, all the jokes, all the gossip behind his back would someday snowball into disaster. Eventually, they would pin something on him. They'd nail him, and they'd nail him good.

All because his father was a crook.

*Thanks, Dad. Thanks a million.*

# 10

*T*he morning sun emerged as a bright orange ball on the horizon as Ryan disembarked from the ship. The same two guards who had taken him to the brig were escorting him down a gangplank to the pier.

Ryan had not slept well in the brig. All night, his mind had simply refused to shut off and go to sleep. Being imprisoned made him think of his dad, and he wondered how his father passed the time, alone on his bunk, nothing to do, no one to talk to, night after night. He probably tried to think happy thoughts, so Ryan tried it, too. He thought of the Bahamas, where he and his dad had shared their best day together ever. It was painful for Ryan to recall those better days, because it only made him wish that his father had never gotten into trouble with the law. But no one could take his memories away from him. Like that day on the motor scooter in the Bahamas. They covered an entire island together—stopping wherever they wanted, resting on a deserted beach, going for a quick swim in turquoise waters. Ryan especially remembered the old man named Rumsey that he and his father befriended. He called everyone "mon," and he somehow worked it into every sentence. "Hey mon, dat's a very nice scooter you got dare.

Hey mon, how 'bout you buy some conch shells from dis old man?" Rumsey had hundreds of shells. Each one was as big as Ryan's head, and when he held it to his ear he could hear the sound of the ocean.

All night long, Ryan had heard the swooshing of the sea. He didn't need a conch shell. But he sure could have used a motor scooter. He would have ditched these turkeys the minute they reached dry land.

*Later, mon.*

The ship was docked at a commercial port. All around him, large cranes lifted cargo from rusty, old barges. Container trucks carried load after load to and from ships. It was a noisy place where workers had to shout to one another over the rattle of huge chains and the rumble of diesel engines. Ryan tried to spot a license tag on a truck or a street sign—anything that might give him a clue as to his whereabouts. Before he could focus, however, a blindfold slipped over his eyes.

"I think you've seen enough," the guard said as he tightened the knot behind Ryan's head.

The guards led him across the dock. Ryan took small steps, since he couldn't see anything. The noises faded in the distance as the guards took him farther away from the center of activity. Finally, they stopped. "Step down," the guard said.

Ryan followed his instructions. The floor beneath him seemed to move with the weight of his step. The men helped him to keep his balance as they lowered him onto a bench seat. There was a rocking motion, followed by something that sounded like the clatter of oars and the hum of a modest outboard engine. They were on a small boat. Ryan felt them push away from the dock. The engine whined and the bow rose as the boat gained speed.

"Where are we going now?" asked Ryan.

"Really now," the man said over the noise of the engine. "Do you think I'd bother to blindfold you if I was going to tell you where you're going?"

Ryan said nothing, as the answer was pretty obvious.

The blindfold made it difficult to gauge time, but Ryan guessed that they skimmed across the waves for about twenty minutes before the engine quieted and they came to a stop. The men helped him out of the boat, and his legs wobbled a bit as he planted himself on the more solid footing of a wooden pier.

"Have a look," the man said as he pulled away Ryan's blindfold.

Ryan's eyes needed a minute to adjust to daylight. Before him was an old stone fort with formidable gray walls. Armed guards kept watch from the turrets. The entire building was surrounded by water—not a thin castle moat, but miles of open ocean as far as the eye could see. This place was a veritable fortress on its own remote island. Ryan was reminded of Fort Jefferson near Key West, Florida, an impenetrable old prison that the Union army had built during the Civil War. His father had taken him there once, too. That was yet another one of those "good old days" that seemed like five-thousand years ago.

"How long do I have to stay here?" asked Ryan.

"That depends on your trial," the man said. "If the jury finds you not guilty, you can go home. If the jury finds you guilty . . . well, then this *is* your home."

Ryan took another look. It was anything but "home."

"And don't even think about trying to escape," the man said as his gaze drifted toward the surrounding sea. "Unless you want to become shark food."

The men took Ryan by the arm and led him toward the fort's main entrance. The iron gate clattered as it rose. The threesome entered, and the gate was even noisier on its way down. They were standing in a center courtyard, and the surrounding stone walls seemed even taller now that Ryan was inside. The fort was divided into two sections. On the east side, the accommodations resembled an old hotel, not exactly cheery but at least comfortable. The west side was three stories of prison bars. Ryan didn't have to ask which side he would be visiting.

The men handed some official papers to a guard at the western entrance. He gave them a quick look. Then, with a simple jerk of his head, he muttered, "Cell C-12."

Ryan hoped that Cellblock C was on the third floor, which might at least give him a decent view of the surrounding sea. Maybe he'd see some birds or ships, anything to help pass the time and break the boredom. To his dismay, they took Ryan *down* three flights of stairs. Cellblock C was three stories below ground. There were no lights, and one of the men had to light a torch to lead the way. The walls and stone floors seemed to sweat with dampness. It reminded him of underground caverns he had once hiked through with his father.

*Why do I keep thinking of him?* thought Ryan, chiding himself. But it was only normal. He was in prison. How could he not think of his father?

The torchlight wasn't very bright, but as far as Ryan could tell, he was the only prisoner down in Cell Block C. He heard not a sound from any of the other cells.

"Do I really have to stay in this hole?" asked Ryan.

"What, you don't like it?"

"I'm not complaining," said Ryan. "It's just that I specifically told my travel agent to book me a suite."

"Wise guy, huh?" He opened the cell door, pushed Ryan inside, and slammed the door shut. "I hate wise guys." The key turned in the lock, and the man shook the bars to make sure they were secure. He lit a torch outside Ryan's cell and mounted it in a bracket on the wall. Aside from the guard's torch, it was the dungeon's only source of light.

"We'll be back later. Let's see if you're still cracking jokes after your flame burns out."

The men turned and walked away. The sound of their laughter echoing off the cold stone walls only served to remind Ryan that this was no laughing matter. Four people were dead, and they wanted to blame Ryan for it. He didn't know why he would make jokes in such a serious situation. It was just his nature. Whenever he was under stress, he tried to make light of it with humor. Strange, but his father had always done the same thing. *The apple doesn't fall far from the tree.* Maybe they were more alike than he cared to admit.

Ryan turned his attention toward finding a dry spot in his damp cell. He crouched in a corner. Moisture seeping up through the soles of his shoes was just something he would have to get used to. He was cold, angry, and trying not to feel depressed. It was difficult. All he needed was a dry place to sit, to think, and to wait. They wouldn't even give him that much. He wondered why they were treating him so badly, but only one answer came to mind. They didn't think he was ever going to leave. After all, his name was Ryan *Coolidge*. Why did they even need a trial? *Of course* he was guilty.

Ryan suddenly felt something scurry over the top of his foot. He withdrew quickly, his heart in his throat. He looked around, but he saw nothing. Whatever it was, it had disappeared in a flash. He hoped it was a large cockroach. He feared it was a rat. He wished his dog were with him. Sam was a gentle giant, but Ryan always felt safer with him around.

"Pssssst."

Ryan froze. He thought he heard a snake hissing.

"Psssst."

There it was again. This time, however, it sounded more human. It was coming from the next cell. "Who's there?"

"Not so loud," she said. "It's me. Kaylee."

Ryan moved all the way to the bars, but he couldn't see her. A solid brick wall separated the two cells. Iron bars ran across the front of Ryan's cell, and they were too close together for Ryan to stick his head out and peer into the next cell.

"Is that really you?" he said, his voice slightly louder than a whisper.

"Yes. They brought me here last night, while you were still asleep in the ship's brig. I was worried about you. I'm so glad you're okay."

"Yeah, I guess I'm okay." He scanned his bleak surroundings and added, "If you call living in a dungeon okay."

She fell silent, and Ryan wondered what she was thinking. Finally, she said, "I'm sorry."

"For what? You didn't do anything."

"I heard that they're planning to put you on trial. For manslaughter."

"Looks that way. Are they putting you on trial, too?"

"No."

"Then why are you here?"

She paused, then said, "You shouldn't be talking to me."

"Why?"

He couldn't see her, but he could hear her sigh in the darkness. "Because this is a trick."

"What kind of trick?"

"The detective put me in the cell next to yours for a reason. I'm supposed to get you talking. He hopes you'll slip and say something incriminating. Then I'm supposed to testify against you at trial and repeat all the damaging things you say."

Ryan scoffed. "It's hard to imagine how I could say anything that would make things worse than they already are."

"Things can always get worse. Take it from somebody who knows."

"I'm not so sure," said Ryan. "This may be one situation where it's about as bad as it gets."

"This is so unfair. You were just trying to save me. Why do I always do this? It seems like every time someone does something to help me, it ends up getting them into trouble."

She sounded genuinely upset. Funny, thought Ryan. When they'd first met in the ER, Kaylee had struck him as the kind of pretty and popular girl whose biggest challenge in her perfect life was trying to figure out what to wear every morning. Sometimes, first impressions could be way off the mark.

Ryan said, "Don't go blaming yourself. I know why they're doing this to me, and it has nothing to do with you."

"What's it about then?"

Ryan took a seat on the floor, his back against the brick wall. The sound of Kaylee's back sliding down the opposite side of the same wall told him that she, too, had taken a seat on the floor. But for the bricks and mortar between them, they would have been sitting back to back. Strangely, Ryan took some comfort in that. "You don't want to know the truth," he said.

"Does it have anything to do with Ryan L'new?"

Ryan bristled. This Kaylee was one smart girl. He drew a circle on the dirty floor with his fingertip. He was just doodling, not sure if he should tell her.

"You can talk to me," she said. "I'm not going to tell those jerks anything."

He spoke softly, trying to bite back some of the anger in his voice. "My father's name is William Coolidge. He's in jail."

They were in separate cells, in almost total darkness, looking in completely opposite directions. Still, Ryan felt certain that she was seeing him in a completely new light. People always did, once they found out that his father was in prison.

Kaylee said, "Do you think they're out to get you because your father is in jail?"

"Of course. That's the way people think. You know that old saying, 'The apple doesn't fall far from the tree?' People know my dad's a criminal, so they treat me like one, too."

"I'm sorry about your dad," she said. "I really am."

Her tone surprised him. It was soothing, as pleasant as it ever had been. She didn't seem to be judging him. Maybe she'd never heard that old expression, "The apple doesn't fall far from the tree." Or maybe she was different from most people.

"Thanks," he said.

"What did your dad do?" she asked.

"He was a journalist. An investigative reporter for the *Tribune*."

"No. I meant, what did he do to end up in jail?"

"They say he stole something."

"What?"

Ryan shrugged. "I don't really want to talk about it."

"Sorry. Didn't mean to be nosy."

"It's okay. That's the way it always is. Once people find out that your dad's in prison, that's all they want to talk about."

"I won't bring it up again, okay? If you want to talk about it, we'll talk about it."

"I don't want to talk about it."

"Then we won't."

"Good." Ryan was glad to have that part of the conversation behind them, but it hadn't gone as badly as it might have. For the first time since his father had landed in prison, he felt as though he'd found someone who understood—someone he could talk to, if he wanted to.

"Ryan, I'm not going to repeat any of this to anyone. You know that, right?"

"I think I do.

"I wasn't trying to get you into trouble when I told them what happened in that conference room. I spoke up only because I thought they were going to give you a medal or a reward. What you did was so courageous. I never dreamed they were trying to build a criminal case against you. You do believe me, don't you?"

He paused, but only because it was his nature to be cautious. He didn't really doubt her sincerity. "Yes, I believe you."

The burning torch was flickering. The dungeon was getting darker. Kaylee's voice tightened. "Ryan, I'm scared. This place is creepy. What if there are rats or snakes?"

He didn't tell her about that thing—whatever it was—that had scurried over the top of his foot. "Try not to think about that."

"I can't stop. I'm afraid."

There was silence, total stillness. Ryan could hear only the distant drip of water in another damp cell.

"Ryan?"

"Yes?"

"Will you hold my hand?"

He glanced toward the bars. There was barely enough light to see his own hand, but hers almost seemed to glow in the darkness. She had reached through the bars of her own cell and slid her hand across the floor toward his. Ryan reached through his bars and took her hand.

It was cold in the dungeon, but her hand felt warm. His heart was beating a little faster, and it was a good feeling. It washed away a lot of loneliness, and not just the loneliness of his cell. It was the loneliness of lost friends at school, teachers who didn't trust him, parents who didn't want him staying in their house for sleep overs with their children. All those terrible things happened when your father was locked behind bars. *This*, however, had a way of making it all disappear.

It was the feeling that nothing else mattered.

They stayed that way, silent, their fingers interlocked. Ryan's thoughts turned to the four unlucky ones: Flu Lady, Sling Man, Head Case, and Coach Jenkins. He'd forgotten their real names, but he would never forget their faces. He said a silent prayer for each of them. He prayed for Kaylee, too.

The burning torch flickered. The flame weakened, fighting for survival. It shrank to almost nothing. Ryan caught his breath. Kaylee squeezed his hand.

The flame went out. Their cells were in total darkness.

Ryan said another little prayer. For courage.

# 11

yan woke the next morning. Or was it the afternoon? He had no way of knowing. The cell was completely dark, night or day. Then he heard noises—faint at first, then louder. Footsteps! And they were coming toward his cell.

It had been a difficult night. Kaylee had made him promise not to fall asleep before she did. Ryan always kept his promises.

The corridor that led to his cell was growing brighter. Someone was coming. He could hear them. He could see the glow of their torch.

"Kaylee," he whispered into the next cell. There was no answer. He tried again, a little louder this time. "Kaylee, wake up."

Suddenly, the glowing torch appeared on the other side of the bars. The flame was harsh on Ryan's eyes, but it was sorely welcome. The iron door opened, and a guard entered his cell.

"Kaylee is gone," he said.

"Where did she go?"

"Detective Malone sent her home. You're the only one charged with a crime."

Ryan felt sad that she was gone, but he knew he was being selfish. Any home, even his own, had to be better than this place. "What happens now?"

"Let's go," said the guard.

"Time for my massage already?" said Ryan. Yet another joke. He was at it again, looking danger in the face and trying to defuse the situation with humor. Just like his dad.

"Time to meet your lawyer," the guard said.

"I don't have a lawyer."

"The court of justice appointed one for you. Now, come on. Move it."

Ryan followed the guard out of the cell and down the long, stone corridor. The thought of climbing out of the dungeon and seeing the blue sky and sunshine made him eager with anticipation, but he was soon disappointed. They weren't going upstairs. The guard stopped at a large wooden door at the end of the corridor. The painted sign on the door read, LAW LIBRARY.

Ryan said, "This is where I meet my lawyer?"

"Yup. This is where his office is."

"IIis office is in a dungeon?"

"The Court of International Justice goes to great lengths to make sure that all prisoners are given a fair trial. There is a law library here on the premises. All court-appointed lawyers are given an office in the library where they can meet with their clients."

"I'd be happy to relocate. I mean, if that would make my lawyer happy."

The guard shot him a nasty look, and then he knocked hard on the door. No answer. The guard grabbed the brass knocker and gave it three loud bangs. They waited. Finally, a reply came.

"Send the boy in!"

"He's expecting you," the guard told Ryan. He opened the door and gave Ryan a little shove. Ryan stumbled into the library, and the door closed behind him. The guard had not come with him. Ryan was alone, and he was simply awestruck by the surroundings.

"Wow, this is so cool." He was speaking to no one. His words were like a reflex.

He was standing in the center of a five-story atrium. It was like one of those cavernous lobbies in the big-city hotels where you could see all the way up to the top floor. Here, however, none of the floors had hotel rooms. Each level had only bookshelves, row after row of bookshelves. They were stacked with books from floor to ceiling. The volumes had to number in the thousands, at least. Ryan felt as though his head were on a swivel. He was looking up and all around, admiring all the books.

"How do you do, young man?"

Ryan turned to greet the voice. "Fine, thank you. You must be the lawyer."

"Yes, that's me. Hezekiah is my name."

"Pleased to meet you. My name's Ryan."

They shook hands, which made Ryan feel good. It was nice to know someone was on his side. Actually, everything about Hezekiah was strangely reassuring, though a bit quirky. He was a very old African-American with bushy white eyebrows that nearly joined at the bridge of his nose. It was as if a long, white caterpillar were crawling across the top of Hezekiah's eyeglasses. The glasses, themselves, were a relic from the past. They were black and horn-rimmed, with thick Coke-bottle lenses that made his eyes seem larger than life. They were dark, expressive eyes that sparkled when he smiled. His hair was a frizzy mess of long, gray strands that practically stood on end. "Wild" was the word that came to mind. The overall appearance was an eclectic cross between Thurgood Marshall and Albert Einstein, two very famous men whose photographs were in Ryan's dictionary. Hezekiah's clothing was only slightly less peculiar. He wore a navy blue suit and a white shirt, which were standard for a lawyer. Hezekiah's suit was completely wrinkled, however, as if he routinely slept in his work clothes. The skinny neck tie was straight out of the old black-and-white movies that Ryan's mother liked to watch on television. The shoes were the biggest surprise of all. Ryan did a double take, but sure enough, the old lawyer was wearing canvas, high-top basketball shoes.

"You were expecting wingtips?" said Hezekiah.

Ryan smiled, realizing that he must have been staring at the man's shoes. "Sorry. I don't know many lawyers who wear basketball shoes."

"That's because there aren't many lawyers like me." He smiled again, then gestured like a tour guide to show off the surroundings. "How do you like the library?"

"It's awesome."

The old man flashed a boyish grin. "It is, isn't it? That's one of the things I like most about handling cases before the Court of International Justice. I just love their library."

"Are these all law books?"

"Yup."

"Why do you need so many?"

"Because that's how our law is made."

"With books?"

"No. Not with books. With people."

Ryan looked up, then down, roaming the shelves with an inquisitive gaze. "All I see are books."

"That's all most people see. But when you've been trained as I have, you see much more. These are case books. Every time there's a legal case, that means someone went to court. Every time someone goes to court, that means somebody wins and somebody loses. Someone goes to jail, someone goes free.

Every single case reported in every last one of these books is a piece of someone's life."

"I never thought of it that way."

Hezekiah shrugged, as if he weren't surprised. "You hungry?"

"Yes."

"How hungry?"

"Enough to eat a book."

"Good. Take your appetite straight back that way, then turn left to the kitchen. Help yourself to the refrigerator. When you've had your fill, you can get out of that hideous orange prison jumpsuit. Your jeans and sweatshirt are in the closet."

"What about my basketball jersey?"

"Darn, I was going to keep that for myself. Goes well with the shoes." He winked to let Ryan know he was kidding. "Come get me when you're finished. I'll be on the second floor. I have a ton of research to do."

"Thanks," said Ryan.

"You're welcome."

Ryan was starting to like this Hezekiah better by the minute. He followed the old man's directions and found the kitchen. His stomach growled as he opened the refrigerator, and he nearly flipped when he saw what was inside. Not only was it packed with food, but it contained only the food he liked. Cheeseburgers, mac and cheese, yellow cake with chocolate frosting. Raisin bread, chocolate milk, and vanilla-flavored cola. Hezekiah even had his favorite sports drink in his lucky citrus-cooler flavor. Ryan grabbed a little of everything, cleared a spot on the table, and then proceeded to eat and drink until the thought of swallowing one more bite made him sick to his stomach. He pushed away from the table and found his clothes in the closet. They'd been washed and were neatly folded. It felt good to put on his favorite jeans, sweatshirt, and sneakers. And the basketball jersey always brought him good luck.

A sudden crash from inside the library wiped the smile from his face.

He ran out of the kitchen and took a quick look around. Everything looked normal, but then he heard another crash upstairs, in the atrium. It sounded like books tumbling to the floor. Finally, his eyes locked on a huge mess on the second floor. One of the bookshelves had been overturned. It was exactly where Hezekiah was supposed to be doing his research. Ryan raced up the stairs and headed straight for the pile of books.

"Hezekiah!" he shouted, fearing the worst.

The pile of books was enormous, taller than Ryan and almost fifty feet long. The entire row of shelving had collapsed. Books were piled on top of books. Somewhere beneath the rubble, Ryan feared, was his new friend Hezekiah. Ryan started tossing books aside, digging furiously.

"Are you okay?" he shouted. No one replied. Ryan kept digging through the pile.

"Hezekiah! Are you—"

The old man's head suddenly popped up through the pile. He was laughing.

"Hezekiah?"

"Oooooh boy. That was a close one."

"Are you hurt?" asked Ryan.

He struggled to push his way up from the bottom of the pile. Ryan helped him to his feet.

"I'm fine, just fine. That happens every now and then."

"What happens?"

"Oh, the re-entry can be a bit rough sometimes."

"Re-entry? What do you mean, re—" Ryan stopped himself.

He noticed Hezekiah's clothes. "How did you get all soaking wet?"

"Research, of course."

"You get wet doing research?"

"Sometimes. It depends on the case."

Ryan made a face, confused. "What are you talking about?"

Hezekiah dug through the pile. He found the right book and turned to a certain page. "Here it is. This is what I was researching."

It was an old case. The pages had yellowed with age. The date was 1842. Ryan read the case name aloud. "United States versus Holmes."

"That's right," said Hezekiah. "I was doing research to prepare your defense at trial. This case—United States versus Holmes—will be very important to your defense."

"Why?"

"Because that's the way the law works. Judges rely on old cases to decide new cases. They're called legal precedents."

Ryan was still confused, but he was also curious. "What is this Holmes case about?"

"Oh, it was a terrible case. Just awful what happened to those poor souls." Hezekiah was trembling as he spoke.

Ryan was almost afraid to probe, but he asked anyway. "What happened?"

"A long time ago, a ship called the *William Brown* was sailing across the North Atlantic Ocean. It was carrying passengers from Liverpool to the United States. It hit an iceberg off the coast of Canada. The ship went down in a matter of minutes."

Ryan thought of the movie about the *Titanic*, another ship that hit an iceberg. It gave him chills. "That does sound awful. But what does a sinking ship have to do with my case?"

"Everything, my boy. That's what I've been trying to tell

you. These cases are about people. To understand them, you have to get in to them. *In* to them, I tell you."

Ryan wasn't sure what to make of the old man. "Wait a minute. Are you saying that the reason you're all wet is because . . ."

Hezekiah nodded slowly, flashing a mischievous grin. "Now I think you're beginning to get the picture."

"Nah," said Ryan, scoffing. "No way. You can get into books, figuratively, I mean. But you can't literally get *in* to them. Nobody can do that."

Hezekiah chuckled to himself. "What do you think happened here, then?"

"Looks like you pulled these bookshelves over and dumped a bucket of water over your head."

"Do you really think that's what happened?"

"I don't know. But that's a heck of a lot easier to believe than you jumping inside a book and getting all wet doing research about a ship that sank in 1842."

Hezekiah nodded, as if he expected Ryan's reaction. "What if I could prove it to you?"

"How are you going to do that?"

"Simple. I'll show you how I do my research."

Ryan took a half step back.

"What's the matter?" said Hezekiah. "You scared?"

"No. I'm not scared."

"Of course you're not. There's nothing to be afraid of, is there, Ryan? I'm just a crazy old man who pulled down the bookshelves and dumped a bucket of water over his head. Right?"

"Maybe."

"Or maybe not," said Hezekiah. "Come with me, Ryan. Do a little research, and learn for yourself."

# 12

*T*he library was a mess, and Ryan offered to help the old man reshelve his fallen books before they went anywhere. It was a polite gesture that would have made Ryan's mother proud. Hezekiah seemed to realize that Ryan was really just buying a little extra time to quiz him. He wanted to know more about these "research trips" before he agreed to go on one.

Ryan picked up one book at a time and handed them to Hezekiah. The lawyer knew exactly where each book belonged. He was standing atop a stepladder, filling the top shelf.

"So tell me one thing," said Ryan as he passed up another book.

"Certainly. Anything you want to know."

"Exactly what kind of a lawyer are you?"

Hezekiah gave a little wink. "I'm the kind of lawyer you want on your side if you ever get into trouble."

"You're that good, huh?"

"Let's just say I have a lot of experience."

"Have you ever lost a case?"

"A few. The law is like anything else in life, Ryan. The right side doesn't always win."

Ryan thought of all the times he'd visited his father in jail, all the times his father had told him that he was innocent. "I suppose that's true."

"It's absolutely true," said Hezekiah. "Judges and jurors are human beings. Sometimes they make good decisions. Sometimes they make bad decisions." He paused, and his gaze slowly swept across his vast library. "And all those decisions— good or bad, right or wrong—are right here."

"Have you read all of them?"

"No. But I've visited many of them."

"Visited?"

"Yes. Like I just told you. As part of my research."

Ryan chuckled. Hezekiah restocked another book and asked, "What's so funny?"

"I just had this crazy image pop into my head. You, with a long flapping cape around your neck standing on top of a spinning globe. Then a deep voice in the background says, 'Look, up in the library! It's Super-Lawyer! Able to soar through time. Able to journey through the dusty old pages of law books and make the cases come to life. Yes, it's Super-Lawyer!"

Hezekiah laughed with him. Then his smile faded, and his expression turned stone-cold serious. "That's exactly what I do, Ryan."

Ryan laughed again, but this time Hezekiah didn't join him. The old man climbed down the ladder and went to work on the lower shelves. Ryan handed him a few more books from the pile on the floor. Hezekiah placed them carefully back on the shelf. They worked in silence for a minute or two. Ryan wondered if he had hurt the old man's feelings.

Finally, Hezekiah looked at him and said, "I was serious when I invited you. Come with me, Ryan. Come on a research trip."

Ryan was skeptical, but he played along, just out of curiosity. "Okay, let's say I agree to go with you. How do we travel?"

"There are two possible answers to that. First, let me give you the one you're not going to believe."

"Okay. This should be fun."

"I travel through legal leapholes."

Ryan started to laugh, then stopped himself, careful not to insult his lawyer all over again. "Through *what?*"

"Leapholes."

"Leapholes? How do you find these leapholes?"

"You earn them. By closing loopholes."

"What's a loophole?"

Hezekiah considered the question, as if trying to think of a way to make the concept understandable to Ryan. His eyes seemed to brighten, then he said, "A loophole is when you find a clever but sneaky way to get around a rule."

"I don't think I follow you," said Ryan.

Hezekiah began to pace as he spoke, like a professor lecturing to his class. "Okay. Let's say you live in Florida. Your mom tells you to be home by five o'clock. You show up at eight o'clock. What do you say?"

"Uh . . . Sorry, Mom?"

"Maybe. Or you might say, 'But Mom, you said be home by five o'clock, and it *is* five o'clock—in Los Angeles."

Ryan thought for a moment. "Oh, right. They're three hours behind us on the west coast. So when it's eight o'clock in Florida, it's only five o'clock in L.A."

"That's right."

"That's a loophole?" asked Ryan.

"Right. Because next time your mother would have to say, 'Ryan be home by five o'clock *Florida* time."

"Or, she could say, 'We don't live in Los Angeles, bucko, you're grounded.'"

"She could. But stay with me on this, I'm trying to make a point here. There are all kinds of loopholes. And there are plenty of lawyers willing to argue about things a lot sillier than whether your mother meant five o'clock Eastern Time or five o'clock Pacific Time when she said be home by five o'clock."

"There are?"

"Yup. And it's all just a waste of everybody's time and money. That's why I close loopholes. And every time I close a loophole, the Society gives me another leaphole."

"What Society?"

"You'll learn more about that later," said Hezekiah. "First, let's just stick with leapholes."

"Okay. So exactly what is a leaphole?"

He smiled and said, "You're not going to believe it. So let me give you the other answer—the one you *will* believe."

"Okay, shoot."

Hezekiah took a seat on the stepladder. Ryan seated himself on a stack of books, facing Hezekiah. The old man leaned closer and said, "When I was a boy your age, I went into the library and I saw one thing. Books. Nothing but books. But if you go into the library these days, you also see . . . what?"

"Computers?" said Ryan.

"Exactly. All libraries are computerized nowadays, including law libraries. So I took it to the next level. I call them Virtual Legal Environments."

"Which means what?"

"I can bring the cases to life. Virtually speaking."

"How does it work?"

"It's a step beyond virtual reality. More like the legal extension of what NASA calls virtual environments. V-Es for short."

"How do you get into these V-Es?"

"They're presented through head-mounted computer-driven displays. Which is nothing more than a medium for man-machine interaction. This one is a bit more advanced, because it operates on a multi-modal interactive level."

"Multi-what?"

"Multi-modal. I know, it sounds like technical mumbo jumbo, but conceptually it's quite simple. The key is a computer that is powerful enough to capture the largest possible part of the human motor outflow. By 'motor outflow' I mean not just your arms and legs moving, but your eyesight, hearing, smell, taste, touch—all sensory perception. Then we need a staging area where human movements are constrained as little as possible. Here, the human receives from the computer a perceptual inflow, which will work only if the different available channels are firing to the max. Finally, the inflow and outflow are optimally tuned in relation to a specific task."

"You're right. It does sound like mumbo jumbo."

"But it works."

Ryan glanced at the water dripping from Hezekiah's clothing. "Obviously. But one thing has me really confused."

"What?"

"If it's a *virtual* environment, that means it's not real, right?"

"That's right. Feels real, but it's not."

"Then why are you all wet?"

He smiled and said, "That's the part that very few people understand. It's the part you're not ready to hear. Maybe one day you will be ready. But not now."

"What are you saying? It's magic?"

"Do you believe in magic?" asked Hezekiah.

"Oh, yeah, sure. As a matter of fact, I just sawed some guy in half yesterday. Waved my magic wand and put him right back together. Didn't even need crazy glue. Good as new. Magic."

"I see you're a skeptic."

"Let's just say I'm skeptical. There's a difference, you know. Skeptics are skeptical about everything. I'm just skeptical about things that don't exist. Like magic."

"It's all right. I was once skeptical myself. Then I learned."

"What do you know about magic? You're a lawyer."

"No better person to know about magic than a lawyer. Magic is rooted in laws."

"Yeah, right."

"It's true," said Hezekiah. "Magic is nothing more than the knowledge of some very special laws of nature. I'm talking about laws that scientists could never understand."

"Why couldn't they?"

"Because scientists are trained to think too rigidly. They want to be able to test the laws of magic the way they test the law of gravity. Well, I'm sorry, folks: If you want to understand magic, you can't just sit under a tree waiting for an apple to fall on your head. You have to think like a lawyer. We understand better than anyone that laws are fluid."

"Laws of magic, huh? That must be the most popular course in college. Right up there with Fairy Godmothers 101."

Again, Hezekiah smiled. "You're definitely not ready for the whole leaphole enchilada."

"You're definitely right."

"But you're in luck, my boy. Leapholes work whether you believe in magic or not."

"Thanks to the computer," said Ryan, still skeptical.

"If that makes you feel more comfortable, then sure. It's the computer. Or is it magic? Only the members of the Society know for sure. The good news for you is that it doesn't matter.

You get to go along for the ride and decide for yourself. Ready?"

"Sure," said Ryan.

"Good. Let's give it a go."

"You mean we do it right here?"

"Yes, of course."

"But you said we need a staging area where human movements are constrained as little as possible."

"You're thinking too narrowly when I speak of human movements. Human movement includes the imagination. That makes the library a perfect staging area. Nowhere is the imagination less constrained than in a library."

Ryan studied the man's expression. Hezekiah was genuinely excited. On one level, Ryan thought this had to be a joke. But if it was a joke, Hezekiah was one heck of a good actor.

"All right," said Ryan. I'll play along. I'll go on your little computer trip."

"That's my boy," said Hezekiah. He hopped to his feet and took Ryan by the hand. "Come now. Quickly. Get ready for the journey of a lifetime!"

# 13

yan followed Hezekiah up and down the stairs in the library. Every now and then, the old man would stop, pull a book down from the shelf, and tuck it under his arm. When he had collected all the books he could carry, he looked at Ryan and said, "This way."

"Where are we going?"

He smiled and patted his stack of books. "Wherever we want."

Hezekiah led him to a conference room, and he laid the books on the table, one next to the other. It was an assortment of law books, some so old that the bindings cracked when Hezekiah opened them. Others were not quite so old. When he had each book opened to the selected page, he stepped back to make sure that everything was in order. He seemed satisfied. Then he went to a large closet in the back of the conference room and brought out a helmet. It looked a lot like the protective headgear that Ryan wore in his BMX races. It had a big plastic shell that covered the entire head. A dark reflective visor covered the face.

"You'll need to wear this," said Hezekiah. "It creates your virtual legal environment."

Ryan had seen gizmos like this in game rooms, so it made sense. "You want me to put this on now?"

"No, not yet." Hezekiah went to the other side of the room. There was a large glass jar on the very top shelf. He reached up and brought it down with great care. Gently, he placed the jar on the table amidst the open books.

"What's that?" asked Ryan.

Without saying a word, Hezekiah opened the jar and laid the lid aside. He reached inside and removed something that looked like a metal bracelet. It was just the right size to fit around a person's wrist, except that it wouldn't have been very comfortable to wear. It had a certain thickness to it, but it was perfectly flat, as if a steamroller had gone over it. If anyone tried to wear it, the edges would dig into the wrist bones.

Hezekiah held it before Ryan's eyes and said, "This is a leaphole."

"Looks more like jewelry for my baby sister's Woodkin dolls," said Ryan.

Hezekiah took aim at one of the open books on the table. He held the leaphole in his right hand, directly above the book. Then he let go. It dropped onto the open page below, landing with a thud.

Ryan's gaze was fixed on the leaphole, partly because he was curious, but mostly because Hezekiah was staring at it so intently that Ryan *had* to watch. He was expecting something exciting to happen. Instead, the leaphole just lay there, flat, like a bookmark. Finally, Ryan said, "I don't see anything happening."

"Put on your helmet," said Hezekiah.

Ryan slipped the helmet on over his head. The instant he flipped down the visor, he did a complete double take. "Wow, cool!"

"Told you," said Hezekiah.

Ryan was watching the very same leaphole, but the helmet allowed him to see something entirely different. An orange halo had formed above the leaphole. It began to swirl, slowly at first, then faster and faster. Within seconds, the printed words on the open page began to rise into the air. They were caught up in the orange swirl like a miniature hurricane. Ryan's eyes widened with amazement. As the words continued to swirl, he began to feel a pull on his body. It was as if someone was trying to draw him into the book with a giant vacuum cleaner.

"This is amazing!" shouted Ryan.

"It's just the beginning," said Hezekiah.

The swirling intensified, and the pull on Ryan's body became stronger. It took every ounce of his strength to keep his feet planted firmly on the floor. It was an unnerving sensation, the feeling of being on the verge of losing control over his own body. He was tempted to pull the helmet off, but it was as if Hezekiah could read his mind.

"Stay with it, Ryan!" he heard the old man shout.

Ryan resisted his impulse to bail out. He kept the helmet in place. The spinning orange swirl rose higher above the book. As it rose, it expanded. At first, it was no bigger than the book, itself. Then it was as large as the table. Then, in another flash of orange, the swirling took over the entire room. At that moment, Ryan felt his feet go out from under him.

"What's happening?" he shouted.

There was no reply, but somehow Ryan knew the answer. In the blink of an eye, it seemed that time was speeding past him. Ryan knew that he was moving, but it wasn't the feeling of moving from Point A to Point B in a car or a bus or even by airplane. He was moving along another plane, another dimension. He was surrounded by something. He was in some kind of tube. Not a tube of metal or glass. It was just an opening through which he could pass safely. Everything else that was out there, everything that was caught up in the orange swirl of confusion, would allow him to pass. It was exactly the way Hezekiah had promised it would be. The laws of nature had suddenly been rewritten to allow Ryan Coolidge to travel wherever he needed or wanted to go. Time was no longer a boundary.

He was entering the leaphole.

It would have been difficult for Ryan to pinpoint the exact moment, but in one inexplicable flash, the orange swirl was gone. The next thing Ryan knew, he and Hezekiah were speeding down a racetrack on the backs of thoroughbred racehorses. Flecks of mud from the clay track were flying up around them. Ryan was hanging on tightly, fearful that he might fall off. It took Ryan a minute or so to get his bearings, but he was in the middle of a tight pack of horses peeling around the final turn and entering the homestretch. The crowd in the grandstands was going wild. Jockeys in brightly colored uniforms were high in the saddles, giving their horses the whip. All except for one jockey—the one right beside Ryan. He was low in the saddle, doing nothing to encourage his horse to run faster.

"That's Guy Contrada," shouted Hezekiah.

"Who?" Ryan shouted back.

"Contrada. He's riding the fastest horse in the race."

"What in the world are we doing here?" Ryan had to shout at the top of his lungs to be heard above the thunder of horse hooves, the noise of the crowd.

"It's in the book!" shouted Hezekiah.

"What book?"

"The law book. This is *United States versus Winter*, a big federal case back in the early 1970s. Guy Contrada was riding the favorite, a thoroughbred called 'Spread The Word.' The horse was raring to go. But the jockey held back and threw the race so that his gambling buddies could make some money. 'Spread the Word' lost by twenty lengths."

It suddenly made sense to Ryan. Then again, it made no sense at all. The books were filled with cases about real people. But how in the world was Hezekiah bringing those people and those cases to life?

*Has to be the computer*, thought Ryan.

The horses crossed the finish line, Win, Place, and Show, followed by the "also-rans." Ryan and Hezekiah were somewhere in the middle. Dead last, as Hezekiah had predicted, was Spread The Word, the fastest horse in the race.

The pack began to slow down on the other side of the wire. Ryan and Hezekiah continued forward, faster and faster, sucked down another leaphole. Ryan was suddenly no longer on a horse. He was back in the tube, the orange swirl all around him.

"Where to now?" he shouted.

No answer, but in seconds Ryan was back on his feet. The landing wasn't quite so gentle this time. Ryan still needed to get used to the idea of shooting through leapholes. He was sitting in a field of grass, and he rose slowly. Again, there were grandstands all around him, and they were filled with baseball fans. Ryan turned around and saw a huge green scoreboard behind the centerfield bleachers. The sign at the top read: WRIGLEY FIELD, HOME OF THE CHICAGO CUBS. They had landed in a professional baseball field. And it was Ryan's turn at bat.

Again, it wasn't something that Ryan fully understood. Somehow, however, he knew what he was supposed to do. He grabbed a bat and headed for the batter's box. The crowd cheered. Ryan stepped into the box. Then he noticed that playing catcher—the man behind the mask at home plate—was his friend, Hezekiah.

"Easy out," said Hezekiah, mocking him.

"What are we doing here?" said Ryan.

Hezekiah pounded his catcher's mitt, then squatted behind the plate. "Mr. Wrigley—the wealthy man who makes all that famous chewing gum—used to own the Cubs. He got sued because he wouldn't put lights in the stadium for night games. He believed that baseball should only be played in the daytime, not at night."

It was late in the afternoon, and the sun was setting. Ryan glanced again at the scoreboard and noticed that the game was in the bottom of the thirteenth inning in the second game of a doubleheader. In a matter of minutes, it would be too dark to play. "A few lights would be nice," said Ryan.

"Now you sound like the people who sued old man Wrigley," said Hezekiah.

"Enough chatter," said the umpire. "Play ball!"

Ryan looked toward the pitcher's mound. A lanky ballplayer wearing a Pittsburgh Pirates uniform was staring straight at him, ready to deliver the pitch. Hezekiah gave the pitcher a signal. The pitcher shook it off. He tried another signal. Suddenly, the ball was speeding through the darkness at Ryan, easily exceeding ninety miles per hour.

Ryan swung in desperation at the screeching fastball. To his delight, the bat connected, and the ball was soaring out of the ballpark. For some reason—again, completely inexplicable—he and Hezekiah were pulled right along with it. Together, they sailed clear over the leftfield wall. An excited fan speared his glove into the air to catch the home run ball, and both Ryan and Hezekiah were sucked into the leather, disappearing from sight, back down into the tube.

They were back in the orange swirl, that cocoon of safety. But not for long. Ryan felt another jolt. A splash of Technicolor appeared before his eyes. He and Hezekiah reappeared in a colorful cartoon, in a dusty canyon in some desert.

The Roadrunner sped past them. *"Meep, meep!"*

Hezekiah and Ryan were stacked inside a cannon, like human cannon balls. A mangy looking coyote suddenly appeared, his pointy ears sticking out of his strange protective helmet.

"That's Wile E. Coyote," said Hezekiah.

"I know who it is," said Ryan. "I've seen the Roadrunner cartoons."

"Yes, but did you know that the coyote sued ACME Manufacturing Company for all those lousy gadgets that blew up in his face every time he tried to catch the Roadrunner?"

"Really?"

"Nah," said Hezekiah. "I made this one up. But it's a fun one, isn't it?"

Wile E. Coyote lit the fuse on the cannon. The whole contraption exploded in his face, sending Ryan and Hezekiah speeding through the air. They were in another leaphole that carried them across a different plane, through another orange swirl.

Finally, they landed in the back of a bus.

"Where are we?" asked Ryan.

Hezekiah was in the seat beside him. "Montgomery, Alabama. City bus number twenty-eight-fifty-seven."

Ryan looked out the window. People on the sidewalks were wearing warm overcoats, and there were Christmas decorations in the storefronts. It had to be December. Ryan spotted a license plate on a parked car. The year was 1955.

The bus stopped. Ryan watched from the rear of the bus as a black woman boarded and paid the driver. She then got off the bus and re-entered through the rear door. The bus continued down the street.

"That's Rosa Parks," whispered Hezekiah.

Ryan asked, "Why is she coming in through the back door?"

Hezekiah's voice seemed lower, sadder. "Colored people can't enter the bus through the front door. That's the law."

Ryan watched as the woman headed up the aisle and took a seat in the fifth row. Ryan also noticed that everyone in the first four rows was white. Everyone in the fifth row and farther back was black.

The bus stopped again. The front of the bus (the white section) was now full, nowhere to sit. A white passenger boarded the bus. He walked up to Rosa, who was seated in the fifth row, and demanded that the black woman give up her seat and move farther back in the bus.

Ryan asked, "What's going on?"

Hezekiah said, "Rosa is breaking the law. Colored people have to give up their seat and move farther back in the bus if a white person has no place to sit."

"What the heck kind of law is that?" said Ryan.

"It's 1955, Ryan. That was the law in Montgomery, Alabama."

Rosa shook her head and refused to move. The white passenger complained to the driver. He stopped the bus and walked down the aisle to the fifth row.

"Ma'am, I have to ask you to get up and move."

Again, Rosa refused. The driver seemed exasperated. He looked at Rosa and said, "Well, I'm going to have you arrested."

Rosa looked at him and said, "You may go on and do so."

The driver went back to the front of the bus, got on the radio, and called for police backup. After a few minutes, a police car pulled up alongside the bus. Two officers came aboard, and the driver explained what had happened. The police came down the aisle.

"They're actually taking her to jail?" said Ryan.

"I told you, Ryan. The law doesn't always prevent bad things from happening to good people."

Again, Ryan thought of his own father in jail, but he was too taken aback by the arrest of Rosa Parks to think about his own situation for very long. One of the police officers had a set of handcuffs with him, and those rings of metal suddenly reminded Ryan of the leapholes he had seen in Hezekiah's jar. Both resembled flat, uncomfortable, metal bracelets. Ryan wasn't sure if the police were going to cuff Rosa or not, but as the light reflected off those shiny metal circles, the swirling sensation resumed. It was as if the leaphole had reemerged before Ryan's eyes. The eye of the miniature hurricane was centered around those handcuffs dangling from the police officer's belt. In a matter of seconds, the spinning was more intense than ever. Ryan had the sensation of being pulled from his seat, pulled through the bus, sucked out the door. His body was turned in such a way that he was facing backwards, yet he could feel the thrust of forward motion. All was a blur, yet he knew that he was headed in the right direction. The power of the leaphole was taking him back to the place where he belonged, back to a place he knew well.

The swirling stopped. His surroundings came into focus. Ryan and Hezekiah bounced onto the floor of Hezekiah's law library.

Ryan pulled off his helmet and looked at Hezekiah with complete disbelief. "That was amazing!"

"You liked that, did you?"

"Totally. This helmet is so cool." Ryan inspected it briefly, then looked quizzically at Hezekiah. "But where's your helmet?"

"I don't need one."

"How come I do and you don't?"

"You don't need one either."

"You're still trying to sell me on that idea of legal magic, aren't you? The secret Society."

"I'm not selling anything, Ryan. When you're ready to step beyond the virtual legal environment of a computer, you will. For now, suit yourself. Grab your helmet, and let's go."

"Where to this time? Do I get to pick?"

Hezekiah shook his head. "Leapholes are not all fun and games. They're not just joyrides or tools to help satisfy our idle curiosity."

"I know, I get it. It's like you said before, these books aren't just a bunch of dusty old pages. These were all real people with real problems."

"And the best lawyers understand people and their problems. No better way to understand a case than with a leaphole."

Ryan was really starting to like Hezekiah, but the old man was suddenly very serious. "Now it's time to prepare for your case," said Hezekiah.

"So, we have to go . . . where?"

"Back to the *William Brown*."

"You mean that ship that sank when it hit the iceberg? The case that got you all wet?"

Hezekiah nodded. "For you, that is the most important case in all these books. The judge will use that case to decide whether you are guilty or innocent."

"How can an old case about a sinking ship help the judge decide whether I'm responsible for those people who died from a disease like BODS?"

"You'll understand when we get there." Hezekiah went to the closet and draped a heavy black cloak around his shoulders. It was the kind of winter garment that Ryan would have expected to see on a man from the nineteenth century. Then Hezekiah found a long wool coat and gave it to Ryan. "Better wear this," he said. "Nighttime in the North Atlantic isn't exactly Miami Beach."

Ryan still didn't believe that they were actually going anywhere. But he pulled on the coat, just in case. It fit perfectly.

"Are you ready?" said Hezekiah.

Ryan took a deep breath and strapped on his VLE helmet. "Ready."

"Then off we go."

# 14

yan landed hard on the wooden deck of a ship. A cold wind was howling, and the icy spray of the North Atlantic broke over the rail. On the opposite side of the deck, men and women were screaming and shouting. They ran in every direction, eyes filled with terror. Almost immediately, Ryan was chilled to the core, shivering in the night air.

"Look out!" someone shouted from above.

Ryan quickly rolled to his left. Hezekiah came crashing down on the deck beside him. If Ryan hadn't moved out of the way, he would have been flattened by the old man.

Ryan said, "Do you have to make these landings so rough?"

"How else am I going to convince you that this is real?"

"It's not real. You said it yourself. It's a virtual legal environment."

"Sure it is," said Hezekiah.

Another wave broke over the bow, soaking Ryan and Hezekiah with sea water.

"That was *virtually* freezing," said Hezekiah.

Ryan rose to his feet, shaking water from his coat. He was about to say something, then stopped short at the sight of a ring-shaped life preserver hanging on the rail directly in front of him. Hezekiah had warned Ryan about their destination. Still, it gave him goose bumps to see the ship's name printed in bold black letters on the white life preserver.

"The *William Brown*," said Ryan, reading aloud. It was as if the full ramifications of their journey had finally set in. "We're on a doomed ship."

"Yes, we are," said Hezekiah. "In less than two hours, this vessel will be resting on the bottom of the Atlantic Ocean."

Ryan and Hezekiah exchanged a look of concern, but a shrill scream from the other side of the ship sent them scampering to see what was the matter. Ryan went first, followed by Hezekiah.

The *William Brown* was nothing like the great iron ocean liners of the later steamship era. With three tall masts, large canvas sails, and a long wooden hull, it was fairly typical of the ocean-crossing ships that sailed in the 1840s. Ryan and Hezekiah climbed over boxes, barrels, and other cargo that was strapped to the deck. Above them, the tattered remains of a huge canvas sail flapped in the windstorm like an old shredded bed sheet. The ship was in peril, completely at the storm's mercy as it rolled from one great ocean swell to the next. At times, Ryan could barely stand on his own two feet against the northeasterly gusts. If the wind didn't soon tear away what little was left of the main sail, Ryan feared that the next great gust might take the entire mast down. They had to cross the deck with caution. The planks were slick with foamy sea water. Rain and sleet were coming down harder by the minute. It was like sliding down an icy hill, as the ship was listing badly to the port side. Clearly, the hull had already taken on too much seawater.

Although it was only a short distance, it seemed to take them a very long time to reach the starboard side of the ship. Perhaps a hundred people were already there ahead of them.

They were pushing and shoving, each one trying to out-shout the other. Another huge wave slammed across the bow. Cold, salty water drenched the crowd. It only fueled the sense of panic.

"Order! We must keep order!" a man shouted above the ruckus.

Three young sailors armed with clubs pushed back against the advancing mob. The crew and some volunteers were trying desperately to hoist a lifeboat into position. It was the sailors' job to keep the most unruly passengers at bay.

"Get back, mates!" another sailor shouted. He was speaking to Ryan and Hezekiah, which Ryan didn't realize until the sailor shoved him hard against the wall.

"What happened?" asked Ryan.

"We've hit an iceberg," said the sailor. "The captain has given the order to abandon ship."

"But where do we go?" said Ryan.

"Same place we're all going, mate. To meet our Maker.'

Ryan felt as if the wind had been knocked out of him, but it was just the weight of the man's words.

"Heave ho!" the sailor shouted. The strongest volunteers had broken into two groups, each of them pulling on a length of thick rope. The pulleys above them creaked and swayed. Slowly, the wooden lifeboat inched downward from its davits. As it neared the deck, the crowd surged forward. It didn't take a genius to see that this lifeboat wasn't nearly large enough to carry everyone to safety. Many would be left behind. It seemed that everyone was willing to fight to be among the lucky few survivors.

The men pulled harder on the ropes. Children clung to their mothers. Sailors moved at the command of their officers. The wind continued to howl. The night air seemed to turn even colder, if that was possible. Ryan wasn't dressed for such brutal weather, and neither were the rest of the passengers. The women were wearing ankle-length dresses, and the men wore heavy coats and capes. The fashion was clearly of another era, which was no surprise. This was, after all, the mid-nineteenth century.

"Grab a line, mates!" a sailor shouted.

Ryan and Hezekiah took hold of the line. They replaced two other men whose hands were bloodied with rope burns. About a dozen volunteers were on their team. At the lead sailor's command, they pulled and released, pulled and released, slowly lowering the lifeboat. It was hovering about five feet above the deck when passengers started climbing up the rail. They grabbed at the ropes and even jumped on top of other passengers. Every last one of them was desperately looking for any possible route to secure a precious place in the lifeboat.

"Order, order!" a sailor shouted. But it was to no avail. In a matter of seconds the situation had turned into utter chaos. The lifeboat was nearly filled before it could even be lowered into position for boarding. Ryan felt the strain on the rope in his hands. With the added weight of passengers, there weren't enough men to secure the boat.

"We can't hold on much longer!" Ryan shouted.

The crowd ignored him. Frightened passengers forced their way forward. There were men as well as women, and even some crying children who had been separated from their parents. They all knew the choices: Get on a lifeboat, or go down with the ship.

"It's overloaded!" someone warned.

Just as those words were spoken, the rope snapped. The main pulley gave way. The lifeboat came crashing down onto the deck. People were screaming. All were frightened. Many were injured, some severely, crushed beneath the weight of the fallen lifeboat.

"Help! Help us, please!"

The men dropped their ropes and ran to the lifeboat. Some tried to help the injured, but many simply fought for their own seat on the boat. The most badly hurt, the ones unable to pick themselves up and slide to safety, were trampled in the human stampede.

"Have you all gone mad?" a sailor shouted. "Stop, stop, I say!"

"Let's get out of here," said Hezekiah.

"But what about these people?" said Ryan.

"We can't save them."

"But—"

"Don't argue with me, Ryan. You said it yourself: This ship is doomed. Come on, now. Let's get to another lifeboat."

It was difficult, but Ryan forced himself to turn away from the crowd and follow Hezekiah. The deck was sloped even more dangerously than before. Ryan had to brace himself against the rail to keep from sliding into the roaring ocean below. Finally, with the wind battering their faces, Ryan spotted another crowd of passengers closer to the stern. The lifeboat had already been lowered into position. Passengers were boarding. The process wasn't exactly calm, but it was more orderly than at the other station. A man was standing at the bow of the lifeboat. From the looks of his uniform, he appeared to be the ship's captain. Perhaps that accounted for the lack of chaos. The boat appeared to be fully loaded. The captain was signaling to his crew to begin lowering them.

"Just two more!" the sailor shouted. "Room for just two more passengers!"

Hezekiah pushed Ryan forward and shouted, "Here, sir! This one is just a boy!"

The sailor took a close look at Ryan, saw his youth, and then waved him forward. "Bring him aboard."

Another sailor grabbed Ryan by the shoulders and lifted him into the boat. Ryan resisted and shouted, "Not without my friend!"

"Sorry, lad," said the sailor. "No room for old men."

"I'm not going without him!" said Ryan as he broke free from his grasp.

"Have it your way, lad. Stay behind and drown."

Another sailor intervened. He shoved both Ryan and Hezekiah onto the lifeboat. "It makes no difference," he said to his fellow crewman. "You think that little lifeboat has a chance in these seas? All of us, young and old—we're all going to the bottom!"

Ryan and Hezekiah squeezed in between two passengers in the boat. At the captain's command, the sailors aboard ship lowered them toward the ocean. Ryan watched with a heavy heart as the other screaming passengers begged for their lives.

"Please, sir!"

"Take my granddaughter, captain!"

"Make room for just one more, please. Don't leave us here to drown!"

Their pleas were in vain. The lifeboat continued its descent. Soon, the screaming and begging had completely given way to the sound of the lifeboat splashing into the ocean. The oarsmen untied the ropes that tethered the lifeboat to the ship. The moment they were adrift, the lifeboat started to roll from side to side. It was pounded by seas as high as twelve feet.

Ryan could hardly move. Hezekiah was pressed against his left side. The woman on his right was sitting so close that Ryan couldn't move his arm. There was some shifting and stirring among the passengers as the oarsmen maneuvered into position and placed the oars in the locks. Slowly, they began to row away from the ship. The rain had finally stopped, and there was a momentary break in the clouds. In the moonlight, Ryan could see just how much trouble the *William Brown* was in. Half of the ship was under water. Some passengers had already slid into the ocean, screaming and splashing in the freezing water. Ryan spotted another lifeboat some distance away, but it was hard to tell how many had finally made it to safety.

"So many left behind," a man said sadly.

"Poor souls," said the woman next to Ryan.

A huge wave smashed into their boat and drenched all the passengers. The rain was letting up, but the wind was blowing even harder.

"We'll be joining our friends in the icy depths soon enough," said the oarsman.

The oarsman pulled with all his strength, but the powerful seas seemed to be winning the struggle. The moon again disappeared behind the clouds. The rain returned. The full fury of the storm was upon them once again. Punishing waves slammed without mercy against the side of their little boat. Ryan gripped the person next to him. One more wave like the last one might send them all tumbling overboard. On impulse, he took one last look over his shoulder.

There was only darkness in the distance. All signs of the *William Brown* had faded from sight.

The captain stood tall at the bow of the lifeboat. His cape flapped in the breeze as the rain pelted his face. He cupped his hand around his mouth like a megaphone and shouted, "We're overloaded!"

Another wave splashed over the side. The boat was rocking and taking on seawater.

"I say, there are too many aboard!" cried the captain.

A monstrous wave slammed the boat and completely washed over them. It was too dark and crowded for Ryan to be able to see his feet, but he could feel the cold water in the bottom of the boat. It was up over his ankles. Yet another wave hit them, and the boat took on more water.

"The plug is out!" a sailor shouted.

The plug was for a small drain in the hull. Normally, it was opened only when the boat was resting on board ship. A pulled plug at sea meant the boat was taking on water.

"Someone, quick, find the plug!"

The water had risen to Ryan's mid-shin.

"Lord, have mercy! We're all going to drown!"

One of the crew stuffed a rag in the hole, and the water stopped rising. The boat, however, was nearly swamped. The wind was whistling. Passengers were bailing water with their bare hands. Frantically they fought to keep the lifeboat from sinking. Several women were crying. A young child near Ryan was shivering and turning purple.

The captain was on his feet again. "Crew, what's the head count?"

The oarsman shouted, "We are a dozen too many, sir!"

"Then twelve must go!" the captain shot back.

Ryan looked at Hezekiah and whispered, "Go *where*?"

The captain stood at the bow and said, "Everyone, listen to me. There are twelve of us too many on this boat. If we do not reduce our load, we all shall perish. Do I have any volunteers? Is anyone willing to abandon this boat and save the rest of us?"

The passengers glanced nervously at one another. No one said a word. Perhaps they were too cold and wet to speak. Perhaps they all hoped to make themselves unnoticeable to the captain.

A black wave seemed to rise out of nowhere. Its foamy whitecap hit the captain squarely in the chest. He was nearly knocked overboard, but he managed to hold on. The water level in the boat had risen above Ryan's knees.

"You leave me no choice," shouted the captain. "We'll draw lots. The winners will stay. The losers must go. It's the only way, mates."

The captain directed two of his crewmen to come forward. Then he reached across his cape and tore off one of the brass buttons. He turned his back to the passengers, and then he wheeled to face them. His arms were extended away from his body. Both of his hands were clenched into a tight fist. He stepped toward the first row of passengers, keeping his crewmen at his side.

The captain looked at the man in the first seat and said, "Choose one!"

"What?" the man said.

"This is the way we shall proceed. Choose a hand. Find the button, and you stay. Choose the hand without the button, and may God have mercy on our souls."

"I refuse," said the man.

"Then you shall be the first to go overboard!"

The crewmen grabbed the man by the shoulders and lifted him to his feet. The man struggled and said, "All right, all right! I'll choose."

The crewmen released him. The man was shaking, Ryan noticed, and with good reason. He was literally making a life or death decision, just as Ryan and the others had been forced to do in the disease control center. It was suddenly clear to Ryan why the *William Brown* was so important to his own trial.

The man pointed nervously to the captain's right hand. "I choose that one, sir."

The captain opened his hand. To the man's great relief, there, in the captain's palm, was the brass button.

"You may stay," said the captain.

The man returned to his seat. The captain again turned away

to hide the button. Then he presented the next passenger with the same unthinkable decision. "Choose," said the captain.

The man stared at the captain's fists. Rivulets of rainwater ran down the man's face. Finally, he pointed and said, "I choose the left."

The captain opened his fist. It was empty. No button.

"Over you go!" the captain shouted.

"No!"

The crewmen grabbed him. The man squirmed in their arms, but the sailors were too strong.

"Someone, help me!" the man shouted. No one moved. The crew heaved him overboard, and the man soared into the air, arms flailing. Ryan looked away, but he heard the splash as the unlucky man met his fate.

"This is sheer madness," a woman behind him whispered.

"It's the only way," another man replied. "Or we'll all go down."

The captain continued down the row, stopping next at an old woman. He gave her the same choice. She made the correct one. He moved to the next passenger. "I choose the left, sir." Wrong choice.

"Over you go!"

The captain and his two crewmen moved methodically through the lifeboat, covering each row of passengers. Everyone was given the same chance. Everyone played by the same rules. The captain treated everyone the same, giving them the same choice. Right or left? Live or die? There were winners, and there were losers. Ryan turned and glanced at the surging seas behind the lifeboat. The losers had already disappeared into the black, churning ocean.

Finally, the captain was standing before Ryan.

"Your turn, son," said the captain.

Ryan took a hard look at the captain's face. His cheeks were red and raw from the winter storm, but there was no emotion in the captain's eyes. He had the self-assured and determined expression of a man who was simply doing his job. He extended his closed fists away from his body, looked at Ryan, and said, "Choose one."

Ryan stared at his choices. Right or left? He tried to make up his mind, but in his gut he felt nothing but revulsion for the whole process. It was the same feeling he'd had back in the hospital. No one had the right to choose who lives or dies.

"This is so wrong," said Ryan.

"Choose one, or you go overboard!"

The crewmen were at the ready, poised to pitch Ryan overboard if he refused to cooperate. It seemed like a contradiction, but Ryan had no choice but to make a choice.

"I choose the right," said Ryan.

The captain breathed a heavy sigh. Ryan couldn't tell if it was a sigh of relief or a sigh of pity. Slowly, the captain opened his right fist and said, "I'm sorry, son."

His hand was empty. Ryan's heart sank.

"Crew," said the captain. "You know what to do."

"Please, no," said Ryan.

The sailors grabbed him and lifted him from his seat.

"Hezekiah!" Ryan shouted.

One of the sailors grabbed Ryan's arm. The other grabbed his ankles. Ryan kicked and squirmed, but the crewmen were too strong. He couldn't believe this was happening.

"It's okay, Ryan," said Hezekiah. "Virtual legal environment, remember?"

His words did nothing to put Ryan at ease. Ryan was a skeptic when it came to leapholes, no doubt about it. But this was unlike anything he'd ever seen any computer ever do. This felt too real. The adrenaline rushing through his body was real.

The pounding of his heart was real. The fear that cut to his core was real.

"Hezekiah, stop this right now!"

"I can't stop it!" said Hezekiah.

The lucky survivors ducked out of the way as the crew carried Ryan above a row of passengers. They were just a few steps away from the side of the lifeboat.

"Hezekiah!" he shouted, kicking desperately as each word left his lips: "DON'T . . . LET . . . THIS . . . HAPPEN!"

"Find the leaphole, Ryan. Just find the leaphole!"

Ryan tried to understand what Hezekiah was saying, but he had no idea what he meant. *Find the leaphole? What leaphole?* Hezekiah had the leapholes in his jar back in his office.

The crewmen raised Ryan up over their heads. Ryan gave one last effort to wrest himself free, but it was pointless. On the count of three, the sailors hurled Ryan over the side.

Ryan was suddenly airborne, caught in the cold north wind. For a moment, he felt as if he were a bird soaring above the ocean. But the sensation of flying soon gave way to the terrifying feeling of falling.

"Hezekiah!" he called out.

The old lawyer grabbed a ring-shaped life preserver from the back of the boat. It was identical to the one Ryan had spotted on board ship. It was white with black letters that spelled out the ship's name, *The William Brown.*

A sailor tried to snatch the life preserver away from him. "That's for the winners, not the losers."

"Nonsense," said Hezekiah. He broke free and heaved the life preserver overboard. It soared through the air like a Frisbee and splashed into the crest of a powerful wave. It came to rest on the surface—exactly where Ryan was about to land.

All of this happened in a matter of seconds, but for Ryan it seemed that the world had switched to slow motion. The life preserver sailing through the air. The white ring coming to rest below him. And Hezekiah's words ringing in his ears: *Find the leaphole, Ryan!*

Suddenly, the life preserver didn't look like a life preserver anymore. Instead of bobbing in the water, it began to turn clockwise. The turning became faster. Soon, it was a swirl—a swirl so large and so swift that the water around it began to turn as well. In the blink of an eye, the swirl was a tight whirlpool.

Ryan tried to change his course and avoid the whirlpool. But it was as if some force had grabbed him in mid air and was pulling him into a hole. He landed feet first. A powerful suction immediately took hold of his entire body, pulling down, down, down, into deep cold water.

Ryan didn't feel cold. Or wet. He knew he was underwater, or at least he knew that he was *supposed to be* underwater. Around him there was only darkness, but there was a light above. It was like staring up at the night sky through a telescope.

The next thing he saw was a pair of canvas basketball shoes plunging through the hole. It startled him at first. Then he recalled his first few moments in Hezekiah's office, when he had been surprised to see the old man dressed in a business suit and wearing basketball shoes. The same shoes were coming toward Ryan now. Hezekiah came right along with them.

Ryan couldn't speak. Everything around him was a blur. The feeling was exactly like the sensation he'd felt when he and Hezekiah had traveled from his office to the race track, to Wrigley Field, and to that bus in Alabama. Hezekiah was with him. They were speeding through a strange tube of some sort.

They were headed straight down another leaphole.

# 15

**W**hen Ryan and Hezekiah finally landed on their feet, they were standing in a long hallway with soaring, cathedral-style ceilings. Tall columns of fluted granite supported sweeping stone arches. The floors were polished marble, and the gloss was so high that Ryan could almost see his own reflection.

Ryan removed his VLE helmet. His clothes were soaking wet. "Where are we?" he asked.

Hezekiah took him by the arm. "Come with me. There's not a minute to spare."

They walked quickly down the impressive corridor to a set of double brass doors. The sign on the door read, SOCIETY MEMBERS ONLY.

"What society?" said Ryan.

"Never mind that," said Hezekiah. "You're not a member. Quiet now. I could get in big trouble for bringing you here." Hezekiah pulled a key from his pocket and unlocked the doors. The heavy door opened slowly. Hezekiah pushed Ryan inside. He took him straight to a locker with an old oak door that bore the name HEZEKIAH. The old man opened it and removed a black robe. It reminded Ryan of a graduation gown.

"Put this on," he told Ryan.

"Why?"

"Just do as I say. We're going to be late!"

"Late for what?"

"There's no time to explain. Just put on the robe."

Ryan removed his wet clothing and pulled the robe over his head. It was a heavy garment made of very fine cloth. Hezekiah helped him with the clasps in back. Then the old lawyer pulled another black robe out of the closet for himself.

"How do I look?" said Ryan.

"No sillier than I, I'm sure."

They shared a quick smile, and then Hezekiah turned serious. "We must go now. Follow me. And hurry."

Hezekiah led the way. They exited through the same set of double brass doors. At the long hallway, however, they headed in a different direction. Ryan almost had to run to keep up with Hezekiah. Finally, they stopped at another set of brass doors at the other end of the hallway. These doors were even bigger and more impressive than the other set.

"What is this place?" asked Ryan.

"The Court of Justice."

"Why are we here?"

"For you, of course."

"Me?"

"Yes. Your trial is about to begin."

Ryan gasped. "My trial! But—"

Before he could finish, Hezekiah pulled him aside, shushing him. "You're ready, Ryan. Trust me. Trust me more than your father and mother did."

Ryan scrunched his face, confused. "What are you talking about?"

"I've been waiting for the right moment to tell you this, but I don't think the right time will ever come. So here goes. I wasn't exactly appointed out of the blue to be your lawyer."

"What was it—magic?" he said, smirking.

"I have good sources at the Court of International Justice. When I heard you were in trouble with the law, I immediately volunteered to represent you."

"Why?"

"I was your father's lawyer."

Ryan's mouth opened, but the words were slow to come. "No you weren't. I saw his lawyer in the courthouse."

"That was his *new* lawyer. Your parents hired me first, but they fired me after a couple of weeks."

"They fired you? Why?"

"Your mother thought I was too old. Your father thought I was too crazy, basketball shoes and all that. So they dismissed me."

"So, you were willing to defend my dad? I guess you aren't one of those lawyers who loses sleep over defending the guilty, huh?"

"You think your father was guilty, Ryan?"

"Well, *DUH!* I was in the courtroom when he pleaded guilty."

"That doesn't mean he was guilty. It's just like someone who enters a plea of 'not guilty.' That doesn't mean they're innocent."

"What does it mean?"

"Courtrooms are as much about proof as they are about truth, Ryan. When people stand up in court and say, 'I'm not guilty,' sometimes what they're really saying is that the prosecutor just doesn't have enough evidence to prove them guilty. Do you understand?"

"I think so. It's like the time I was in a crowded elevator with my friend Sweaty Colletti. Sweaty let out a real silent but deadly one. Everyone was looking around, trying to figure out who was the silent stink bomber. When I told Sweaty I knew it was him, he didn't deny it. He just laughed and said 'Prove it.'"

"Crude," said Hezkiah, wincing, "but you appear to have grasped the concept. A plea of not guilty is like saying 'Prove it.'"

"But a man who pleads guilty, like my father, is a totally different situation. What could he possibly be saying other than 'I admit it: I did it.'"

"Usually he is saying, 'Yes, I did it.' But maybe once in a while there are other things involved."

"Like what?"

"I can't talk about that, Ryan. Even though your father fired me, I was still his lawyer for a period of time. Everything a lawyer and his client talk about is completely confidential. I can't discuss it with anyone. Not even you."

"But you're the one who started this. You can't just open this box and then slam it shut. Are you saying my father pleaded guilty to something he didn't do?"

The old man considered it, but he was clearly struggling. "I can tell you this much, Ryan. Had I remained his attorney, I would have advised him to plead not guilty."

"Is that because he was innocent? Or because you thought the prosecutor just didn't have enough evidence to *prove* that he was guilty?"

"Like I said, Ryan. That's all I can tell you."

They locked eyes, but it was clear to Ryan that Hezekiah would never say another word about it.

"Enough about your father," said Hezekiah. "Let's deal with your case now. Are you ready, my boy?"

"Ready as I'll ever be, I suppose."

"Great. Let's go."

# 16

**H**ezekiah opened the door and guided his client inside. Ryan was immediately in awe of the most amazing courtroom he'd ever seen. The ceilings were at least twenty-five-feet high, and they were coffered with elaborately carved woodwork. There was a row of floor-to-ceiling windows on either side of the courtroom. Beyond several rows of public seating was the judge's bench. It was as big as a house, made of dark mahogany. The judge was presiding over the courtroom in his high-back leather chair. His black robe was similar to the ones Ryan and Hezekiah were wearing, except that he had some kind of embroidery around the collar, which seemed to identify him as a judge. He looked even older than Hezekiah, probably because of the wig. It was powder white, with row after row of tight curls that hung down to his shoulders. It reminded Ryan of the old horsehair wigs that men wore in Early-American history books.

The judge was scowling, which Ryan did not take as a good sign.

"You're late, Hezekiah," the judge said in a gravely old voice.

"My apologies, Your Honor. My client and I were . . ." He seemed at a loss for the proper explanation.

"Stuck in traffic?" the judge suggested.

"Yes," said Hezekiah. "You might say that."

"Come forward, and make quick of it. As you can see, we are quite ready to proceed."

"Yes, Your Honor."

Hezekiah nudged Ryan forward. Side-by-side, they walked up the center aisle. They were headed toward what lawyers called "the well" of the courtroom, which was the open area directly in front of the judge's bench. Ryan remembered that from the time his father was arrested. His mother had told him that it was sometimes helpful to think of the courtroom as a stage where the lawyers and witnesses performed. The judge was like a director who made sure that everything went smoothly and fairly. The audience, of course, was the jury, which was positioned off to one side. The analogy wasn't perfect, however. In showbiz, they always said that "The show must go on." In the case of Ryan's father, there was never any "show." He had pleaded guilty to the crime and was sentenced to jail without a trial. From that day forward, he somehow expected Ryan to believe that he was innocent.

*Makes no sense*, thought Ryan. Not even after what Hezekiah had just told him in the hallway.

The bang of the judge's gavel startled Ryan. This was no time to think about his father. He had his own trial to worry about.

Ryan took a seat at the table beside his lawyer. They were on the right side of "the well," an area commonly reserved for the defendant and his lawyer. To their left was another mahogany table, and the prosecuting attorney was seated behind it. She was easily young enough to be Hezekiah's granddaughter. She showed little expression as Ryan and Hezekiah settled into their chairs. Ryan tried to avoid looking at her. It was traditional that the prosecutor sat near the jury, and this courtroom was no exception. Just on the other side of the prosecutor, to the far left of the well, was the jury box. Twelve people had been selected to sit in judgment of Ryan. Ryan counted seven women and five men. They watched impassively as Ryan and Hezekiah gave them a casual once-over.

The judge peered out over the top of his wire-rimmed spectacles and said, "Good morning, everyone."

"Good morning," the lawyers replied. Ryan and the jurors were silent.

The judge said, "We are here today on the criminal case against one Ryan Coolidge. Mr. Coolidge, before we begin, allow me to read the charges against you, which are serious indeed. You are charged with four separate counts of manslaughter. It is alleged that six human beings were exposed to the deadly BODS virus. There was enough vaccine to save only five. Those six persons, yourself included, agreed to cast lots to determine which five would receive the vaccine. The lots were cast. Then you refused to abide by the agreement and insisted that it be shared among all six."

Hezekiah rose and said, "Judge, I think it is fair to point out that Mr. Coolidge was not the loser. He refused to abide by the results out of principle, not sour grapes."

The judge cast an angry glare. "Hezekiah, you will have your turn to dispute the evidence. I am simply reading the charges."

"My apologies, Your Honor." Hezekiah returned to his seat.

The judge continued, "As I was saying, it is alleged that

the defendant refused to abide by the agreement. He took the five vaccines and tried to stretch them into six. It is alleged that, as a result, the vaccines became ineffective. Four of the six persons died. It is further alleged that if Mr. Coolidge had abided by the agreement, those four persons never would have died."

The judge rubbed his nose and laid the printed indictment aside. "Those are the charges. How do you plead, young man?"

With a little prodding from his lawyer, Ryan rose and said, "Not guilty, Your Honor."

"Then we shall proceed to trial. Ms. Baldwin, is the prosecution ready?"

The young prosecutor rose and nodded respectfully. "We are, Your Honor."

"Is the defense ready?"

Ryan took a breath. He'd never done this before, so he wasn't sure what it felt like to be "ready." But he knew that the time for research and preparation had ended. Ready or not, the trial was going to begin.

"Ready, Your Honor," said Hezekiah.

"Splendid," said the judge. "We will begin with opening statements. The prosecution shall have the first opportunity to state its case to the jury. We will then follow with a statement from the defense. Ms. Baldwin, if you please."

"Thank you, Your Honor."

The prosecutor seemed very sure of herself as she approached the jury. She wore a powdered wig, just like the judge, but she somehow managed to look distinguished and presentable in it, not silly in the least. She stopped a few feet before the jury, and even before she opened her mouth, she seemed to command their respect. The trial hadn't even begun, and already Ryan was worried sick.

"Ladies and gentlemen of the jury," she said in a voice that filled the cavernous courtroom. "To understand what Ryan Coolidge did wrong, you need only look at the case of the *William Brown.*

"It is an old case, a reliable legal precedent. On the nineteenth day of April, in the year 1841, the American ship *William Brown* hit an iceberg in the North Atlantic while en route from Liverpool to Philadelphia. It was loaded with Irish and Scottish emigrants. Roughly half the passengers went down with the ship. The rest piled into two lifeboats. One was so badly overloaded that it began to sink. Faced with crashing waves and a driving rainstorm, the captain knew that if he didn't do something to lighten the load, they all would drown. It may have been his intention to cast lots to determine who should go overboard. We don't know for sure. But we do know that the system broke down. The crew started throwing passengers overboard without casting lots. In all, fourteen men were tossed into the sea and died."

Ryan was momentarily confused by the prosecutor's version of events. Then he realized that the system of casting lots must have broken down *after* he was thrown overboard.

The prosecutor stepped closer to the jurors. "When the survivors were rescued, a crewman was brought before the court on criminal charges. The prosecution argued that the crew had no right to throw anyone overboard. The court agreed, and the crewman was found guilty. The crime, however, was not in throwing passengers overboard. It was in *the way* the crew had done it. They failed to abide by a system of casting lots. I'll read you the words of the very learned judge in that case: 'When the selection has been made by lots, the victim yields to his fate. If he resists, force may be employed to coerce his submission.'"

Ryan felt butterflies in his stomach. The prosecutor spoke so eloquently, so forcefully, seeming to have the jury in the palm of her hand.

She continued, "The point here, ladies and gentlemen of the jury, is simple. Ryan Coolidge was in the Infectious Disease Control Center with five other people. All of them had been exposed to the deadly BODS virus. The doctors had enough vaccine to save five. The group agreed to select the survivors by lot. As the very wise judge stated in the old case of the *William Brown*, 'when the selection has been made by lots, the victim yields to his fate.' Ryan Coolidge broke that law when he refused to enforce the results of the lots that had been drawn. He broke the law when he tried to turn five vaccines into six. Because he broke the law, four people are now dead. I ask you, therefore, to find Ryan Coolidge guilty of manslaughter."

Ryan felt numb. Having heard those words from the prosecutor's lips, he couldn't imagine what his own lawyer might say in his defense. He had, of course, understood the significance of his travels to the *William Brown* with Hezekiah. The point had been impressed upon him as soon as the captain ordered the passengers to cast lots. From that moment forward, he had known that this old case was the entire basis for the charges against him.

Only now, however, seated in a court of law, did the full weight of the potential consequences come crashing down upon him. He still believed that he had done nothing wrong. Yet he couldn't possibly see how a jury could acquit him. He had done exactly what the prosecutor had accused him of doing. He refused to accept the results of the lots they had agreed to cast.

The prosecutor returned to her seat. The judge looked across the courtroom, his gaze coming to rest on Ryan's lawyer.

"Hezekiah?" the judge said in a stern voice. "What statement do you wish to make for the defense?"

"None, Your Honor."

Ryan did a double take. He was certain that his lawyer had misspoken.

"Excuse me?" said the judge. He, too, seemed confused.

Hezekiah glanced at Ryan, then looked back at the judge. "I intend to let Mr. Coolidge present his own case."

Ryan nearly gasped. He didn't want to argue his own case. Surely he was no match for the skilled prosecutor. But Hezekiah seemed to be entirely serious.

"A bit unorthodox," said the judge. "But certainly not against the rules. Mr. Coolidge, you may address the jury."

Ryan rose slowly and faced the jury. He felt certain that his movement was stiff and amateurish compared to the prosecutor's glide.

Hezekiah whispered, "Move closer to the jury, Ryan."

Hezekiah gave him a nudge of encouragement, but Ryan's feet wouldn't move. He spoke between clenched teeth and said quietly, "What the heck am I supposed to say?"

"Say what you felt when you were in that hospital."

Ryan still didn't move, and it seemed to take a moment for Hezekiah's wisdom to sink in. But finally, it did. It was as if a warm blanket had suddenly wrapped around him. It took away his goose bumps and made him feel at ease. Hezekiah's advice made such good sense. *Say what you felt when you were in that hospital.*

Ryan approached the jury slowly. He still wasn't sure what he was going to say. But he remembered clearly how he felt when they had decided to cast lots. He remembered the look on Kaylee's face when she learned that she was the loser— when she learned that her fate was to die as a teenager. No, he didn't know what he was going to say. But, somehow, he knew where to find the words. Hezekiah had shown him the way.

Ryan looked straight at the jurors and spoke from the heart.

"The prosecutor is right," said Ryan. "We did cast lots. And I refused to go along with it. But why did I do that? The reason is simple. We all know right from wrong. This *felt* wrong. I know what the judge in that old case of the *William Brown* said. But was that old judge sitting in that lifeboat with those passengers? Did he look into the eyes of the people who were thrown overboard? Was he there in that disease control center with me? Did he look into the eyes of a teenaged-girl who had lost the game we were playing—a game of life and death?

"No," said Ryan. "That judge was not there. The prosecutor wasn't there either. That's why they are able to think the way they do. But there's another way. We all agree that saving ourselves is only natural. But sometimes the bravest thing we can possibly do is to save others. Even at the risk of sacrificing ourselves."

The courtroom was stone silent. Slowly, right before his eyes, the strangest thing started to happen. Ryan blinked once, and again, not quite believing his eyes. He noticed a change among the jurors. At first it was subtle, a mere adjustment in their facial expressions. But then he realized that the change was more profound. The appearance of each juror was actually changing. They weren't simply looking at him differently. They literally *looked* different. Their faces changed. Their hair changed. Even their clothing changed. It wasn't just one or two of them. It was all of them. Right before Ryan's eyes, all twelve members of the jury had physically transformed into passengers from the *William Brown*—twelve of the fourteen "losers" on the lifeboat who were thrown overboard to their deaths.

Ryan turned and looked at Hezekiah. "How did *that* happen?"

Hezekiah smiled proudly. "You did it, Ryan."

"What did I do?"

The judge interrupted, but he too, was smiling. "Very powerful argument, young man. And a very important lesson for all of us. Just because a case is old does not mean it's right. Sometimes, legal precedent is wrong. Casting lots to save lives is a horrible thing. It appears to me that you have persuaded this jury on that point. You have made this jury stand in the shoes of the victims of the *William Brown*. There is no better way to rip a wrongly decided case from the law books than to see the world from a victim's point of view. The eyes of the victim are the law's immortal soul. This case is dismissed."

The prosecutor jumped to her feet. "But Your Honor, I haven't even presented any evidence yet."

The judge shook his head, then gestured toward the new jury—twelve people whom Ryan had completely transformed. They were still wearing the immigrant clothing of the victims of the *William Brown*. They still bore the pitiful faces of twelve innocent victims. "You've lost the case before it has even begun," the judge told the prosecutor. "This boy is a true Legal Eagle."

With a bang of the gavel, the case was over. Ryan was acquitted.

"Yes!" shouted Hezekiah, his voice filling the courtroom like a pipe organ.

"I won?" said Ryan.

"Justice prevailed," said Hezekiah.

"You're such a nerd."

"I can't help it. I'm a Legal Eagle." He put his arm around Ryan's shoulder. "Come on. Let's you and I go celebrate."

# 17

yan and Hezekiah left the courtroom together. On the first floor of the courthouse was a noisy cafeteria with booths and counter space. They found a booth in the back where they could talk privately over french fries and chocolate milkshakes.

"You were fantastic, Ryan. Even the judge thought so."

Ryan chuckled. "Yeah, what did he call me? A real Legal Eagle."

"That was quite a compliment," Hezekiah said in a serious tone. "What he was really saying is that you are definitely a potential candidate for the Society."

"The Society?"

"The Society of Legal Eagles, of course. I'm a member. That old judge is a member. You have to be a member in order to earn leapholes."

Ryan plunged an extra straw into his thick milkshake and took a double-barreled mouthful. "Society of Legal Eagles, huh? Sounds kind of goofy to me."

"Sure it's goofy. On the laugh-out-loud meter, it's right up there with the Mouseketeers. But it shows we have a sense of humor. Believe me, Ryan: You don't ever want to meet a lawyer who takes himself or herself too seriously."

"Like the prosecutor in my dad's case. Boy, was that guy ever full of—"

"Watch your language, young man."

"*Himself.* I was going to say he was full of himself."

"Oh, of course. A lawyer like him would never be invited into the Society."

"He still won the case. He got my father to confess. Dad's in jail now."

"I'm sorry about that."

Ryan waited for him to say more, hoping that perhaps Hezekiah would continue the discussion they'd started in the hallway before trial. But the old lawyer was stone silent. Ryan said, "Why would my father have confessed if he wasn't guilty?"

Hezekiah selected a french fry from the plate, but he didn't eat it. He just wagged it like an extra finger as he spoke. "My guess is that this is something very hard for him to explain."

"I'd love to hear him try."

"Have you told him that?"

Ryan shrugged. "Yeah, sort of."

"I'm serious, Ryan. Have you sat down with your father and told him you want to understand what he did? Have you given him that chance?"

Ryan was silent, staring down into his milkshake.

Hezekiah said, "Or have you been too angry to even listen?"

"I just can't understand why he would have done that. People don't confess to things they didn't do."

"It's not unheard of, Ryan."

"It just doesn't make sense."

"The system isn't perfect. You proved that today. You showed the judge that the *William Brown* was a bad decision. Just because a case went one way or the other doesn't always mean it went the *right* way. There are bad decisions handed down every day."

"How does that happen?"

"Sometimes mistakes are made. Those are bad, but those aren't the ones that worry me the most."

"What *do* you worry about?" asked Ryan.

The old man's eyes seemed to glisten like two burning embers. "What I'm about to tell you is very important. It's something you must never forget. My friends and I may kid around a little, give ourselves a corny name like the Society of Legal Eagles. But the other side is no laughing matter."

"What other side?"

"Just as sure as there are Legal Eagles in the world, there is also Legal Evil. That's where the worst decisions come from."

"Are there worse decisions than the *William Brown*?"

"Oh, yes," said Hezekiah. "Much, much worse."

"Like what?" asked Ryan.

Hezekiah said, "Perhaps your father's case. If he's telling you the truth, perhaps his case was worse."

"Do you think he was innocent?"

"I have no way of knowing for certain. I wasn't there when the crime was committed."

"But he must have said something to you."

"Like I told you before, I couldn't share that with you even if I did know. The point is, your father wants to talk to *you*, not to me. Only you can find out the truth."

"I want to know more about this Legal Evil."

"Oh, this is far too happy an occasion to dwell on Legal Evil. We should be celebrating your victory."

"I want to know," said Ryan. "What's the worst, most awful decision out there?"

Hezekiah's face turned very serious. "The worst decision ever . . . this is just my opinion. The worst decision ever is where Legal Evil lives."

"Where is that?"

Hezekiah was clearly reluctant to say more. Finally, he seemed to conjure up a satisfactory answer. "Legal Evil lives where the brood follows the dam."

"Huh?" said Ryan. "Sounds like some kind of riddle. Where is that?"

"It is the most horrible, dark place in legal history."

"Can I see it?"

"Not now," said Hezekiah. "Like I said. We must celebrate. You have passed the test."

Ryan suddenly had brain-freeze from his milkshake. Or was it something that Hezekiah had just said? *A test—is that what he said?* "What *test* are you talking about?" asked Ryan.

"Oh, me and my slippery old silver tongue. But you were bound to find out sooner or later anyway." Hezekiah leaned closer. It was clear from the expression on his face that he was dying to share a secret with Ryan. "Do you ever wonder how you ended up in the hospital in the first place?"

"Of course I do. I wonder about a lot of things. Mostly what I think about are those poor people who died of the BODS virus."

Hezekiah narrowed his eyes and said, "No one actually died."

"Say what?"

"We sort of placed you in that whole situation. Kaylee was in on it as well. So was everyone else you met there. As a matter of fact, Kaylee is one of the newest members of the Society of Legal Eagles. She's going to be a real firecracker."

Ryan could barely speak. "Why would you do that to me? Is that how you get your kicks?"

"Look at me," said Hezekiah. "I'm very old. It's time for me to retire. In order to retire from the Society of Legal Eagles, a member must find a younger replacement. I've chosen you as my replacement."

"So you decided to torture me?"

"Not torture you. *Test* you. I had to make sure you have what it takes to be a loophole closer. As a matter of fact, you were in a leaphole from the minute you were knocked off your bicycle and hit the pavement."

"You mean the whole fire at the hospital—that was from an actual legal case?"

"Stacy versus Truman Medical Center. Missouri Supreme Court, 1992. We brought you out of the leaphole when you were swinging through the elevator shaft at the end of that rope you and Kaylee made."

"Is that why all that wind was blowing up through the shaft and into the hallway?"

"That's right. There was no leaphole to the Infectious Disease Control Center. The Society had to stage that part of the test on its own."

"And the trip to the prison, the night in the dungeon?"

"We staged that, too. Sorry about leaving you and Kaylee in those dark cells all night. With our latest budget cuts, an old fort with no electricity was all we could afford to rent."

"You could have afforded a stinking candle."

"You're right. All I can say is that the Society takes its tests very seriously. Sometimes our members go a little overboard."

"What were you testing?"

"Character, of course. And courage. Each step presented a different question. First: would you run out of the hospital when you saw Kaylee running the wrong way, or would you go back to save her? You went back. Second: would you share the vaccine with others, putting your own life at risk in the hope of saving all? You did. Third: were you willing to travel back to the *William Brown* to discover bad precedent? You were. Finally: did you learn how to abandon bad precedents, to make the jury see through the eyes of the victim? You did."

"I don't like being tested," said Ryan.

"But you passed, boy. You have what it takes to become a Legal Eagle."

"Who says I want to be one?"

Hezekiah was taken aback. "What did you say?"

"You think this is all a big joke, the way you tricked me?"

"It wasn't a trick, Ryan."

"Of course it was. It was you and Kaylee and the judge and probably even all those jurors who made themselves look like the passengers on the *William Brown*. You all got together and decided to make me run through this maze like a rat after cheese."

"Don't be angry."

"I have a right to be angry. Sure, it's nice to know that no one actually died in the hospital because of a lack of vaccine. It was all just a test. But that doesn't excuse what you did. You just jerked me around."

"I did nothing of the sort. This is an honor. I *chose* you."

"Well, maybe I choose not to be chosen."

"You must accept, Ryan. Not everyone is given the opportunity to become a Legal Eagle."

"Maybe you should rethink the way you deliver your invitations."

"Please, Ryan. I'm old, and my skills are fading. I don't have the time or the energy to scout out a new candidate. Don't do this to me."

"So, it's all about you. Is that it?"

"No. It's about the future of our Society. It's about the battle against Legal Evil."

His repeated mention of the battle against Legal Evil set Ryan to thinking. From the day his father was taken away to jail, Ryan had thought his father was nothing but a liar. He'd lied to Ryan's mother when he said everything was going to be all right. He'd lied to Ryan and his sister when he said they had nothing to be ashamed of. He'd lied again when he said he was innocent. Ryan wasn't so sure anymore. Maybe those weren't lies. But he was dead certain of one thing: Hezekiah *had* lied to him. Ryan didn't like being tricked. He didn't like being lied to or deceived. The fact that Hezekiah said it was all for a good cause didn't make Ryan feel any better.

"I want to go home," said Ryan.

"But you're so close to becoming a member. Just a few more—"

"I don't want to be a member. My mom must be really worried about me. I just want to go home."

Ryan pushed away from the table and started toward the cafeteria exit. Hezekiah hurried after him. "You're making a terrible mistake, Ryan."

Ryan kept walking down a long corridor that led to the main lobby of the courthouse. On either side of him were two rows of towering columns, each one easily four stories in height. They made him feel so small, like a tiny ant among a forest of redwoods.

"Do you hear me, Ryan? I say, you're making a mistake!"

"I can live with it," said Ryan. He was headed toward a set of massive wood doors. His heels clicked against the polished marble with each footfall. As he neared the exit, it suddenly occurred to him that he didn't know where the courthouse was located. He didn't know the street, the city, the state. He didn't even know what *country* he was in. But it didn't matter. He'd had enough of this legal fantasy land. He wanted out. He wanted to go home.

"Ryan, don't open that door!"

Ryan ignored him and pushed on the handle.

"Ryan, don't!"

He pushed once more, but to no avail. Then he pulled— and it was as if he'd unleashed a hurricane. The door flew open with so much force that it was nearly ripped from its hinges. It slammed against the wall, and a tremendous wind rushed in. Ryan was swept from his feet and thrown back into the lobby. Somewhere in the background he heard Hezekiah calling to him, but it sounded as if he were a mile underwater. Ryan tried to move forward, toward the door, but the screaming wind was too strong. He turned to find another way out of the building, and what he saw stunned him.

The columns were moving.

Massive pillars of stone were on the verge of teetering back and forth. It was just a few inches of movement, but they were indeed moving, he was sure of it. It was a side-to-side motion, like that finger wagging in his face when that man with the flat face had carried him to his ambulance. The courthouse lobby was a wind tunnel, and the only things in it were Ryan and two rows of columns. Everything was a blur. The courthouse itself had seemed to fade from existence. Back and forth, back and forth the columns swayed.

Then Ryan left his feet, and everything went black.

# 18

**R**yan woke to the sound of his own heartbeat. He was lying on his back in a hospital bed, but the mattress was angled upward so that he was nearly in a sitting position. A tangle of wires and tubes connected him to some kind of machine that made his pulse audible.

*Beep. Beep. Beep.*

His gaze swept the room. Slats of sunshine were streaming through the blinds on the window. The shadows made a funky zebra-like pattern on the floor. There was a television, but it was turned off. A woman was seated in a chair at the end of the bed. She was slouching, and her chin was resting on her chest. She appeared to be asleep. Finally, Ryan's vision came into focus.

"Mom?" he said.

Her eyelids fluttered. She seemed dazed at first. Then her gaze met Ryan's, and her face lit up. "Ryan, are you awake?"

It was a simple question, but it still confused him. He was feeling a bit disoriented. "I think so."

His mother rushed to his side. She threw her arms around him and hugged him so tightly that the heart monitor actually did a *beep, beep-beep, blip*. She switched off the volume on the machine and said, "I can't believe you're back."

"Where am I?"

"Mercy Hospital. They brought you into the emergency room yesterday afternoon."

"You mean I've been gone less than a day?"

"No, no. You were missing for three days. Teddy Armstrong and his friends told the police that you tried to race your bike against their car. They saw you get hit by a station wagon. The driver stopped, and the boys thought he was taking you to the hospital. But you never made it to a hospital. You never showed up anywhere." Her eyes welled with tears. "Oh, Ryan. I'm just so glad you're back."

Ryan hated to see his mother cry. He'd seen her cry too often since his father went to prison. "It's okay, Mom. I think I'm okay."

"Thank God."

She wiped away her tears, and they shared a little smile. It actually felt good to be back. But this was all so confusing. "So, how did I get here yesterday?" he asked.

"It's the strangest thing. Someone found you lying on the side of the road where you had your accident three days ago. They called for an ambulance, and there you were."

"Who called?"

"Nobody knows. The person didn't leave a name, and when the ambulance arrived there was nobody there but you. Think hard, Ryan. Do you have any idea how you got there?"

He sighed, thinking aloud. "The last thing I remember is opening that courthouse door. All that wind rushed in, and those tall, stone columns started going back and forth, and . . ." He stopped himself, seeing the incredulous look on his mother's face.

"Courthouse?" she said.

"Yeah. I was in the Court of International Justice."

She laid her hand on his forehead and checked for a fever. "Do you even remember the bike accident?"

"Of course I do. But that seems like such a long time ago. So much has happened since then. When I woke up, I was in the emergency room—a place a lot like this one. Then a fire broke out, and I met a girl named Kaylee and some other people. We tried to escape from the fire, but we ended up in a disease control center that was top secret and . . ."

The concern on his mother's face stopped him in mid-sentence. "This all sounds crazy, doesn't it?" he said.

"You poor boy. It's just like the doctor said. You must have bumped your head pretty badly in the accident. You couldn't even find your way home. He thinks you may have been wandering around aimlessly for the last few days in some state of temporary amnesia."

"No, Mom, that's not what happened."

"It's all right, darling."

"Mom, I'm telling you the truth."

"Please, just rest, son. The police are going to want to take a statement from you. But I want you to rest until you're able to tell the difference between what's real and what's not real."

He wanted to explain more, but he feared that she would only think that he had really lost his mind. "How's Ainsley?" said Ryan.

"She's fine. Misses her big brother."

"And Sam?"

"If he could talk, he'd say it wasn't very nice the way you left him frozen in the *stay* position when you bolted out of the house on your way to the bike accident."

Ryan felt bad about that, but it also made him proud to have such an obedient dog. *Good boy, Sammy.*

They sat in silence for a minute, and then his mother took his hand. "Ryan, why *did* you leave the house that morning?"

He struggled for the right words, but there was no way to say it without shame. "Because I didn't want to go visit Dad in jail again."

"I wish you would give your father a chance."

"I know."

"Your anger is understandable," she said. "No child wants to have to visit his father in prison. But if your father tells you he's innocent, I wish you would at least consider the possibility that maybe, just maybe, he isn't lying to you."

Ryan took a moment to think about all he'd been through over the past few days. He had seen with his own eyes that bad things can happen to good people. Good people could even find themselves trapped by bad laws, like those passengers thrown overboard on the *William Brown*. Or like that woman on the bus who was arrested because of her skin color.

Ryan wondered if his father was like them.

"Okay, Mom. As soon as I get out of here, let's go visit him."

"You mean it?"

"Yes. I want to hear what Dad has to say. I really do want to know why an innocent man would confess to a crime he didn't commit."

"I'm sure he'll tell you if you seem willing to accept the truth. But remember. You still may not like what your father has to tell you. The truth is sometimes hard to swallow."

"I understand."

"Good," she said as she squeezed his hand.

Ryan smiled a little, then said, "I'm starving. Would you mind getting me something to eat?"

"Sure. I'll check downstairs in the cafeteria. Why don't you try to get a little more rest while I'm gone?"

"Okay, Mom."

She kissed his forehead and left the room, leaving the door open on her way out. Ryan's head sank back into his pillow. This truly was bizarre. Hit by a car. Gone missing. Found three days later in the exact spot where he'd had his accident. Could he possibly have been wandering around the city all that time, not sure who he was? Could he have imagined the hospital, Kaylee, the casting of lots for a vaccine? He supposed it could have been a dream or some sort of delusion. Except Hezekiah. That lawyer had seemed too real to him. He couldn't have been a dream.

Because Ryan really missed the old geezer.

Ryan suddenly did a double take as a man passed his room in the hallway. He was eerily familiar. He looked exactly like the driver of that car that had hit Ryan on his bicycle. It was the man with the incredibly flat face. Slowly, Ryan slid out of bed. His bare feet came to rest on the cold tile floor. He felt dizzy for an instant, but he soon got his bearings. He disconnected the wires that tethered him to the heart monitor. Then, one step at a time, he walked toward the door.

He stopped, poked his head out, and peered down the hallway. A nurse got onto the elevator. An old woman was being taken to her room in a wheelchair. No sign of Flat Face anywhere. Maybe Ryan had imagined it. Maybe he'd imagined everything. He closed the door, turned and started toward his bed, then stopped short.

Flat Face was sitting on the edge of his bed.

"How did you get in here?" asked Ryan.

"With ease," he said.

Ryan took a half-step back. "What do you want?

"Don't be afraid. My name's Jarvis. I've come on behalf of Hezekiah."

The mention of Hezekiah caught him off guard. If the last few days had truly been nothing but a dream, how did this Jarvis know about the old lawyer?

"You were *not* dreaming," said Jarvis.

"How did you know I was wondering about that?"

"I would be happy to elaborate, but I know how you reacted to Hezekiah's explanation of how leapholes really work."

"You mean the computerized virtual legal environments?"

"No. I was referring to his other explanation."

"You mean magic?" said Ryan.

"That would be the one," said Jarvis. "I know you don't believe in legal magic."

Ryan gave it a moment's thought. Talk of magic still seemed like something out of fairy tales. But the computer and virtual legal environments sure did seem to leave many things unexplained. "Let's just say I'm still skeptical."

"No problem. I was too. Before I met Hezekiah, I was just a greedy lawyer headed in the direction of Legal Evil. I was what they refer to in the profession as an ambulance chaser."

"What's that?"

"That's another name for a sleazy lawyer who chases after injured people in ambulances. Before they even got to the hospital, I would convince them to sue the person who hurt them. That's how I used to get my clients. And that's how my face ended up this way."

Ryan had been afraid to ask about his flat face. Now that the man had mentioned it, he felt free to inquire. "It *is* amazingly flat."

"Never chase a parked ambulance," said Jarvis.

Ryan tried not to laugh, so it came out like a snort. Jarvis didn't seem too offended, and Ryan figured it was because he was just kidding anyway.

Suddenly, the door to Ryan's room flew open. Kaylee rushed inside and shut the door behind her. "You found him!" she said to Jarvis.

"Yes, I told you I would," he said.

Ryan looked at Kaylee and said, "What are you doing here?"

"We need your help. Jarvis didn't want me to come along and ask you any favors, because he thought you might be mad at me. But I thought you might be too frightened by him to agree to anything. So I followed him here on my bicycle."

"Well, I guess you're both right. No offense, Jarvis, but you are a little scary looking. And I suppose I am a little mad at you, Kaylee. You did trick me that night we were in those dark cells next to each other. The way you pretended to be afraid and all that."

Kaylee said, "I'm sorry about that. But we can sort that out later. Right now, Hezekiah needs your help. He's in big trouble."

"Did something happen to him?"

Jarvis said, "Oh, I suppose it was inevitable. Hezekiah wasn't kidding when he told you that he's getting old and needs to retire. He really shouldn't be working on so many cases. Anyway, after you left, he was back in his library doing some research."

"You mean leaphole research?"

"Exactly. He used one of those leapholes to check out an old case. And now . . ."

"What?" said Ryan.

Jarvis had a lump in his throat, as if all choked up. "He can't get back."

Ryan folded his arms, his skepticism rising. "Wait a minute. You're trying to tell me that Hezekiah got trapped in a virtual legal environment? You can't get trapped in a *virtual* environment. It isn't real. There's nowhere to go."

"Maybe it isn't as virtual as you think it is."

"So you're trying to tell me that Hezekiah is lost?"

Kaylee said, "He's definitely not lost. No one knows his way in and out of cases better than Hezekiah."

"Did he run out of leapholes?"

"Are you kidding?" said Kaylee. "Nobody has earned more leapholes than Hezekiah."

"Then why can't he get back?"

Kaylee and Jarvis exchanged glances, as if coming to a silent agreement that Kaylee should do the rest of the talking. "I don't think it's really a matter of not being able to come back. I think he's too *ashamed* to come back."

"What does Hezekiah have to be ashamed of?"

"It's like Hezekiah told you," said Kaylee. "He is about to retire. You were his chosen replacement. He selected you from millions of other kids. And you refused. He failed at the most important mission in his life, which is to preserve the future of the Society."

"I wasn't trying to embarrass him."

"I'm afraid you have," said Kaylee. "Now it's really up to you to show him that he didn't fail."

"You mean I have to agree to become a Legal Eagle?"

"At least tell him that you'll think about it," she said. "Give him enough hope to draw him back. Let him save face."

"And then what happens?"

"You'll restore his confidence. No one can be a Legal Eagle without self-confidence. Hezekiah has to start believing in himself again. Then he can get back through the leaphole."

"And if I don't do it?"

"I'm afraid he'll be trapped there forever. And I just pray that he doesn't bump into Legal Evil while he's in this weakened state."

Ryan smiled knowingly. "Now I see where this is headed. Is this some kind of ploy that you and Hezekiah cooked up to get me to come back and join his Society of Legal Eagles?"

"It's not a ploy," said Kaylee. "Jarvis and I didn't come here to argue with you about whether leapholes are real or virtual. All I can tell you is that this is a *real* emergency. Somebody has to help Hezekiah."

"Why don't you two help him?" Ryan asked.

"First of all, Jarvis is not a Legal Eagle."

"You're not?" said Ryan.

Jarvis shook his head. "I'm not even a candidate for the Society. When Hezekiah gave me the test, I failed miserably. But you passed, Ryan. That means you can use Hezekiah's leapholes and bring back Hezekiah."

Ryan looked at Kaylee and said, "You can do it. Hezekiah said you're the newest member of the Society. Just go find him and tell him that I'm thinking about becoming a Legal Eagle."

"He'd never believe it unless he sees you and hears the words come from your own mouth."

"Do you actually expect *me* to do this by myself?" said Ryan.

"No. Jarvis and I will go with you. We just need your help in convincing Hezekiah that he isn't a failure. That he has nothing to be ashamed of."

Ryan thought about it. He still didn't know what to make of these leapholes, whether they were real or virtual. But the questions were starting to pile up, and he remembered what Hezekiah had told him about Legal Evil. If leapholes were real—or if there was something about them that he still didn't quite understand—he hated to think of Hezekiah stranded someplace, possibly a bad place, unable or unwilling to save himself.

Ryan asked, "How long will this take?"

"Not long."

"What about my mom? She looks like she hasn't slept since the last time I left. She'll freak if I disappear again."

"Why don't you try being honest with her?" said Kaylee. "Explain what you have to do. Trust me. After everything she went through when your father was sent to jail, she'll understand that you're doing the right thing."

"She'll never believe it. I started to explain, and she thought I had a fever."

"Then don't tell her," said Kaylee.

"I have to tell her."

"No, what I meant was, don't tell her, *show* her. That's what I did with my parents. Jarvis can take you and your mother to Hezekiah's office. You can show her Hezekiah's leapholes. She can decide for herself whether to let you help."

Kaylee was making it hard to say no. Ryan said, "Let me think about it."

"There's no time to waste. This is urgent."

Ryan really did admire Hezekiah, and he didn't like the angry terms on which he'd left. Beyond that, perhaps this was his golden opportunity to sort out these leapholes, virtual legal environments, and the so-called magic that Hezekiah had talked about. Most intriguing of all, it might even be a chance to solve Hezekiah's riddle about Legal Evil—"Legal Evil lives where the brood follows the dam."

The more he thought about it, the more impossible it was to refuse.

"All right. I'll give it a try."

"Great," said Kaylee. "Now, the first thing you have to do is convince your mother that you're ready to leave the hospital. Do it today."

"Fine. I can't wait to get out of this place anyway."

Jarvis handed him a business card. "As soon as you get home, dial this number. We'll set up a meeting with your mother at Hezekiah's office."

"Okay," said Ryan.

"Thank you," said Jarvis.

"Yes, thanks a ton," said Kaylee. Then she and Jarvis started out of the room.

"One more thing," said Ryan. Jarvis continued down the hall, but Kaylee stopped in the doorway. "What is it, Ryan?"

"You know, I really was mad at you. I understand that everything you said and did was part of the test Hezekiah designed for me. But it still wasn't very nice the way you tricked me. Especially that night we spent in the dungeon, when you pretended to be so scared. The truth was, you could have gotten up and left anytime you felt like it."

"I'm sorry, Ryan."

Ryan wasn't sure if he should say everything that was on his mind, but he couldn't stop himself. "And it's not very nice to hold someone's hand if you don't mean it."

"You're right about that," she said as she lowered her eyes. "But there's one thing you should know. Just because I tricked you into thinking I was scared doesn't mean—"

A blaring announcement over the intercom—"Dr. Blanco, please report to the O.R. immediately"—completely drowned out Kaylee's words. Ryan watched her lips move. He could have sworn she said *doesn't mean I didn't want to hold your hand.*

"Doesn't mean what?" Ryan asked.

She looked away, seemingly too embarrassed to repeat "Nothing. I'm just sorry about that whole thing, okay?"

He was curious to know if he had read her lips correctl but he didn't press it. He was already feeling less anger towaı her. "Okay."

She gave him a little smile and said, "I'm glad you're goin to help us find Hezekiah."

"Me, too," he said. And he truly meant it.

# Part II

---

# *The Brood Follows the Dam*

# 19

From a very early age, Kaylee knew she was different. Kaylee was just a toddler when her mother started fighting off the modeling agencies. Your daughter should be in commercials, they told her. Maybe even movies. She had perfect features. A natural beauty. *Cha-ching, cha-ching.* Her mother was smart enough to realize that the only thing those people cared about was the sound of a cash register ringing.

Kaylee was no dummy herself. In fact, she was so intelligent, it sometimes scared people. Once, when she was a little girl, she tagged along to the doctor's office for her mom's annual checkup. Her mom sat on the examination table. She was so pretty, looking exactly like the woman Kaylee dreamed of becoming. Kaylee watched intently as the nurse rolled up her mother's sleeve and checked her blood pressure.

"Very good," said the nurse, reading from the gauge. "One-twenty over eighty."

"One and a half," Kaylee volunteered.

"One and a half what?" her mother asked.

"One-twenty over eighty. That equals one and a half."

The nurse looked up from her chart and almost dropped her pen. "How old is that child?"

"Six," said her mother. "Well, *almost* six."

The look on that nurse's face was unforgettable. Over and over, throughout her childhood, Kaylee would see that same spooked expression. Hearing the amazing things that came out of her mouth, adults would guess that she was just small for her age. "You're special," her mother would tell her. She always made Kaylee feel that way.

It had taken Kaylee's mother a while, but finally she warmed up to Hezekiah and his leapholes. Some parents would freak out if an eccentric old man told them that their daughter has what it takes to become a Legal Eagle. Kaylee, however, had been pursued all her life, whether it was the modeling agencies or top private schools. Her mother checked out Hezekiah carefully. Eventually, she came to see him as a private tutor of sorts, though her affections ran much deeper than that. He was like family to her, and she adored him like a grandfather. It was difficult for her to accept the fact that Hezekiah was gone.

Naturally, her heart fluttered when Jarvis called her with the good news.

"Ryan and his mother are driving to Hezekiah's office right now," he said into the telephone.

"Awesome!" said Kaylee. She was speaking from her bedroom on an encrypted satellite telephone that the Society had given her. Secrecy was at the core of the Society. "What time are you meeting them?"

"Three o'clock."

"Do you want me and my mother to come over? Maybe it would put Dr. Coolidge more at ease if she met my mother."

"It's best if I handle the first meeting by myself."

"Why?"

"Because we can't trust Ryan or his mother yet. Your membership in the Society is secret. I can't run the risk of exposing your identity until I know more about Dr. Coolidge. You and I will be dead meat if she shows up on the nightly news talking about the secret Society of Legal Eagles."

Kaylee fretted for a moment. She didn't like leaving this in the hands of Jarvis, but he had a valid point. "All right. As soon as you develop a level of trust, call me. It will be easier to convince Ryan's mother to let him go looking for Hezekiah if my mother is there to reassure her."

"No problem."

"Oh, and just a reminder: Don't even think about taking Ryan by yourself to search for Hezekiah without me. That would be way too dangerous. You're not a Legal Eagle. Ryan may have what it takes to be one, but he doesn't fully understand leapholes yet."

"Yes, I'm fully aware that I'm not a Legal Eagle, that you are, and that Ryan probably will be. Is there anything else you'd like to rub my nose in?" He sounded quite annoyed.

"Sorry," said Kaylee. "I wasn't trying to put you down. I just want to make sure that this is done right and that we get Hezekiah back."

"Then we're all on the same team."

"Good. Don't forget to call me."

"I won't."

She said goodbye and hung up. But the tone of his *"I won't"* made her wonder. Did he mean *I won't forget*?

Or did he mean *I won't call*?

# 20

**R**yan's mother was no fool. No one knew that better than Ryan.

Sharon Coolidge had graduated at the top of her medical school class. She did her residency (a form of training for doctors after med school) at the most prestigious children's hospital in the country. She was a respected pediatrician. As Ryan had learned at a very early age, it was extremely difficult for a child to pull the wool over the eyes of a pediatrician. His friends could often skip school by faking illness in the morning. Not Ryan. One time he held the thermometer over the light bulb so that it would register a phoney fever. This same kind of stunt worked every time for his friend Sweaty Colletti. Ryan's mother just looked at the thermometer and said, "Either someone put a match to this thing, or you died twenty minutes ago."

No, it wasn't easy for Ryan to fool his mother. So, as he stood in Hezekiah's law office, listening to Jarvis talk, he had a sinking feeling. He knew that his mother wouldn't easily buy into the notion of lawyers who could make law books come to life.

"Leapholes, huh?" she said with a hefty dose of skepticism.

"Yes ma'am," said Jarvis. "That's what we call them."

"It's not really magic, Mom," said Ryan. "It's computerized. They're called Virtual Legal Environments."

"Is that so?" she said.

She didn't seem persuaded. Ryan was beginning to wish he had explained more to her during the car ride. He had gone missing almost three full days to take Hezekiah's test. Both Ryan's hospital physician and his mother were convinced that Ryan's accident had caused temporary amnesia. Their theory was that Ryan had walked around aimlessly for three days before someone finally brought him to the hospital. Had Ryan tried to tell her about leapholes and magician-like lawyers, she probably would have readmitted him to the hospital—maybe even the psychiatric ward. So he decided to let Jarvis do most of the explaining. Perhaps that was a mistake.

Ryan said, "Jarvis, why don't you take my mom to Hezekiah's library?"

"Good idea. Come right this way, Doctor."

Ryan was eager to see if Hezekiah's personal library was as impressive as the one in the old fort where they'd first met. It wasn't. The prison library had clearly been designed to impress Ryan. This one had just as many books, but they were scattered everywhere. Piles and piles of books stood in random stacks around the room. Some of the stacks were taller than Dr. Coolidge. It was as if Hezekiah had long ago given up hope of building enough bookcases to shelve all his books. Ryan couldn't imagine how anyone could find what he was looking for in this mess, which only confirmed his continuing belief that the key to Hezekiah's leapholes was the computer, not the books.

"This is where Hezekiah does his research," said Jarvis.

Dr. Coolidge walked several paces, then stopped. The look of disapproval on her face was all too familiar to Ryan. It was usually accompanied by the words *You call this room* clean, *young man?*

"Show her one of the VLE helmets," said Ryan.

"Sure." Jarvis went to the closet and rummaged through it. He returned with a black helmet with a visor, which he placed on the table.

Ryan said, "That's exactly like the one I wore, Mom. It was the most amazing thing. I put on that helmet, and suddenly Hezekiah and I were racing on thoroughbreds, playing baseball in Wrigley Field, and riding on a bus through Alabama. We even went on a ship that was hit by an iceberg!"

His mother looked at him with concern. "You poor dear."

"No, it's true, Mom. All I had to do was put on this helmet."

"Ryan, I'm sure you *think* this happened, but—"

"It *did* happen. Just watch. Jarvis will show you."

Her expression said it all. It was bad enough to think of her son wandering around lost for three days. But his mother seemed even more distressed by the possibility that Ryan may actually have been cooped up with the likes of Hezekiah (who was nowhere to be found) and his flat-faced sidekick.

"If it really happened," she said, "then exactly where is this Hezekiah?"

"That's why we need Ryan's help," said Jarvis. "He disappeared."

"Where did he go?" she asked.

Jarvis shrugged. "I don't know, exactly. But I have a pretty good idea."

"You do?" said Ryan.

"Yeah. Follow me."

They zigzagged through several towering piles of law books. Jarvis took them to a small study area behind an overloaded bookcase. There was only one chair at the rectangular oak table. It was empty. The tabletop was clear, except for a single law book. It lay open.

"This is where he was working when he disappeared," said Jarvis.

Ryan stepped forward and took a closer look. "Eighteen-fifty-seven," he said, reading the date from the case caption. "That's an old case."

"It's not the age that concerns me," said Jarvis. "It's the time period. Eighteen-fifty-seven was one of the darkest years in American legal history. It was near the height of legal conflict over slavery—before that conflict turned into the Civil War. If Hezekiah went there, he could be in some real trouble."

"Why would he go there?" said Ryan.

"No," his mother said sternly. "The better question is *how* would he go there. I am just about fed up with this nonsense, Ryan."

Jarvis didn't say a word. He simply reached under the oak table, lifted a large jar from the floor, and placed it on the table. "That's how," he said.

"What's that?" she asked.

"Leapholes," said Ryan. "I'm not exactly sure what they are, Mom. But there is something about them that creates the virtual legal environment."

"Right," said Jarvis, smirking. "For people who insist that this is nothing more than an ultra-hi-tech computer, that's what leapholes are. Keys to virtual legal environments."

"Are you suggesting that they're something else?" said Dr. Coolidge.

Jarvis paused, seeming to choose his words carefully. "I'm not the best person to explain it to you, ma'am. All I can tell you is what I think, which is this: I think the best lawyer I've ever known used one of these leapholes to bring himself face-to-face with Legal Evil."

Ryan glanced at the open book on the table. A chill came over him. "Are you saying that's where Legal Evil lives? That's where the brood follows the dam?"

Jarvis gave a solemn nod.

"But why would he go there on his own?" said Ryan.

"Because you shamed him. He invited you to be a Legal Eagle, and you rejected him. The only way he can save face is to take on Legal Evil himself."

"Can he do that?"

Jarvis shook his head. "He's too old, Ryan. Way past his prime. He'll be slaughtered."

"What will happen to him then?"

Jarvis lowered his head, as if he couldn't bring himself to say it.

Ryan's mother could hold her tongue no longer. "What in the world are you two talking about? I'm no computer genius, but nobody disappears into a virtual environment."

"That's what I told him," said Ryan.

"Good for you," she said. "I'm glad you haven't completely lost your marbles. And as for you, Jarvis: What have you and this Hezekiah character been doing with my son for the past three days?"

"We haven't done anything," said Jarvis.

"Maybe you should tell that to the police." She took her cell phone from her purse and punched out the number.

"Mom, what are you doing?"

She waved him off and spoke into the telephone. "Yes, Detective Spessard? This is Doctor Sharon Coolidge. I've heard enough. I think it's time for you to come inside."

Almost immediately after she hung up, there was a tremendous pounding on the office door. "Open up! Police!"

Ryan looked at his mother in disbelief. "You told them to follow us here, didn't you?"

"Ryan, this is giving me the creeps. It seems like some kind of cult."

"You had this planned all along. You think Hezekiah abducted me."

"I'm doing this for your own safety, Ryan."

Jarvis's eyes filled with rage. "You double crossed me! Now we'll never find Hezekiah."

The pounding at the door grew louder. "Open up, or we'll bust the door down!"

Ryan said to Jarvis, "Give me the VLE helmet."

"You don't need the helmet."

"Yes, I wore it when I was with Hezekiah."

"The helmet is worthless. It doesn't do anything. It's all in the leapholes, Ryan. When are you going to believe?"

"Ryan!" his mother shouted. "Stop talking to that man!"

The door crashed open. A SWAT team burst into the office. In a matter of seconds, a half dozen men dressed in black combat fatigues, weapons drawn, were approaching the library at full speed. In the stampede, they smashed into a row of bookshelves and knocked it over. The toppling of the first row of shelves created a domino effect. One bookshelf fell onto the next one, and so on. It was like an earthquake in Hezekiah's law library. Thousands of books came smashing to the floor. The advancing SWAT team members were buried in the avalanche of falling books.

Jarvis grabbed a leaphole from Hezekiah's jar. "Let's go now, Ryan!"

Dr. Coolidge snatched it from his hand. "You're not going anywhere."

"Mom, don't touch that!"

Another row of bookshelves toppled, and the domino effect suddenly reached Ryan and his mother. The bookcase crashed onto the table where Hezekiah's research book lay open. The book fell to the floor—and it opened to a *different* page.

Ryan's mother backed away. Another falling book knocked the leaphole from her grasp. It rolled on its edge and landed on Hezekiah's book.

Ryan dove for the leaphole and grabbed it. He noticed immediately that the old book was open to a different page than the one Hezekiah had been studying. But it was too late. His entire hand was glowing bright orange. The leaphole inside his tightly clenched fist was already doing its work.

"Oh boy," Ryan said nervously. He could feel the pull of the leaphole. For the first time, he realized that maybe Jarvis and Hezekiah had been telling the truth. Maybe he really *didn't* need the VLE helmet.

The suction was tremendous. It was more power than Ryan had ever felt. He tried with all his strength to release the leaphole, but his fist was locked shut. He tried to turn the pages back to Hezekiah's exact destination—back to 1857. There seemed to be no way to change the leaphole's course once the journey began.

The noise was deafening, a swirling, swooshing sound like a hurricane. "Mom!" he shouted at the top of his lungs, "I'll be back as soon as I can."

"Where do you think you're going?" she asked in a panic.

"I don't know. I think it's someplace close to where the brood follows the dam."

Suddenly, it was as if a rocket had fired. Jarvis grabbed Ryan by the ankles. In a final orange flash, they were sucked into the pages, zooming down the leaphole.

Ryan had no idea where they might end up.

# 21

**R**yan hit the ground so hard that he nearly bit his tongue. It was the roughest landing yet, by far. He chalked it up to the fact that he wasn't traveling with Hezekiah. Or perhaps it was because Jarvis was still holding onto Ryan's ankles. He was like a baby chimp clinging to its mother.

"Uh, you can let go now," said Ryan.

Ryan's new surroundings were completely foreign to him. There were no cars and no traffic lights. He didn't even see bicycles. Telephone wires and electric-power lines were nonexistent. Ryan could have stared up into the bright blue sky all day long and never seen an airplane. He heard no music blaring from boom boxes. Skateboarding down the bumpy cobblestone streets would have been impossible.

"Outta the way!" a man shouted.

Ryan quickly rolled to one side. A horse-drawn carriage rolled past him, nearly flattening him in the street. "Did you see that?" Ryan said.

"You were expecting a Hummer?" said Jarvis.

Ryan picked himself up off the ground and brushed the dirt off his clothes. He was wearing what he usually wore: Blue jeans, sneakers, and a baggy sweatshirt with an NBA jersey underneath. Earlier that morning, he had decided to switch out of the white "home" jersey for the black "away" jersey. It turned out to be the right call. He was nowhere near "home," and there was no telling how long this road trip would last.

Ryan and Jarvis walked for several blocks, just taking it all in. The sidewalk was made of bricks, not concrete. Most of the buildings were also made of red brick, though some had iron or stone facades. The tallest buildings were perhaps seven-stories high, but four or five stories were much more common. Old-fashioned gaslights were spaced at even intervals along the sidewalk. The smell of burning coal lingered in the air. A horse-drawn trolley bumped along the street. It rode on wagon wheels, not rails, and the passengers seemed quite uncomfortable. People on the sidewalks were dressed very differently from Ryan. Many wore fashionable hats and capes, but Ryan hardly noticed. He was too busy reading the hand-painted signs on storefronts and the stone-chiseled markers on buildings, trying to figure out where he was. He saw the Barnum Hotel, St. Paul's Episcopal Church, and the William Barr Dry Goods Company. He spotted several more churches, a public park, a library, and a bank. He found a barbershop and a blacksmith, and many other places of interest. As they passed a dentist's office with a big wooden tooth hanging in the window, a shrill scream startled Ryan. Inside, some poor guy was probably getting a molar yanked out by the roots with a pair of pliers and no anesthetic. Ryan prayed that he wasn't going to be in town long enough to get a toothache.

After several minutes of exploring, Ryan and Jarvis stopped outside a bakery. The smell of fresh bread made them both very hungry.

"Let's buy something to eat," said Ryan. "You got any money?"

"Even if I did, I don't think they take bills from the twenty-first century."

"Oh, right," said Ryan. "Any idea where we are?"

"Not yet."

"Why don't we just ask someone?"

"Because they'll think we're two crazy people who should be locked up."

"I guess you're right. We must look totally weird to them as it is."

Jarvis looked away, as if his feelings were hurt.

"Sorry, I wasn't talking about your face," said Ryan. "I meant the way we're dressed. We look so different."

"Like a couple of clueless clowns," said Jarvis. "We don't even know what day, month, or year it is."

As best Ryan could figure, it was early spring. He had no coat, but it was warm enough that he didn't need one. Some of the windows along the street had flower boxes, and the lilacs looked ready to bloom. Even the stray dogs seemed to have spring fever. A couple of yelping mutts were chasing chickens down an alley. It was the first time Ryan had watched hens try to fly. They weren't very good at it. Ryan could have soared higher and longer on his BMX bicycle.

They passed a theater on Third Street. At Fourth Street they found another large hotel called Planters House. They were on Olive Street, Ryan discovered, and there they spotted the most impressive building yet. It was made of red brick with a big dome on top. The stone marker above the entrance told Ryan exactly where he was. It read: CIRCUIT COURT, ST. LOUIS MISSOURI. An American flag was flying in front. It looked slightly different from the one Ryan saluted at school every morning. He counted the white stars against the blue background.

There were only thirty-eight.

"Holy smokes. We're in St. Louis, Missouri in the middle of the nineteenth century. How can that be?"

"The leaphole, of course. The case in Hezekiah's law book was from 1857."

"But I wasn't wearing the Virtual Legal Environment helmet. All we had was a leaphole."

"That's all we needed. That's all you *ever* needed. It's like Hezekiah told you. You are Legal Eagle material. Nice driving, kid."

Ryan looked around. The town was like a movie set, only real. He still wasn't sure about the power of the leapholes, whether it was magic or computers or something in between. "I just thought of something," said Ryan. "If I'm not a Legal Eagle yet, why do you suppose that leaphole worked for me?"

"Because you have what it takes to become one. You'll only get better with experience."

"I'm not so sure about that. But answer me this: Once a leaphole is used, can you use it again?"

"It has to be re-energized first."

"How does that work?"

"You have to charge it up with another leaphole."

"Do you have another leaphole?"

"Nope. I'm not a Legal Eagle, so I don't have any."

"Yeah, and like I just said. I'm not one either. Not yet."

Jarvis stopped cold. The significance of Ryan's words seemed to hit him like a mule kick. "We have no return leaphole," said Jarvis.

"We sure don't," said Ryan.

"What do we do about that?"

Ryan tucked his spent leaphole into his pants pocket. He looked off to the distance, toward the endless stretch of prairie that marked the edge of town. "Looks like finding Hezekiah is even more important than I thought."

# 22

*D*r. Sharon Coolidge sat in silence at her kitchen table, her fist clenched tightly around a moist tissue. Ryan's dog Sam lay at her feet, seeming to sense her sadness. Two detectives from the local police station were seated across from her. The older one was heavy-set with a large, fleshy nose. Whenever he furrowed his brow, the skin folded into little steps that led up to his salt-and-pepper hair. The younger man was more handsome, more athletic looking. His clean-shaven head glistened like a polished bowling ball beneath the kitchen chandelier. They were waiting for Ryan's mother to dab away the tears and regain her composure.

"I'm sorry, gentlemen," she said in a voice that quaked.

"Take your time, ma'am."

Just three hours had passed since Ryan and Jarvis disappeared down the leaphole. Dr. Coolidge was not holding up well. She was still recovering from Ryan's first disappearance. Those three days he had gone missing could only be described as a mother's worst nightmare. The only information the police could give her was that a high-school boy had seen Ryan's bicycle collide with a white car. He wasn't in any of the hospitals. No one called to say he was okay. Worst of all, her last words with her son had been an argument over their weekly visit to his father. Three sleepless nights later, the hospital called to say that Ryan had turned up in the emergency room. She vowed never to let him out of her sight again. Then, just a few hours after leaving the hospital, he was gone again.

It was the worst day of her life—even worse than when her husband had gone to prison. At least she knew where her husband was.

The lead detective blew his nose into his handkerchief, then checked his notes. His name was Jorge Gonzalez, and he had a heavy New York accent. A toothpick dangled from the corner of his mouth, and it wagged like the tail of a dog when he spoke. "So let me get this straight, Dr. Coolidge. You're saying that one minute your son and this flat-faced character were standing in the library. The next—*poof!*—they disappeared into a book."

"Yes."

The detectives exchanged glances. Dr. Coolidge could almost read their minds. "You don't believe me," she said.

"People don't just vanish, ma'am."

"I can't explain it. I'm telling you what I saw. The SWAT team raced into the library like a stampede of elephants. They knocked over all the bookshelves. Next thing I knew, I was struggling with Ryan and this flat-faced man for a metal bracelet that they called a leaphole. And then they were gone."

Detective Gonzalez worked his pencil between his fingers like a miniature baton. "Let me ask you this, ma'am. Other than yourself, is there anyone who can say for certain that your son and this other man were actually in this building?"

"The SWAT team, I'm sure."

He shook his head. "I'm afraid not. No one from SWAT saw anyone inside the office but you."

"That's not surprising. With all the bookshelves falling down, they probably couldn't see all of us. Ryan and that man disappeared just a few seconds before the SWAT team reached the study area."

The younger detective spoke up, the one with no hair. "Let's back up a second. How did you find this building in the first place?"

"My son took me to it. He said it was the office of a lawyer named Hezekiah."

"That's very interesting," said Detective Gonzalez. "We checked this out. No one named Hezekiah has ever been a tenant at this address. It was last rented to a law firm called Dewey Cheatam and Howe. They vacated the space about three weeks ago."

"So, the law books belonged to them?" she said.

"Yes," said Gonzalez. "And according to their office manager, no one has ever disappeared into any of their books before."

"I don't understand this," she said.

Detective Gonzalez leaned into the table and looked her straight in the eye. "I've seen this a hundred times, ma'am. I know how difficult it can be for a mother to admit that her child has run away from home."

"Ryan didn't run away."

"Has he ever run away before?"

"No."

"What about last week? You told the police that you and your son had an argument. He was supposed to visit his father. You came into the kitchen and he was gone."

"Well, I wouldn't call that running away."

"Ma'am, he took off on his bicycle and didn't come home for three days."

"He was in an accident. The doctor thinks he could have had temporary amnesia."

Gonzalez looked at her skeptically. "You're a doctor. How many cases of temporary amnesia have you seen in your entire career?"

"Very few," she admitted. "Maybe a couple."

"A couple. Now, I'm a cop. I probably see a dozen kids a year who claim to have temporary amnesia. Funny thing is, they're all faking it. These kids are just afraid that their parents will punish them for running away from home. So they make up a story."

"Ryan knows he can't fool me. He's not a faker."

"Lady, he disappears for three days. He comes back telling you that he and some magic lawyer traveled back in time to a sinking ship from another century. He may get points for imagination, but he's still a faker."

"You don't believe anything I've told you, do you?"

The detective rubbed his big nose again. "Look, I'm not calling you a liar. You seem like a nice person. I'm sure Ryan isn't running away from *you*. But kids do this kind of thing when their dad ends up in prison."

"Are you suggesting that this is somehow my husband's fault?"

"All I'm saying is talk to your son. Maybe he's getting teased at school. Kids can be cruel. Ryan's a pretty easy target with his dad in jail."

She folded her arms tightly, a purely defensive gesture. "Ryan knows he has nothing to be ashamed of. His father is innocent."

"I'm sure you and his father tell him that. But innocent men don't plead guilty. Ryan is old enough and smart enough to know that. Believe me, for a boy his age, there's plenty to be ashamed of."

The anger was boiling up inside her, and she feared that she might say something unwise. She rose and said, "Get out of my house."

The men pushed away from the table without a word. Dr. Coolidge showed them the way out.

Standing in the open doorway, the old detective glanced back over his shoulder and said, "Just so you know, we'll be treating this case as a runaway. I'm sure your son will turn up. Probably as soon as he gets hungry."

She watched as they climbed down the front steps. Detective Gonzalez turned and looked back at her one last time before getting into his car. He was shaking his head.

*How dare he*, she thought as she closed the door. *How dare that old detective say that about my son.* She felt another surge of anger, but her feelings were more complicated now. As much as she hated to admit it, the detective had managed to plant a tiny seed of doubt in the back of her mind.

Maybe Ryan *had* run away.

# 23

ever before had Ryan seen a river so big. He now understood why they called it the Mighty Mississippi.

In the mid-nineteenth century, a levee extended along the Mississippi's right bank for nearly six miles. At old St. Louis, it rose to a limestone bluff almost forty feet high. Wharves, warehouses, and other structures stretched all along the bank, serving a city of over 150,000 people. Ryan and Jarvis watched from a high point on the bluff, looking down on the river. This was the golden era of river boats. Still, the sheer amount of traffic on the waterway surprised Ryan. He stopped counting at 170 vessels, but he saw still more. There were paddle boats, sailboats, steamboats, and fishing boats. Ferries operated between Illinois and Missouri, as there was no bridge. Coursing between the larger boats were rafts, canoes, and rowboats. Some were purely pleasure craft. Others were commercial. They ranged from the old and barely seaworthy to floating palaces with fine Victorian carpentry. They headed up river and down river. At the levee, dozens more unloaded cargo and passengers, making St. Louis one of the busiest ports in the country, second only to New York in tonnage.

Ryan and Jarvis were seated on the grass, eating little green crab apples that they'd picked straight from a tree alongside the road. The sour juices made Ryan wince as he chewed. They weren't exactly tasty. Funny how the mind works, but Ryan seemed to recall from his summer reading that even Huck Finn swore off stealing them. In fact, it was right when Huck and Jim's raft floated past St. Louis that Huck said "crab apples ain't ever good." Huck was probably right. But Ryan was starving, and his belly was grateful for anything that would fill it.

Ryan nibbled his eighth apple down to the seeds. He pitched the core into the river. He was still thinking about Huck and his friend Jim, who was a slave. "Hey, Jarvis. Was Missouri a slave state or a free state back in 1857?"

"Slave, I think. Wasn't that the whole issue with the Missouri Compromise?"

Ryan strained his brain to recall the things he'd learned about the Civil War and the events leading up to it. Disagreements over slavery threatened to tear apart the Union. Missouri was admitted to the nation as a slave state, and Maine entered as a free state. Congress approved the so-called "Missouri Compromise" to maintain an equal number of slave and free states.

Ryan said, "What do you think the case we fell into was about?"

Jarvis swallowed the rest of his apple, seeds and all. "I don't know. Considering the time and the place, I'd guess the Missouri Compromise, maybe."

"Sounds boring."

"Yeah. Most of the law sounds boring. Until you look through a leaphole. You have to see the people and how it affects their lives. That's the interesting part."

"That's what Hezekiah used to say." Ryan glanced toward the flowing river. His belly was full from the apples, but just mentioning the old lawyer's name brought back an empty feeling inside. "You think we'll ever find Hezekiah?" said Ryan.

Jarvis didn't answer. He was on his back, snoring. Ryan was getting sleepy, too. He reclined on the grassy slope. With his hands clasped behind his head, he looked up at the clouds. As a kid, he and his friends used to find clouds that looked like cars or trains or even elephants. He hadn't played that game in a long time. In fact, he hadn't seen any of those friends since his father went to jail. Their parents wouldn't let them hang out with Ryan anymore.

Ryan rolled on his side and felt a lump under his ribs. It was an apple, which made him smile. But it was a sad smile. It reminded him of that old saying: "The apple doesn't fall far from the tree."

His eyelids were growing heavy. He was thinking about his dad. The day that marked the beginning of trouble for Ryan's family had been a day much like this one. It was sunny and warm, the kind of day when nothing should go wrong. As a patch of puffy white clouds moved across the bright blue sky, Ryan's thoughts drifted back to the past. Or was it the future? It was getting complicated. He was in 1857 now, so technically speaking, Ryan Coolidge hadn't even been born yet. But to Ryan, his memories would always be "the past," even if the power of leapholes had landed him on the banks of the Mississippi River in the nineteenth century. At that particular moment, one of those memories came flooding back to him. With his eyes closed, he could see himself on a beach not far from the Coolidge house. He could see himself in the twenty-first century again, but it was long before Ryan would meet Hezekiah. It was before he would watch his father plead guilty in court. It was even before his father would be arrested. It was the innocent beginning—the *very* beginning—of a story with a terrible ending.

A balmy breeze was blowing in from the bay. Ryan could almost taste the sea salt in the air. Crandon Park on Key Biscayne was always full of beach lovers on Sundays, and on gloriously sunny days like this one, the park was packed. The Coolidge family did a barbecue every weekend. Their favorite spot was about a hundred yards from the beach, a little picnic area beneath the shade of a huge banyan tree. Ryan's father would cook hamburgers and chicken breasts on the grill. His mother made the salads and snacks. Ryan always got to bring a friend along. This time (as usual) he brought his best friend, Leddy "Sweaty" Colletti. They headed straight for the beach.

Ryan and Leddy were lying flat on their backs. Above them was only blue sky. Ryan could feel the warm, wet sand beneath him. Anyone could leave a handprint in the sand, but Ryan liked to leave full-body prints. In a rhythm that seemed to have no end, the white foam of breaking waves rode up the shoreline. They reached as far as Ryan's knees before receding back into the ocean. It was the most relaxing feeling imaginable.

A seagull soared overhead. It was coming closer. Too close. Ryan sat up quickly. He would never forget what had happened to his friend Leddy the last time they were lying on the beach. Seagulls had some deadly aim.

Ryan looked left, then right. It was the most beautiful beach he had ever seen. The sand was like powder with a pinkish cast to it. Palm trees dotted the shoreline. Some were forty or fifty feet tall, with long, skinny trunks that reached for the sun. It reminded Ryan of a brontosaurus's neck.

Around him, sun worshipers had spread out their blankets. Beach chairs and colorful umbrellas dotted the landscape. Ryan's gaze drifted toward the cabana behind him. It was shelter for three generations of females—a grandmother, a mother, and a little girl about two years old. The girl seemed fascinated by her grandmother's jewelry. She tugged on the necklace and drooled on the bracelet. Ryan smiled wanly. The days when he could do absolutely anything he wanted and still be adorable had long since passed.

The mother and grandmother were deep in conversation. The two year old was obsessed with the jewelry. She was especially fascinated by the ring. It was one of those obnoxious, rich-old-grandma rings with an emerald stone as big as an acorn. It must have looked tasty to the toddler. She started licking it. Grandma didn't seem to care. She just kept talking, and the little girl kept licking. The ring was still on the old woman's finger, but grandma didn't notice as the girl started sucking on the big stone like a pacifier.

Suddenly, the child started choking. The grandmother screamed. The stone was missing from her ring. The child had worked it loose from the setting. That huge, green stone had come off the ring and was now lodged in the child's windpipe. The grandmother tried to reach into the child's throat, but it would not come out. She screamed for help.

Ryan leaped to his feet and ran to them. "She swallowed the stone! I saw it. I saw it happen!"

"We know!" the grandmother screamed. "Do something!"

Ryan shouted to his friend. "Leddy, call the lifeguard!" Then he looked at the grandmother and said, "My mom's a doctor. I'll get her!"

In a flash, Ryan raced across the beach. He found his mother back at the picnic area. She had a camera bag around her neck, and she was busy photographing red and yellow hibiscus flowers.

"Mom, come quick! A baby's choking!"

Dr. Coolidge didn't even have time to drop her camera bag. She ran with Ryan across the sand to the cabana. A crowd had gathered to watch. The onlookers had formed a semicircle around the mother and grandmother. The lifeguard was on his knees, and he was holding the little girl in his lap. His attempt to perform the Heimlich maneuver was finding no success. It was clear that he'd never practiced on a child so young. The child's face was turning blue. Her mother and grandmother looked horrified, fearing the worst.

"I'm a pediatrician!" Dr. Coolidge shouted as she broke through the crowd. "Let me try."

The lifeguard handed the child over to her. Something had to be done quickly. The girl was fading from lack of oxygen. Ryan's mother dropped her camera bag and gathered the child into her arms. She placed one hand on the girl's back and the other on her tiny abdomen. Quickly but gently, she pushed. But nothing happened.

She tried again.

Still nothing.

"Please, please!" the grandmother cried.

She tried a third time, and it was like uncorking a bottle of champagne. The emerald stone popped from the child's mouth and flew through the air. It landed in the sand, right next to the doctor's camera bag.

The child was crying, like a newborn drawing her first breath.

Her mother and grandmother screamed with relief. The onlookers applauded. Dr. Coolidge continued to massage the child's chest, trying to make her breathe regularly. Just then the paramedics broke through the crowd. Ryan's mother helped them give the child oxygen from a tank. When she seemed satisfied that her young patient would be okay, she didn't stand up and take a bow. She didn't wave to the crowd of onlookers like some kind of hero. She simply whispered something into the mother's ear—something that wiped away much of the anxiety from the young mother's face.

And then Dr. Coolidge quietly slipped away, melting into the crowd of onlookers.

Ryan had never been so proud of anyone in his entire life. For that brief and wonderful moment, it felt like a badge of honor to have the last name "Coolidge."

# 24

"Hey, what do you think you're doing over there?"

Ryan was only half awake, and he didn't recognize the voice. Somehow, however, he realized that the man was talking to him.

Ryan wiped the sleep from his eyes. Part of his brain expected to see the palm trees and sandy beaches along Biscayne Bay. Those images, however, were only in his memories. Instead, he saw the glisten of sunshine dance across the flowing waters of the Mississippi River. He saw Jarvis sound asleep on the grassy bank. And he saw a very large man on a very high horse.

Ryan rose to his feet and faced the stranger. "We're just resting, sir."

The man climbed down from his horse and stepped closer. A beard and thick sideburns covered most of his face. A bushy walrus-like mustache concealed his lips. Ryan hadn't noticed before, but the man was wearing a star-shaped badge on the pocket of his blue shirt. It read METROPOLITAN POLICE. A gun was holstered on his right side, and he carried a nightstick in his left hand. Ryan braced himself for his first encounter with the law of the nineteenth century.

"You boys aren't from around here, are you?" said the police officer. He seemed intrigued by Ryan's clothes. The blue jeans and sweatshirt weren't totally out of place, but his sneakers were unlike any footwear for the time period.

"No, we're from—" Ryan stopped himself. The less said, the better. "We're from out of town."

"When did you get in?"

"This afternoon."

He spotted the remains of their crab-apple meal scattered across the grass. His gaze returned quickly, and his icy-blue eyes made Ryan shiver. "Where did you get those *apfels*?"

"*Apfels*?" said Ryan.

"I mean *apples*," the officer said, correcting himself. The lapse into German pegged him as one of the city's many immigrants.

"Oh, do you mean these apples?" said Ryan, stalling.

"We found them," said Jarvis, rising.

Ryan did a double take. He had thought Jarvis was still sleeping. It was a relief to let someone else do the explaining.

"Found them, huh? You didn't happen to *find* them on Mrs. Emerson's tree, did you?"

"I wouldn't know anything about a Mrs. Emerson," said Jarvis.

"Is that so? I'll have you know that those are winter crabs you're eating. We had ourselves a mild winter, but Mrs. Emerson's got the only trees in town with fruit hanging in March. So what have you to say about this, boy? You want to tell me whose tree you raided?"

"Ryan, don't say anything," said Jarvis, his voice barely above a whisper.

The sour taste of crab apples was rising in Ryan's throat. If he got into trouble now, he might never find Hezekiah. "I'm not going to lie. We were going to pay for them, as soon as we figured out how to get some money. We took them from—"

"Hey, Conradt!" another officer shouted. He was on horseback, stopped on a street that led down to the river.

The other officer—Conradt—shouted back at him. "What you want, Brooks?"

"Need your help on Main Street. The posse is back in town. They got six runaway slaves with them."

Officer Conradt pointed toward Ryan and said, "Can't you see I'm busy here?"

"Forget about them!" said Brooks. "We gotta get this crowd under control, or we'll have a riot on our hands. Every available officer, right now!"

Conradt shook his head, frustrated. He looked at Ryan and Jarvis and said, "Guess this is your lucky day, fellas." Then he jumped back on his horse and rode back into town.

The minute he was gone, Ryan said, "Let's get over to Main Street."

"What?" said Jarvis.

"Didn't you hear what that other cop said? A posse is bringing runaway slaves into town. People are up in arms. It's the slave owners versus the slavery opponents. This could be it!"

He started running. Jarvis gave chase, but he was nowhere near as fast.

"Could be what?" said Jarvis.

Ryan was at full speed, headed for Main Street. He glanced back and shouted, "That place Hezekiah was looking for. The place where the brood follows the dam!"

# 25

ight fell as the posse rode into town on horseback. An unruly crowd lined both sides of Main Street. Slave owners stood on one side, opponents on the other. Hand-held torches lit up the night, casting a yellow-orange glow on a sea of angry faces. People shouted back and forth, tempers flaring, words running on top of words. It was impossible to discern any single voice, any coherent sentence. There was just a noisy, collective rumble of discontent.

Ryan and Jarvis pushed their way through the crowd, but it was tough-going. The sidewalks were jammed, and people were spilling into the streets. Ryan noticed black faces and white faces on his side of the street. On the other side, he saw only white. He wanted to be closer to the action, but it was like trying to push his way to the front row of a sold-out concert. Hundreds of people had already staked out their position. Suddenly, two men gave up their spots and headed for the tavern. Ryan and Jarvis maneuvered forward and took the openings.

"Look!" said Jarvis.

A dozen men on horses approached from the east. All of them were white. Each was armed with a pistol and rifle. One was belting back a bottle of whiskey. People on the other side of the street shouted in celebration. Those on Ryan's side hissed and jeered.

"Sinners!" one woman shouted.

"Slavery is immoral!" cried another.

Tempers were on the verge of explosion, and the growing crowd swelled farther into the street. Ryan climbed atop a barrel near the hitching post for a better view. He had a clear line of sight, but he nearly lost his balance when he saw what the posse was bringing into town.

Six black men walked in single file, right down the center of the street. Their hands were bound at the wrists. A heavy chain connected their ankles, and it rattled with their movements. Two of the men were old and appeared to be on the verge of collapse. The rest were much younger, perhaps even teenagers. All of them were singing. *Singing.* Their tune was slow yet moving, a powerful old spiritual:

*Go down, Moses, Way down in Egypt's land,*
*Tell old Pharaoh, Let my people go!*

It amazed Ryan that these men could be brought into town like animals, paraded down a crowded street, and still find the courage *to sing.* As they passed, Ryan noticed the long rope that tethered one man to the next. They were spaced evenly apart, each man a few feet behind the man in front of him. They sang loud and with feeling. Even though crowd noises drowned out most of the lyrics, Ryan could feel the power of their voices. As they trudged forward in their shackles, the rope slackened and drooped between them. It seemed to join them together like a string of sad smiles.

"I have to talk to them," said Ryan.

"Are you crazy?" said Jarvis.

"I need to know if we're in the right place."

"What are you talking about?"

Ryan pushed forward. He squeezed between people and crawled on hands and knees around others. Finally, he was standing on the street. He waited for the right moment. The men on horseback were waving to the pro-slavery side of the street, receiving a hero's welcome. When no one from the posse was looking in his direction, Ryan broke away from the crowd and approached one of the slaves.

"Do you know a man named Hezekiah?" he asked, his voice racing.

"No," the man answered. "Not one of us by dat name."

"But do you know him?" said Ryan. "Have you ever met anyone named Hezekiah?"

"Uh-uh," he said. Then he started singing again.

Ryan dropped back to the second in line. "How about you? Do you know Hezekiah?"

The man shook his head. Ryan moved to the next one, and then to the next, asking the same question. *Do you know Hezekiah? Have you ever met him?*

No one could help him. Then another thought came to him. He ran ahead to the front of the line and caught up with the first slave.

"Sir, do you know where Legal Evil lives?"

The man didn't answer. His eyes were nearly closed, and he was singing in a loud voice.

"Please, can you help me?" said Ryan. "Do you know a place where the brood follows the dam?"

No answer. The slaves kept walking and singing. Ryan stopped, frustrated. "Does *anybody* know—"

Ryan was suddenly on the ground. One of the posse

members had shoved him aside with the butt of his shotgun. "Back away there, boy! This ain't your property."

*Property*? Ryan thought. It was the first time he'd ever heard people referred to as "property."

The posse moved on. The slaves went with them. Their singing faded as the march continued down Main Street. Many of the onlookers moved alongside them. Others dispersed, disappearing into the tavern or walking home.

Ryan stood silently in the street, not quite believing what he'd just seen. He looked around for Jarvis, but he didn't see him. He hoped they hadn't gotten separated in all the confusion.

"You all right, son?" a woman asked him.

Ryan turned to see a gentle but unfamiliar face. She appeared to be his mother's age, though it was difficult to tell. She was wearing a hooded cape. The torchbearers had moved on with the posse. The only light was from the moon, the flickering gaslight on the street corner, and a few oil lamps hanging in the windows behind them.

Ryan said, "I'm all right. Thank you."

"What's your name?"

"Ryan." Even in the nineteenth century, he left off the surname.

"I'm Abigail. Abigail Fitzsimons."

As they shook hands she said, "Are you looking for someone?"

Ryan glanced toward the sidewalk, the spot where he'd last seen Jarvis. "Yes, I'm looking for—"

"Hezekiah?"

Ryan froze. "Yes. How did you know that?"

"I heard you asking the other slaves if they knew a man named Hezekiah."

"Oh." He shrugged and said, "None of them could help."

"Maybe I can," she said.

"Do you know Hezekiah?"

"It's not the kind of name you hear every day. But I just saw a man named Hezekiah two days ago."

"Where?"

"Right here in this street."

"Are you serious? Where was he? I mean exactly."

"He came in behind the posse. Just like tonight's slaves."

Ryan's heart skipped a beat. "Are you saying that the posse brought him in as a runaway slave?"

"Him and three others. Yes."

"But that's not possible. Hezekiah is not a runaway slave."

"Well, none of these are runaways, technically. This all has to do with the Dred Scott decision."

"The *what?*"

She looked at him curiously. "The whole country's been talking about it since the Supreme Court released its opinion on the sixth of March. Where have you been, boy?"

"I guess I've been . . . traveling. But I don't understand. What does a Supreme Court decision have to do with posses bringing slaves into town?"

"Dred Scott was a slave here in Missouri. His master took him to Wisconsin and Illinois for twelve whole years. Slavery is illegal there. So Dred Scott sued his master and asked the court to say he was a free man. It took another twelve years in the court system. The case went all the way to the United States Supreme Court in Washington, D.C."

"What did they decide?"

"They ruled in favor of slavery. The court said that slaves are property, not people. Even if the owner takes his slave into a free territory, the slave is still a slave."

Ryan thought for a moment. He still didn't understand the meaning of the riddle "The brood follows the dam." But this

Dred Scott decision sounded a whole heck of a lot like Legal Evil at work.

"So Dred Scott was forced to become a slave again?" asked Ryan.

"Yes. And so did all these other men you saw paraded down the street tonight. Ever since the Supreme Court made its decision, slave owners have been going back into Illinois and other free states, looking for their property. If they find them, they bring them back."

"And you say a posse brought back a man named Hezekiah two days ago?"

"That's right."

"But it can't be. Hezekiah was never a slave. What did he look like?"

"Very old. Kind of wild hair and bushy white eyebrows. He had on strange clothes, too. And shoes—unlike any I've seen before. They look something like yours."

Ryan glanced at his sneakers, and he recalled the canvas basketball shoes that Hezekiah had worn around the office. It was a painful realization, but Ryan could reach no other conclusion: They were indeed talking about the very same Hezekiah. "This is terrible," said Ryan. "Hezekiah is not a slave. He's my friend. I have to get him out of here."

She smiled with her eyes. "I might just be able to help you there, young man. Bringing people out of slavery is my life's work."

"It is?"

She leaned closer and whispered into his ear. "I'm an abolitionist."

Ryan thought he knew what she meant, but he didn't dare ask for an explanation. From the expression on her face, he was certain of this much: "Abolitionist" was a dangerous word to utter on this street.

"When can we get started?" asked Ryan.

"As soon as you like. Why don't you come on over to my house for dinner. We can talk about it."

Once again, Ryan scanned the street, searching for Jarvis. "I'd like to. But I came here with a friend. I don't see him anywhere."

"What's he look like?"

"Kind of hard to miss," said Ryan. "Big guy. And his face is really flat, kind of like he ran into a brick wall or something."

"Is that him over there?" she said.

Ryan spotted a gathering outside the tavern across the street. People were laughing and celebrating, eating fried chicken, sucking down cold drinks. In the middle of the crowd stood Jarvis. He was gnawing on a barbecued rib.

"Yes, that's him," said Ryan.

"What on earth is your friend doing at the slave owners' party?"

Ryan took a hard look at Jarvis, his eyes clouding with concern. "That's what I'd like to know."

# 26

"I was hungry," Jarvis told Ryan. "That's all there is to it."

They were riding in the back of a horse-drawn wagon. Abigail was at the reins. A struggling old mare with a sagging backbone was pulling them down a dark, rutted road.

Ryan had done his best to avoid making a scene at the street party outside the tavern. He took Jarvis by the arm and quietly pulled him away. Even so, Jarvis did manage to stuff three more barbecued ribs and a grilled chicken leg into his pockets on the way out. Ryan waited until they were well out of town before speaking his mind. First, he told Jarvis what the abolitionist had said about Hezekiah. Then he laid into him about crossing over to the slave owners' side of the street.

"Do you realize that you were partying with the same people who took Hezekiah into slavery?" said Ryan.

"I wasn't partying with anyone," he said, still chewing a mouthful of chicken. "I was just eating their food."

"Did you see me eating their food? Did you see Abigail?"

"Lay off, will you, Ryan? I haven't eaten anything but those crab apples since we got here. These folks were giving away food. I smelled barbecue, and I couldn't resist. What's the big deal?"

"We're with the abolitionists now. We can't go to parties and rub elbows with the slave owners."

"Nice fancy word there, smarty pants. I bet you don't even know what an abolitionist is."

"I do so."

Abigail spoke up. "An abolitionist is someone who fights to abolish slavery. Some of us speak out in public. Some of us work behind the scenes. A few of us will even risk our lives to help slaves like your friend Hezekiah find freedom. Now, if you two don't quit arguing and help me hatch a plan, your friend Hezekiah is gonna be stuck in slavery for good. You understand?"

"Yes ma'am," they said in unison.

The moon rose in the night sky as the wagon bounced farther down the dirt road. They were out of the city and well into the countryside. It was getting chilly, and Ryan wrapped himself in a coarse blanket. The old wagon creaked. A hoot owl called to them from the twisted limbs of an old oak tree. The ride to Abigail's house was taking longer than Ryan had expected. People in the nineteenth century obviously had a different notion of what "Just down yonder" meant.

The wagon stopped. Ryan looked up, but Abigail shushed him.

"Hold still," she whispered.

A shot rang out. Ryan ducked down and said, "What was that!"

Abigail chuckled as she laid down her shotgun and climbed out of the wagon. "Dinner."

They ate rabbit stew that night at Abigail's cottage. She skinned and dressed the animal herself. She added some onions and roots, then boiled it all in an iron pot that hung in the fireplace. Ryan thought her stew was delicious. Over dinner, he managed to keep the conversation mostly about Abigail and her work as an abolitionist. Inevitably, she started down her own line of questioning. Where were they from? How did they get to St. Louis? His responses were vague, but she didn't seem to care. She was an abolitionist, and all that really mattered to her was getting Hezekiah out of slavery.

That was all Ryan cared about, too.

"We'll leave at sunrise," said Abigail.

"Where to?" asked Ryan.

"There's a plantation south of here, near Jefferson Barracks. The slave owner who took your friend Hezekiah lives there."

"I guess we better get some shut eye then," said Jarvis.

"You two can sleep in the loft," she said.

They thanked her. Ryan started to help clear the dinner plates, but she stopped him.

"Never mind that," said Abigail. "You two look exhausted."

Jarvis yawned into his fist. "We are. Goodnight, ma'am." He went up the ladder and climbed into the loft.

"You too, boy. Git."

Ryan started toward the ladder, then stopped with one foot on the bottom wrung. "Abigail, can I ask you a question?"

"Sure. What is it?"

"This plantation we're going to. Where my friend Hezekiah is. Have you ever heard anyone say it was the kind of place where the brood follows the dam?"

"Hmmm, no. Can't say that I have. Why do you ask?"

"Just wondering. Good night."

"Okay, 'night."

Ryan climbed up to the loft. Jarvis was already snoring. Ryan settled in beside him and stole back half of the big, warm quilt that Jarvis was hogging. Ryan was dead tired, but his mind was too busy to let him sleep.

*Where the brood follows the dam.*

This was sizing up to be one tough riddle. And he might have to solve it with no help from anyone.

# 27

*T*he cock crowed as the wagon pulled away from Abigail's house. A silver moon was fading against a bluish-black sky. The sun was but a glowing orange sliver beneath the clouds on the horizon. The prairie grass smelled of fresh morning dew.

Their wagon was packed with everything they would need for the long journey south, which wasn't much. Abigail had run rescue missions before, and she knew the importance of traveling light. Their canteens were filled with drinking water, and they had more dried biscuits and beef jerky than Ryan cared to eat. They each wore a cowboy hat to block the sun. They would sleep on blankets. Beyond that, they had just the clothes on their backs and determination in their bellies.

"How long you reckon 'til we get there, Miss Abigail?" said Ryan.

"*Reckon?*" said Jarvis, mocking him. "Yet another fancy word. You're a regular abolitionist now, aren't you, kid?"

Both Ryan and Abigail ignored the sarcasm. Jarvis had been grouchy all morning, ever since Abigail's goat had relieved itself on his boot. Abigail said, "Two days. Maybe more, depending."

"Depending on what?"

"Dependin' on whether I'm right or not."

They traveled all day, stopping only to give their horse a rest. Ryan rode at Abigail's side. She let him take the reins, and it was fun to have the power of a horse at the control of his fingertips. The dirt road shadowed the river, so it was impossible to get lost or bored. Life along the Mississippi was a nonstop show. Ryan saw foxes, bears, and more deer than he could count. Hawks streaked down from the sky and snatched unsuspecting trout from the eddies. The little towns along the way were straight out of the history books. All afternoon, steamboats churned up and down the river. Ryan half expected Huck Finn and Jim to come floating by on a raft any minute. He imagined his dog Sam running happily along the banks and swimming in the river. Then he shook off that thought, trying not to make himself homesick.

That night, they slept under the stars. They woke the next morning and continued due south. Their course took them away from the river, which jogged southeast. By mid-morning, the seemingly endless prairie had turned to farmland. The first plantation came into sight.

"What do they grow here?" asked Ryan.

"Whatever they can," said Abigail. "That there's a cotton field."

It didn't look anything like the amazing photographs Ryan had seen of snowy-white cotton fields ready for harvest. Spring was the planting season, and the fields were bare by comparison.

"What's that smell?" said Ryan.

"Freshly turned dirt. That smell to a farmer is like blossoms to a bumblebee. They can't stay away from it. Don't matter how bad last year was. They might have worked sun-up to sundown, March to October, then lost the whole crop to boll weevils or bad weather or just plain bad luck. Don't make no never mind. They smell that dirt, and they is right back at it the next year. Farmers are a special kind of people."

She brought the wagon to a stop with a tug on the reins and a gentle *Whoooooa*. She climbed down and told Ryan and Jarvis to follow her up the hill. When they reached the top, they were in a cluster of trees and bushes, looking out over another cotton field.

"This was all useless prairie not long ago," she said. "Now look at it."

Ryan said, "You sound like you admire farmers."

"I do." Then her gaze drifted toward a group of black men in the field, about two-hundred yards on the other side of the fence. "Except when it comes to slavery."

Concealed by the bushes, Ryan counted a dozen slaves scattered across the field. It was mostly stoop labor. Some were planting seeds, while others tended to seedlings and sprouts. Two strong men rode behind a plow mule that was tilling the dark topsoil.

The lone white man was on horseback with a shotgun in his arms. His horse was pulling a small flatbed wagon down a working road that ran alongside the field. On the wagon was a tub of water. The man wore a large black cowboy hat and a black vest over a red flannel shirt. His smokey-gray beard was so long and gnarled that Ryan almost wondered if small animals might be living in there. Despite his advanced years, he sat upright in the saddle. The most striking thing about him was his eyes. They were cold, black, and piercing—the kind of eyes a diver might see just a split second before the Great White shark removes a hunk of flesh.

If Legal Evil had a human host, Ryan imagined that he'd have eyes like these.

Ryan watched as the two plowmen unhitched the mule from the harness and led it to the old man's wagon. The animal drank eagerly from the tub. When the mule had taken its fill, the old man handed the slaves a battered tin cup.

Then the slaves drank from the mule's tub.

One by one, they came to the wagon, dipped their cup into the tub, and took a drink. They looked very thirsty, but they seemed to know better than to ask for a refill. It was a well-worn routine. Each slave trudged across the field, drank, and immediately returned to work. The two big men working the plow were first. The women and girls were next. The boys followed. Finally, from the farthest corner of the field, came a tired, old man.

Ryan watched him carefully. He was at least a hundred yards away, but that gait was familiar. That mop of gray hair was unmistakable. And those basketball shoes were a dead giveaway.

Ryan could barely speak. "That's Hezekiah."

"I knew he'd be here," said Abigail. "This here's the Barrow farm. Old Man Barrow lost a whole bunch of slaves last year when he rented them out to a farmer in Illinois. Slavery is illegal there, and an Illinois judge gave them all their freedom. But now with the Dred Scott case, the U.S. Supreme Court said slaves is property who can never be free. So Mr. Barrow sent out posses to fetch his slaves back."

"But Hezekiah was never his slave. He was never anyone's slave."

"It probably came down to Mr. Barrow's word against Hezekiah's. Guess who the police are going to believe?"

For a brief instant, Ryan was thinking of his father again. Could that have been what made him plead guilty, the futility of one man's word against another's? No way, thought Ryan. This situation was completely different. This was slavery in the nineteenth century. Hezekiah was truly the innocent condemned.

"Let's git," said Abigail. "Before they see us."

She led them down the hill, back toward the wagon. Ryan trailed behind and pulled Jarvis aside. He didn't want Abigail to overhear. When she was far enough ahead of them, he said, "This is going to be tougher than I thought. I just realized something."

"What?" said Jarvis.

"We need a leaphole to get back. I don't have any. You don't have any. And Hezekiah doesn't, either."

"How do you know he doesn't?"

"Think about it. Would he be busting his back working in a cotton field, drinking from a mule's bucket, if all he had to do was pull a leaphole from his pocket and pop himself back to the twenty-first century?"

Jarvis didn't answer, but Ryan saw no inkling of disagreement.

They caught up with Abigail and climbed into the wagon. With a clipped *giddy-up*, Abigail had them rolling forward again. She pulled a U-turn around a tree, and they retraced the ruts in the road from their own wagon wheels.

"Why are we going back?" asked Ryan.

"There's an old barn in the next county. Belongs to an abolitionist. We'll rest there till nightfall. When it's good and dark and everyone's asleep, we'll come back on foot for Hezekiah."

*Then what?* thought Ryan. He had no leapholes. They had no way to get back to the twenty-first century. Ryan said, "Sounds like a good plan."

"Oh, yes. A girl's got to have a plan."

Ryan looked away, thinking. "This boy could sure use one, too."

# 28

*T*heir wagon stopped at the fork in the dirt road. A girl was standing in front of them, blocking their path. Behind her, the setting sun was hanging low in the sky. Ryan squinted, but he couldn't make out the face. Blasts of bright orange and yellow sunshine nearly blinded him.

"Ryan L'new? Is that you?" she said.

Ryan recognized the voice, but he could not believe his ears. "Kaylee?"

"Is there anyone else on this planet who calls you Ryan L'new?"

It seemed too good to be true. Ryan jumped down from the wagon. He ran to her, but they stopped short of hugging one another. For a split second, a big, friendly embrace had seemed like a good idea, but somehow he lost his nerve. He simply smiled and said, "Boy, are we glad to see you!"

Abigail asked him, "She a friend of yours from back home?"

"Uh, yeah, right," said Ryan. "Back home." *As in another place, another time, more than a 150 years from now.*

Abigail decided it was time to let the horse rest a spell before the final push to the abolitionist's barn. Jarvis gave Kaylee a clipped hello, then pulled his hat over his eyes and caught some shuteye in the back of the wagon. While Abigail tended to the horse, Ryan and Kaylee sat beneath a big oak tree and talked, just the two of them.

"What are you doing here?" said Ryan.

"I promised your mother that I would find you."

"You talked to my mother?"

"Yes. After you and Jarvis disappeared, your mom told the police that you were kidnapped. I begged my mom to take me to your house so that we could assure your mother that Hezekiah is no kidnapper. My mom refused to let me get involved, but I couldn't let your mom suffer like that. So I snuck over and talked to her myself."

"Did my mom tell the police about leapholes?"

"Yes. But they didn't believe her. As far as they're concerned, it's all a bunch of nonsense. The cops think you ran away, and they think your mom is too ashamed to admit it."

"So, you told my mom I didn't run away?"

"Of course. I felt so bad for her. The rumors around town were just awful. I wanted her to know that you didn't run away."

"Does she believe you?"

"She didn't at first. But I bet she does now. I used my leaphole right in front of her."

"How?"

"She had the book that you and Jarvis used. She showed me the page you were on. I went to the same page and, well, here I am."

Kaylee removed the law book from her backpack and gave it to Ryan. "I brought it with me," she said. "Hezekiah never does that, because he's an expert on return leapholes. But for a rookie like me, the easiest way to return safely is to bring the book along."

Ryan turned to the marked page. It was definitely from Hezekiah's library. But now that Ryan had seen those slaves marching down Main Street, bound and chained, the book seemed almost holy. The name of the case was printed across the top of the page: *Scott v. Sanford.* That was the Dred Scott decision. It was like Hezekiah had told Ryan the first time they'd met: These books were filled with real people. Dred Scott had lived his life in slavery. Sanford was the man who had owned him. Case books were so much more than words on paper.

Ryan closed the book. "It's a long case. Over fifty pages. I guess that's how we all ended up here, even though Hezekiah entered through a different page."

"Right. Different page, but it was still the same case."

"But you should have landed in St. Louis. How did you know to look for me here?"

"The first thing I did when I landed in St. Louis was buy a newspaper. The story of Hezekiah was on page three of the *Daily Morning Herald.* It said he was taken back to the Barrow plantation. I knew you'd be looking for Hezekiah. This is the only road to the Barrow plantation. So I caught a ride in the back of a feed wagon, got off here, and waited."

Ryan was so glad to see her that he almost forgot the most important thing. Then it came to him—the trip home. "You do have a return leaphole, right?"

"Of course. Never leave home without one."

"Whew," said Ryan. "Jarvis and I don't have any. And we don't think Hezekiah would still be planting cotton if he had one in his back pocket. Can we all use yours to get back?"

"Sure. That's what I'm here for."

"Awesome!"

She turned serious. "But I should warn you. This is the only one I have left. When you become a Legal Eagle, you get one leaphole for the journey out, and one to come back. I can't earn any more until I get my law degree. Those are the rules."

"Where is it?"

"In my backpack. For safekeeping."

"So that's it? You have just the one leaphole?"

"Yup. Just one."

Ryan gave her a little smile. "That's perfect. One is all we need."

Darkness had fallen by the time their wagon reached the abolitionist's barn. It was an old, abandoned structure, no good for anything except as a place to hide the wagon. They rolled the wagon inside, then set up camp outside. No one wanted to sleep in a hundred-year-old barn that might come crashing down with the slightest puff of wind.

"Why do we have to go to all this trouble of hiding the wagon anyway?" asked Jarvis. He was sitting on a tree stump, across the campfire from Abigail. Orange sparks twirled like fireflies between them in the rising curls of smoke.

Abigail said, "We can't take the wagon with us when we go back to get Hezekiah."

"Why not?"

"Once old man Barrow discovers that one of his slaves is missing, every slave owner between here and the Illinois border will be riding up and down this road, checking the wagons. We have to escape on foot and head for the woods. Hide out for a while. We'll come back for the wagon when things settle down and the road is safe again."

Kaylee asked, "What happens if we get caught with Hezekiah?"

"Mr. Barrow might turn us over to the marshal. We could go to jail. Or the boys in his posse might take matters into their own hands."

"Which would be worse?" asked Jarvis.

"The posse, without a doubt. They don't take kindly to abolitionists and runaway slaves in these parts."

"What could they do to us?" asked Kaylee.

"Hopefully just rough us up a bit, teach us a lesson. Hezekiah is the one I'm most worried about. The posse already captured him once before. This would be considered his second runaway. They'll do far worse to him."

"How much worse?" asked Ryan.

Abigail's gaze drifted toward the strong, sprawling limbs of the old oak tree. She paused, as if reluctant to elaborate. "If he's lucky, they'll only shoot him."

Abigail's words just hung in the air, drawing only silence.

Ryan poked at the fire with a long stick, stirring up a few glowing embers. "I sure hope none of us ever has to meet this old man Barrow."

"Why is he so mean?" asked Kaylee.

"It's just his nature," said Abigail. "He was the same way when he was a judge."

"He used to be a judge?" said Ryan.

"Yup," said Abigail. "That's what he did before he retired and went back to the Barrow family farm. He was one of the most pro-slavery judges the South has ever known."

Ryan suddenly recalled those shark-like eyes and that cold expression on old man Barrow's face. He still didn't know how to find the place "where the brood follows the dam," but perhaps Legal Evil was closer than he'd thought.

They ate dinner around the campfire—more beef jerky and dried biscuits. Kaylee had a chocolate candy bar in her pocket from the twenty-first century. She shared it with Ryan. Candy had never tasted so good. Like it or not, she'd just earned herself a friend for life. After dinner, they spread out their blankets around the fire and retired for the night. Jarvis was the first to snore. Minutes later, Abigail was snoring even louder.

Slowly, the campfire burned itself out. Venus was shining brightly in a star-speckled sky. Ryan was still wide awake. He could hear the wind blowing lightly through the cracks in the old, decrepit barn. He opened his eyes and looked up at the stars. It was funny the way stars seemed to swirl in the sky if you stared up at them long enough.

"Ryan, you okay?" asked Kaylee.

He rolled on his side to face her. He couldn't quite see her face in the moonlight, but he could see the outline of her long hair draped over one shoulder. She had propped herself up on one elbow, a dark silhouette in the night.

"I'm okay, I guess," he said. "Just can't sleep."

"Are you worried about Hezekiah?"

"Aren't you?"

He could hear Kaylee sigh. "Hezekiah is an amazing person," she said. "He's the smartest man I've ever met. He can handle almost anything."

"I know."

She waited for him to say more, but he didn't. She added, "That's not what's keeping you awake, is it?"

He rolled onto his back again. The stars had stopped swirling. "Actually, I was thinking about my dad."

"Oh."

"Yeah," he said. "A big 'oh.'"

Kaylee said, "When we were in prison that night, I promised not to ask about your dad anymore. But if you feel like talking . . ."

Ryan hadn't opened up to anyone about his feelings toward his dad since the day he went to prison. For some reason, he felt like he could talk about those things with Kaylee— important stuff. Especially in the darkness. He suspected that some of the most honest conversations in the history of the world had occurred beneath the blanket of nightfall.

"Whenever I visit my dad in prison, he tells me he's innocent. And every time he tells me that, I say, 'But if you're innocent, why did you plead guilty?'"

"What's his answer?"

"He says he can't tell me. Which makes me so mad. If he's innocent, why can't he tell me why he pleaded guilty?"

"I wish I could answer that for you, Ryan."

"I wish *somebody* would answer that."

Ryan couldn't see Kaylee's eyes in the darkness, but he sensed her sincerity. Finally, she asked, "What are you thinking?"

He clasped his hands behind his head, still staring up at the night sky. "I'm confused. I mean, what if he *is* innocent? What must it be like to be in prison for something you didn't do?"

"Horrible," she said without hesitation. "Every day, you must think about being free. And every day ends in disappointment."

"Like being a slave," said Ryan.

"Yeah. Like being a slave."

"Except I can't really be sure that my father is as innocent as these slaves."

"For what it's worth, when I talked to your mother, she told me that your father was innocent. It seemed like she really wanted me to know that."

"No," said Ryan. "She wanted you to *believe* it. I don't think we'll ever *know* it."

She seemed to understand the distinction. Then she lowered her head and nuzzled against her blanket. "Try to get some sleep, okay? Big day tomorrow."

"Yeah," said Ryan, his eyes still wide open. "Huge."

# 29

yan refused to open his eyes. He ignored the gentle nudge in the small of his back and the repeated announcements that it was time to rise and shine. He just rolled over and buried his face in his blanket.

"Mom, there's no school today," he said, grumbling. "Honest. It's a teachers's workshop."

"What?" said Abigail.

Ryan sat bolt upright. He was now wide awake, suddenly realizing that he wasn't in his bed at home and that this woman poking him in the back wasn't his mother. "Uh, nothing," said Ryan. "I must have been dreaming."

It was two o'clock in the morning, and the team was ready to put their rescue plan into action. They had to reach the Barrow plantation on foot, grab Hezekiah, and disappear into hiding before sunrise. There was no time to waste. Before they broke camp, Abigail shared some words of wisdom.

"You have to remember just two rules on a rescue mission. One, the important things are always simple. And two," she said as a wry smile creased her lips, "the simple things are always hard. Let's move."

They hiked for one hour. The wagon remained hidden at

the barn, but Abigail brought her horse to carry supplies. That lightened their load, but it was still difficult to trek through the woods in the dark of night. There were no roads, not even a footpath. Every few minutes one of them would stumble over a fallen log or a rock. The others would stop and look with concern, as if to ask *Are you okay?* It went without saying that this was no time for a sprained ankle. The stakes were way too high.

They stopped to rest at the edge of the woods, where the canopy of spring's new buds and leaves gave way to the cotton field. Abigail tied her horse to a tree deep within the forest, so that it couldn't be seen from the farm. As they took their last sips of water from the canteen, Abigail gave the final instructions.

"This is the danger zone," she said in a whisper. "From this point forward, we move quickly and in silence, and only on my command. Understood?"

They nodded.

Abigail pointed fifty yards to the east, across a stream. "See those shacks yonder?"

It was dark, but Ryan's eyes had completely adjusted to the starlit night. He saw three shacks—four, if you counted the little outhouse behind them. They had sagging roofs, and the walls were made of roughly hewn logs. The two on either end were small, but the middle one was twice as big. It was the only one with a chimney. Spring was chilly enough, but winters had to be awfully cold for anyone who wasn't lucky enough to claim a spot by the fire in the big shack.

"Those are the slave quarters," said Abigail.

"How many slaves are there?" asked Ryan.

"Don't know for sure."

"Which shack is Hezekiah in?" asked Kaylee.

"The small one on the end. If you look at the tools hanging on the side of the shack, they're all for planting. The other shacks are for house servants. Hezekiah is a field worker, so he's got to be in that nearest one. The one with the woodpile behind it.

"When I say so, the four of us will run across the field to that woodpile. Then Ryan and I will sneak into the shack and get Hezekiah. Kaylee and Jarvis, you'll be our lookouts. If you see a dog coming at us or an oil lamp light up in the main house, or if you hear footsteps or anything else that worries you, I want you to make a sound like a hoot owl. Can you do that?"

They tried. *Woo-hoo, woo-hoo.* It sounded pretty authentic.

"Good," said Abigail. "Now, I'm not sure what hour of the night it is in heaven, but I suggest we all bow our heads and make sure the Lord is fully awake and on our side." They joined hands, and Abigail led them in a quick prayer. When they finished, she looked up and said, "Let's do it."

Like a sprinter out of the blocks, Abigail led the way across the open field. The others followed right behind her, moving swiftly and in silence. It seemed to take forever, but in reality it was only a matter of seconds before they were huddled next to one another outside the nearest slave shack. They were hiding behind the woodpile. Jarvis was huffing and puffing. The others were stone silent. Abigail raised a finger to her lips, as if to say *Shhhhhhhh.* When Jarvis got his loud breathing under control, Abigail gave a quick signal. Kaylee and Jarvis, the two lookouts, remained in hiding. Abigail led Ryan away from the woodpile.

They made a quick dash to the shack and crouched at the front door. Slowly—as carefully as Ryan had ever seen anyone move—Abigail turned the handle and nudged the door open. With the jerk of her head, Abigail signaled Ryan to follow her inside.

Two small windows on opposite walls welcomed a fair amount of moonlight. Ryan counted ten wooden bunks with straw mattresses, five on either side of a narrow center aisle. The chorus of loud snoring was a testimonial to how hard these men worked all day. They were in deep sleep. Ryan took a quick look at each bunk—a bald man, a young man, two big men who could have played football in a later century. Finally, Ryan spotted the mop of gray hair in the bunk at the end of the row. He signaled to Abigail.

That's him, he said without words.

Ryan and Abigail crawled down the aisle on hands and knees. Hezekiah appeared to be sound asleep, curled beneath a smelly old horse blanket. Just the sight of him made Ryan want to jump up and down and shout with joy. He was so glad to have found him, but they had a long way to go before it was time to celebrate. Ryan debated how best to wake him. He was about to flick the old man on the end of the nose when, to his surprise, Hezekiah grabbed his wrist and whispered, "What took you so long, Ryan?"

They shared a smile, then Hezekiah turned deadly serious. He put his lips to Ryan's ears and whispered, "The bald slave closest to the door is an informant for the master. If you wake him, he'll run straight to the house and tell him there's an escape. There might be other informants, too. I don't know."

Ryan nodded, and he fully understood: If there had been any hope of taking additional slaves with them, the prospect of informants among them squelched those plans.

Quietly, Hezekiah peeled back the blanket and rolled out of his bunk. He and Ryan inched across the floor, following right behind Abigail. Just as they reached the door, they heard a noise from outside: *Wooo-hooo, wooo-hooo.*

The threesome stopped cold. It sounded a little like a hoot owl, but it sounded even more like Kaylee. It was a warning from their look outs.

For a moment, Ryan felt paralyzed. Earlier that night, back at their campsite, Abigail had told them how dangerous this mission was for Hezekiah. She'd warned them that if the posse caught him, the old man would be lucky "if they only shoot him." Ryan didn't want to risk Hezekiah's life. On the other hand, he didn't want to leave him behind in this shack to live in slavery. In the darkness, he glanced at Hezekiah. He, too, seemed to have recognized Kaylee's voice in the *wooo-hooo* from behind the woodpile. He surely knew the dangers of an attempted escape. But Ryan saw only one message in Hezekiah's eyes.

Keep going.

Without speaking a word, the team became of one mind. Crawling, Abigail led the way to the open door. Ryan was about to follow, but the bald man—the slave that Hezekiah had said was the master's informant—stirred in his sleep. He grunted once, as if something was lodged in his throat. Ryan and Hezekiah pasted their bodies to the floor, lying perfectly still, trying not even to breathe. Finally, the informant fell quiet. Ryan hurried out the door, and Hezekiah was right behind him.

Abigail waved them over to the woodpile. Ryan and Hezekiah rose from their hands and knees and ran in her direction. They rounded the corner at full speed, past the planting tools. Behind the shack, Ryan spotted the collection of shovels spread across the ground, and he easily avoided them. Hezekiah didn't see them until it was too late. Tripping over a pile of tools would have been like sounding an alarm.

Somehow—perhaps it was the twenty-first-century basketball shoes—Hezekiah did a last-second sidestep, pulled a complete three-sixty in the air, and cleared the stack of tools. Ryan looked on with amazement. It was a maneuver worthy of a BMX bicycle champion.

Or of a slave in search of freedom.

They were halfway to the woodpile, speeding past the outhouse, when the door flew open. They stopped in their tracks. They were face to face with a young woman.

"Hey, what—" she started to say, but Hezekiah grabbed her. He covered her mouth with one hand as he took her behind the woodpile. Ryan pulled up behind them.

Kaylee whispered, "That's what we were *wooo-hoooing* about! Somebody went to the bathroom. We were trying to warn you!"

Hezekiah kept his hand over the woman's mouth. She was a young slave with beautiful almond-shaped eyes. At the moment, however, those eyes were wide with fright. Her belly moved up and down with each breath. It was a huge belly, and then Ryan realized: This young slave was extremely pregnant.

Hezekiah spoke in a calming voice. He knew her by name. "Hannah, don't you worry none, okay? These are my friends. They've come to get me. Do you understand?"

She nodded.

"Now, if I take my hand off your mouth, you're not going to scream, are you?"

She shook her head.

Hezekiah's hand slipped away. She looked up at him, then glanced at the others. She didn't scream, but her voice shook as she said, "Take me with you."

No one answered right away.

"Please," she said. "You gotta take me. Please don't let my baby be born a slave."

"When's your baby due?" asked Hezekiah.

"Any day now, they tell me."

Jarvis groaned. "How are we supposed to escape through the woods with a woman who's so pregnant that she can't even see her own feet?"

"We can't just leave her here," said Ryan.

"She'll slow us down if we take her," said Jarvis.

"No she won't," said Ryan. "Abigail's horse is hitched to a tree in the woods. Hannah can ride."

Hezekiah held the woman's hand. "Ryan's right. We can't leave her. Or her baby. We'll find a way, Hannah."

"Thank you, sir. I thank every one of you."

"Which one of the slaves is your husband?" asked Abigail. "We should bring him, too."

The young woman's eyes filled with sadness. "My husband got sold six months ago. I don't know where he is now."

Ryan said, "Old Man Barrow sold your husband after you were expecting a child?"

"He sure did."

"That man is just plain evil," said Abigail.

"Yes, he is," said Hezekiah. "Evil with a capital E."

Ryan wondered if that could mean Evil as in *Legal* Evil, but this was not the time to be sorting out riddles—especially not in front of Hannah and Abigail.

"It's agreed, then," said Hezekiah. "Hannah comes with us."

Jarvis drew a breath. "When we all get caught, I'll try not to say I told you so."

"We won't get caught," said Abigail. "But we have to leave now. Let's move it!"

The run for the woods almost proved Jarvis's point. It was more like a brisk walk. Hannah was going as fast as she could, which was not very fast at all. Finally, all six of them crossed the field and reached the cover of trees and bushes. They stopped briefly to rest—mostly for Hannah's benefit—then continued deeper into the woods. Hannah might not have made it but for the promise of a ride. Minutes later, they found Abigail's horse where she had left it, hitched to a tree. Ryan removed some supplies from the horse's back to make room for Hannah. Hezekiah and Jarvis lifted her into the saddle. She smiled, and everyone seemed happy, as if the most difficult part of the journey was behind them.

The sound of barking dogs immediately told them otherwise.

"Them's bloodhounds," said Abigail.

"On us already?" said Jarvis.

Hezekiah said, "We must have awakened that informant. I bet he turned old man Barrow's dogs loose."

"Obviously they got our scent," said Abigail. "We gotta run for the creek. It's the only way to throw them off the trail."

"It's not the only way," said Kaylee. "We can use a leaphole."

"Leapin' what holes?" said Abigail.

There was no time to explain to outsiders. Hezekiah responded directly to Kaylee, as if Abigail and Hannah weren't even there. "I don't have any leapholes, Kaylee. That's why I'm a slave."

"We can use mine. I still have my return."

Hezekiah seemed tempted. "No good. We can't use it now. We can't leave Hannah behind."

"What are y'all talking about?" said Abigail.

The barking was getting louder. The dogs were drawing closer.

"Those dogs are inside of a quarter mile," said Jarvis. "I told you we should never have brought Hannah with us. Just leave her."

"We can take her with us," said Ryan. "We'll link together, the way Jarvis and I did when we came here. It's like a human chain."

Jarvis grimaced. "You want to take a pregnant nineteenth-century slave to the twenty-first century? That's very dangerous, Ryan."

"It can't be more dangerous than running through the woods and being chased by dogs."

"Oh, yes it can be," said Jarvis.

"Here's the plan," said Ryan. "We take Hannah with us just long enough for her to get away from these slave catchers. We go back to Hezekiah's office. He grabs another leaphole from his stash, and then he immediately turns around and brings her back to 1857. Only this time he brings along a leaphole to get himself back to where he belongs."

Abigail's face was chalk white, as if she'd seen a ghost. "Who in the heck are you people?" she said, her voice quaking.

"Ryan's plan could work," said Hezekiah.

"Then let's do it!" said Kaylee. "Everyone link arms."

Jarvis elbowed his way into prime position, right beside Kaylee. "I better go next to Kaylee," he said. "I'm the only one strong enough to hang on to all of you."

"That's fine," said Hezekiah. "Kaylee first, since it's her leaphole. Jarvis is next. Then me, then Ryan, and then Hannah."

"What about Abigail?" asked Ryan.

"No, sir. I ain't going nowhere with you crazy people," she said.

"It's us or the dogs," said Hezekiah.

The hounds were close enough to be heard breaking through the brush. Abigail considered it for a moment, then said, "Okay. I'll go. I'd rather take my chances with you crazy loons than end up being dog food."

They each took their positions, standing shoulder-to-shoulder. Kaylee opened her backpack and removed the old case book that she'd borrowed from Hezekiah's library. She turned to the Dred Scott decision, finding the exact page through which she had entered the leaphole. Finally, she removed two leapholes from her pocket, the spent leaphole that had brought her here, and the return leaphole that would take her home.

The barking was more intense. The dogs were hot on their trail.

"Hurry," said Jarvis.

"I'm hurrying," said Kaylee. She ran her finger along the page, searching for the precise spot where she had placed the leaphole for her initial journey. She placed the return leaphole exactly in the same place, and then laid her spent leaphole on top of it.

Nothing was happening.

Ryan said, "Are you sure this is going to work?"

"It'll work," said Hezekiah. "Just give it a minute."

The dogs sounded like they were just on the other side of the bushes. Ryan wished Sam were with him, though it was doubtful that his Golden would have been a match for those hounds. "We may not have a minute," said Ryan.

Suddenly, an orange glow appeared around the book.

"Here it goes," said Kaylee.

Ryan felt a warm current of energy rushing through his body. It wasn't scary, but it was definitely inexplicable. The warmth became a vibration, and Hannah was suddenly trying to wiggle free.

"What's happening?" she said.

Ryan tightened his grip on her elbow. "Stay with it, Hannah!"

Slowly, Ryan felt himself moving forward. Kaylee was turning like an axle. The others moved around her in circular fashion, like the sweeping secondhand of a huge clock. They walked slowly at first, then faster. The orange light grew brighter, and soon they weren't walking at all. They were propelled in the same clock-like, circular motion. It reminded Ryan of those Ice Capades shows, where the skater at the fulcrum whips a long line of other skaters around her.

"Holy smokes!" shouted Hannah, but Ryan could barely hear her. They were gaining speed quickly. Suddenly, just as the barking dogs came into sight, the surroundings became a blur. All sounds of the forest evaporated. Then darkness turned to light, and Ryan felt the pull of the leaphole.

"Hold on!" shouted Hezekiah.

Ryan squeezed Hannah's arm with his left hand. He held Hezekiah's arm with his right. Beyond that fading sense of human touch, there was just the intense light of the leaphole, the amazing pull that was its power.

Then something went wrong. The smooth swirling motion of the leaphole gave way to a strange and disturbing sensation of uncontrolled flying. Ryan felt as though they were tumbling and twisting in no particular direction at all. He tried to get his bearings. He told himself that nothing was wrong, but he knew that something was *very* wrong. He knew, because he could hear the concern in Hezekiah's voice. The old man was shouting at the top of his voice. Ryan couldn't understand him at first. As the flying began to feel more like falling, Ryan finally made out the words.

"Stay together!" shouted Hezekiah. "Everyone, just stay together!"

# 30

*T*hey landed in a meadow at sunrise. Low-hanging clouds to the east seemed to be floating on a purple-orange sea of calm. As the sun broke the plane, the chill of night started to burn away. Dew drops glistened on waves of spring grass and an endless field of yellow blossoms.

The forest was gone. The dogs were gone.

And so was Kaylee.

Ryan rose and counted heads once more. To his left were Hannah and Abigail; to his right, Hezekiah and Jarvis. Apart from looking as if they'd emerged from a wind tunnel, they were unharmed. Ryan was more worried about his missing friend. "What happened to Kaylee?" he said.

"Our human chain must have broken during take-off," said Hezekiah.

Jarvis lowered his head in shame. "I'm sorry, everyone. I just couldn't hold on."

Ryan tried not to get angry, but his concern for Kaylee left him somewhere between alarmed and agitated. "What do you mean you couldn't hold on? Everyone else managed to hang on. You're stronger than any of us."

"Yeah, but I was the only one who had the weight of four people pulling on my arm. Hezekiah had only three, you had two, and Hannah had only one. Once that leaphole started to swirl, it was like trying to hold on to four people in the middle of a hurricane."

"All right, fine," said Ryan. "But can somebody please tell me where Kaylee is?"

"She's a sharp girl," said Hezekiah. "She knows well enough to stay with the leaphole and ride it out. I'm sure she's home by now."

Hezekiah's reassurance put him somewhat at ease. But he suddenly had a new worry. "If Kaylee's at home, then where are *we*?"

Hezekiah's gaze swept the meadow. The sun was now completely above the horizon, making the field of wild yellow flowers even more bright. "I have no idea," he said. "Abigail, Hannah—how about you? Does this place look familiar?"

"Not in the least."

"No, sir," added Hannah.

"Then what are you saying?" said Ryan. "We could be . . . anywhere?"

"No, I wouldn't say anywhere. We broke away from the leaphole during take off, which means that we're probably not very far from where we started."

"But we have no leapholes," said Ryan. "So wherever we are, it means—"

"We're stuck," said Jarvis, finishing the thought. "And it's all my fault. I can't believe I blew it for everybody."

He had indeed let them down, but finger pointing never did any good. Hezekiah laid a consoling hand on his shoulder and said, "Don't blame yourself, big guy."

"It's okay, Jarvis," said Ryan. "It would have taken the strongest man in the world to hang on to four people in that leaphole."

"You really mean that?" said Jarvis.

"Sure," said Hezekiah. "We'll figure something out."

Abigail rose and brushed the droplets of morning dew from her pants. "I don't know what in tar-nation you people are talking about, and I don't want to know. But we ain't never gonna figure out where we is just sittin' around moping. Let's git."

"Which way do we go?" asked Ryan.

"North," she said. "As far north as we can take this runaway slave."

Hannah held her belly. "I'm feeling kind of funny."

Abigail said, "You just hang on there, momma. We don't want that baby popping out till we know we're in a free state."

Hannah grimaced with pain. "I dunno if I can wait. I think all that swirling and twirling maybe got this baby a little excited."

"You want your baby to be born free or born a slave?"

"Free. 'Course I want him free."

"Then you tell him to calm right down and wait a spell, honey. Abigail's in control now. I'll get you and that little one to freedom. We'll be having no more fancy leapholes, or whatever you folks call those things. It's time for me to take y'all on a little ride."

"What kind of ride?" said Hannah.

She smiled and said, "From here on out, we'll be traveling by railroad. The *underground* railroad."

As Ryan soon discovered, the underground railroad was neither underground nor a railroad. The term actually referred to the secret routes that runaway slaves traveled when fleeing north to freedom and the loose network of assistance they received along the way. It started after the American Revolution and became more organized as opposition to slavery swelled in the mid-nineteenth century. The lines of secrecy cut through rivers and swamps, across meadows, over mountains, and down dusty roads. The whole system worked because people who hated slavery were brave enough to risk their own lives in the hope that others would find freedom. Over the years, perhaps a 100,000 fugitives from bondage escaped through the underground railroad.

Sadly, Ryan was beginning to have serious doubts as to whether Hannah would be one of them.

"Just a little bit farther, honey," said Abigail.

"I can't go no farther," said Hannah.

They'd been walking for two hours, due north. Abigail's horse had been left behind in the leaphole disaster, so they had to travel on foot. They stopped only three times, once to drink from a stream and fill their canteens, and twice more to hide Hezekiah and Hannah in the weeds. Because they didn't know where they were, the safest bet was to assume that any sign of life on the horizon might be a slave-catching posse. Fortunately, both scares had been false alarms. The first time it was a herd of deer crossing the meadow. The second time was sheer paranoia. Hannah had only thought she'd seen some men on horseback in the distance.

The sod house straight ahead was no mirage, no false alarm. It was as real as the sweat on Ryan's brow. A sod house was exactly what the name implied: a house constructed from chunks of sod cut from the ground. It blended into the surroundings like a grassy knoll on the prairie, which made it a perfect place for runaway slaves to hide from the dangers of daylight.

Unless its owner was pro-slavery.

"Oh, my!" Hannah shrieked. She fell to her knees. Ryan felt her fingernails digging into his forearm as she struggled to endure her sudden surge of pain.

"Another one?" said Ryan.

Hannah nodded, unable to speak.

Abigail said, "She's having some mighty powerful contractions."

"Is that a bad thing?" asked Ryan.

"That's a body's way of telling a woman that her baby's coming. It'll pass."

Slowly, some of the tension seemed to drain from Hannah's body. Her back and shoulders were less stiff, but she appeared exhausted. The intense abdominal pain had indeed passed. From the look on her face, however, the repeated episodes were beginning to take their toll.

"You okay, honey?" asked Abigail.

Hannah caught her breath. "This is wearing me out."

"Your contractions are coming about every ten minutes now. They're getting stronger, aren't they?"

"Yes, ma'am."

"Won't be long now," said Abigail.

Jarvis looked at her quizzically. "What do you mean it won't be long?"

"That baby is coming before sundown. I bet my life on it."

"We need to get her to a hospital," said Ryan.

"A hospital?" Hezekiah said with a chuckle. "This is 1857, Ryan. That sod house up ahead will have to do."

Hannah managed to take a few steps forward, but she'd already done too much walking on too little rest. It was clear that she couldn't make it the full fifty yards to the sod house. Ryan ran ahead and brought back a wood plank from the ramshackle fence around the sod house. Jarvis and Hezekiah each took an end, and they used it like a stretcher to carry Hannah the rest of the way. As they drew closer, Ryan went to the front door and knocked, but he heard only a hollow echo.

He tried again, but it was obvious that no one was home. He pushed the door, and it creaked as it opened. A racoon ran over Ryan's feet, startling him. He collected himself and stepped inside.

There was just a single room, if you could call it a room. It had all the charm of a hole in the ground. The walls were dirt, and so was the floor. The sod roof was supported by rotting timbers. They were sagging in places, and perhaps one or two more winters would trigger a complete collapse. The only furniture was a chest of drawers in the corner and an old wooden table up against the wall. The whole place smelled foul, like an outhouse for racoons. No human being had lived there for quite awhile, but it was the best the prairie had to offer.

Ryan stepped outside and shouted, "Looks great! Come on in!"

They carried Hannah inside and laid her on the table. She was in terrible distress, and Ryan wasn't sure how to console her. He was glad Abigail was with them. Herself a mother, Abigail knew exactly what to do. She sent Hezekiah out to gather sticks and branches for a fire. Ryan searched the chest of drawers for some matches, but of course "safety matches" were not widely available in 1857. Ryan settled for a piece of flintstone that the previous occupants had left behind. After many failed attempts, he and Hezekiah finally produced a spark big enough to light the dry grass and twigs. Minutes later, they had a roaring fire. Ryan and the men stayed outside and kept it burning. Abigail stayed inside with Hannah. All was silent, save for the occasional crackling of the fire and the periodic screams from the mother to be.

Hannah's last cry had been particularly shrill.

"What's going on in there?" said Jarvis.

"Pain's a natural part of childbirth," said Hezekiah. "No way around that. At least not in the middle of the nineteenth century."

The door opened. Abigail emerged, her sleeves rolled up and a panicky expression on her face. She knelt beside the fire and heated the blade of her pocketknife until it was glowing red. Then she handed Ryan her canteen and said, "Boil me some water!"

Ryan didn't know anything about birthing babies, but he seemed to recall from the movies that when someone said "Boil some water," the baby wasn't far off.

"Yes, ma'am," he said.

"I need you in here," she told Hezekiah. She took him by the arm, and the two of them disappeared into the sod house.

Ryan emptied the canteen into an old metal pot that he'd found inside the sod house. Just as the water came to the boil, he heard another one of Hannah's cries from inside the sod house.

"Push!" ordered Abigail.

"I can't, I can't!" screamed Hannah.

Ryan ran to the door with the boiling water, but he stopped short of entering. He suddenly felt like an intruder and that it wasn't his place to watch. He listened from outside the closed door.

"I see the head!" said Abigail. "One more push, girl. On three! One . . . two . . . threeeee!"

The scream that followed was unlike anything Ryan had ever heard in his entire life. It was filled with pain, filled with relief, filled with life, itself. And then there was only crying— a baby's crying. Hannah was crying too, but these were happy tears.

"It's a boy!" shouted Abigail.

Ryan smiled. All was well.

Abigail said, "Ryan L'new, where on earth is that boiled water I told you to fetch?"

Ryan hurried inside and handed her the pot. Abigail sterilized her bandana in the boiling water. She waved it in the air to cool it just a bit and wiped the naked baby clean. Then she handed the infant to his mother, who cradled him in her arms. Ryan had never seen more love in a young woman's eyes.

Hezekiah approached tentatively. Hannah motioned him forward. None of them had known Hannah long, but Hezekiah seemed to swell with a grandfather's pride as he approached.

"What are you going to name him?" he asked.

Hannah held her baby tight, considering it. Then she glanced at Ryan and said, "I'm gonna name my boy after this brave young man right here."

Ryan blushed. Abigail nodded and said, "Ryan's a nice name."

"Not Ryan. L'new. I like that name. L'new."

They all smiled, and Ryan tried not to laugh. He didn't want to break Hannah's heart and tell her that L'new came from LNU—last name unknown.

"That's a good name, too," said Ryan.

They watched in silence as the young mother kissed and stroked her newborn's face, whispering his name. "L'new. I love you, L'new."

Ryan could not stop watching them. It reminded him of the way his mother looked at his baby sister Ainsley, and he imagined that she had once looked at him the same adoring way. He was suddenly feeling the pain of separation from his own family—until Jarvis entered the sod house.

"Someone's coming," he said in a solemn voice.

Hezekiah took charge. "Abigail, you stay here with Hannah and her baby. Ryan, Jarvis, come with me."

He led the way out of the sod house. Standing by the campfire, they spotted the cloud of dust rising on the horizon. It was perhaps two miles off, though distances were hard to gauge on the ocean-like flatness of the prairie.

"Definitely looks like riders," said Hezekiah.

"Lots of riders," said Jarvis. "No way one or two horses kicks up that much dust."

"Kill the fire," said Hezekiah. "No sense sending up smoke signals to guide them to us."

Ryan pitched fistfuls of dirt onto the fire until it was extinguished. "You think it could be a slave-catcher posse?"

"No way to tell just yet. All we can do is wait," said Hezekiah, his voice trailing off. "And be ready for the worst."

# 31

he cloud of dust in the distance was no longer moving toward them. Slowly, like a ship on the horizon, it faded off to the west and dissolved into the setting sun. As dusk fell over the prairie, the dust cloud completely disappeared. In its place was a gentle wisp of white smoke that curled into a dark purple sky.

"They set up camp for the night," said Hezekiah.

"I wish we knew who *they* were," said Ryan.

"One way to find out." Hezekiah suddenly looked like a man with a plan. "Jarvis, you stay here and help Abigail watch over the new momma and her baby. Ryan and I have a little spying to do."

Taking only a water canteen with them, they walked side-by-side in a west-northwest direction. This was new terrain, as they had reached the sod house earlier from the south. It all looked the same, however—waves of prairie grass dotted with wild yellow blossoms, well-suited for a sod house. It was an especially dark night, which made it difficult to see. Occasionally, the skies would brighten as spears of moonlight broke through the shifting clouds. They walked at a strong, steady pace for about ten minutes, and then Hezekiah started to limp.

"Are you okay?" asked Ryan.

"I'm fine," he said. But his voice had a slight edge. He didn't sound fine.

They walked for another half hour, and Hezekiah was noticeably tired. His limp was worsening. Ryan suggested that they stop to rest. Hezekiah didn't object.

"You sure we're going the right way?" asked Ryan.

Hezekiah put his nose in the air. "Don't you smell that smoke? That's their campfire. We're definitely headed in the right direction."

Ryan opened the canteen, and they each took a long drink. Hezekiah reclined in a thick of prairie grass. Ryan watched him for a moment, then said, "Can I ask you something?"

"Sure."

"How did you end up in St. Louis?"

"Same way you did. I used a leaphole through the Dred Scott decision. March sixth, 1857. St. Louis, Missouri."

"I understand that much," said Ryan. "I was wondering *why* you were researching the Dred Scott decision."

He drew a breath and let it out slowly. "Because I'm running out of time."

Ryan felt a rush of concern. "You mean you're . . ."

"No, no. I'm not dying. No lawyer can die before he golfs at Pebble Beach. It's against the rules. I'm just retiring. I told you that before."

"So, you're running out of time to do what?"

"I'm a good lawyer, Ryan. I've been doing this for more years than I can count. Soon, it will be time for me to move on. That's why I picked you as my replacement. You have a lot of years ahead of you."

Ryan didn't say anything. Kaylee had already told him how

much he'd hurt Hezekiah by rejecting the invitation to become a Legal Eagle.

Hezekiah continued, "When you turned me down, I didn't know what to do. I had a terrible feeling inside that I was leaving no one in my place to continue the good fight. That left only one thing for me to do."

"What?"

His expression turned very serious. "I decided to come face to face with Legal Evil myself. Right at its root."

"That was Kaylee's guess," said Ryan. "She asked me to come with her and find you. She was afraid you would be overpowered, that something horrible might happen to you."

"Obviously she was right. I ended up a slave."

"She hoped that if I came and told you that I was reconsidering your offer, maybe you'd come back."

The old man raised one bushy white eyebrow. "*Are* you reconsidering?"

Ryan paused, not because he didn't know the answer, but only because he wanted his words to have the proper impact. "Yes, I am," he said firmly.

Hezekiah smiled. "That's exactly what I wanted to hear."

"Of course, not that it makes much difference anymore. None of us has any leapholes."

Hezekiah shook his head. "That's the strangest thing of all. My entire career, I have always carried an emergency leaphole. But when I landed in St. Louis, I had no return leaphole, and no emergency back up. I guess that's just one more sign than it's time to retire. I'm starting to forget the most important things."

"Maybe it will turn up."

"Maybe," said Hezekiah. "Leapholes are powerful things."

They each took another sip of water, and Ryan packed away the canteen.

"Come on," said Hezekiah. "We got a campsite to spy on."

As they traveled farther west, the landscape began to change. It was a far cry from a forest, but Ryan saw more trees and bushes, and even a few rolling hills. The cloud coverage was blowing east. Soon, the stars twinkled in the black sky above them. Hezekiah continued to follow the scent of campfire smoke. His nose took them west, then northwest. Finally, they reached an east-west trail. It looked well traveled, and Ryan was tempted to take it.

"No way," said Hezekiah. "A well-traveled road like this is no place for a slave on the run."

They cut across the trail and continued toward the campsite. As they climbed another hill, Hezekiah's limp was worse than ever. Ryan was about to ask if he was okay, but Hezekiah staved off the question before the words could cross Ryan's lips.

"I told you I'm fine, Ryan. Don't ask me again."

Despite his protests, Hezekiah had even more trouble going down the hill. They stopped at a swift stream that curled around the foot of the hill. Hezekiah was steadily deteriorating. He was lying on his side near the stream. Ryan watched, curious, as the old man lifted his shirt and splashed handfuls of cold water onto a sore spot on his lower back.

"What's wrong?" said Ryan.

"Nothing," said Hezekiah.

Ryan went to him and took a closer look. An open gash stretched across Hezekiah's back. It was yellow with infection.

"Let me see that," said Ryan.

Hezekiah tried to resist, but he was too weak. Ryan pulled up the old man's shirt and saw a half dozen thick welts across Hezekiah's back. Ryan couldn't speak at first. Finally, the words came like a reflex.

"They beat you, didn't they?" said Ryan. "They beat you like an animal."

Hezekiah smiled, but it was a weak smile. "You don't think I let them drag me into slavery without a fight, do you?"

"You need a doctor."

"I'll be fine."

Ryan wanted to believe him, but like any Legal Eagle, he couldn't ignore the facts. The beating from the posse, the forced servitude, the leaphole disaster, the miles of hiking—it was all taking a terrible physical toll. "We should turn back," said Ryan.

"No," he said as he forced himself onto his feet. "I've come this far. We need to know if those are slave catchers on the other side of that hill."

Ryan understood his point, but that didn't make it any easier. "Look, you have to save yourself. I'll go with Abigail and make sure Hannah and her baby find their way on the underground railroad. But you are in no condition to keep running."

"How can I not run?"

"You're a lawyer, not a slave. We have to figure out some way to make these slave catchers understand that. Even under the twisted laws of Legal Evil, they had no right to take you into slavery. You were never a slave in the first place."

The old man drew a breath, then let it out. "That's not exactly right, Ryan. I was a slave."

"What?"

"I was a slave at one time in my life. So if I'm recaptured, I go back into slavery. At least that's what the Supreme Court said in the Dred Scott decision."

"Wait a minute. Slavery ended with the Civil War. How could you have been a slave? How old are you?"

"Time travel slows the aging process, but I'm still much older than you think. That's why I need you to take my place. The battle isn't over, but I'm old and tired."

Ryan didn't know what to say. He was honored, he supposed, if only because he was so taken with the old lawyer's sincerity and integrity. There was much he didn't understand, but he found himself wanting to be like Hezekiah.

"Okay," said Ryan. "But if I'm going to take over this fight, I need to know more. I need to know where leapholes come from. I need to know where *you* come from."

A somber expression came over his face. He wasn't looking directly at Ryan as he spoke. He was looking past him, and the words seemed to come from somewhere deep within him, some place rich with tradition.

"I was born a prince," said Hezekiah, "in a land now known as the West African nation of Burkina Faso. My father was the tribal ruler. When I became a man, I was given a bracelet that had been handed down from generation to generation within our tribe. Many centuries ago, the first slave hunters came to West Africa to capture slaves. They put men and women in iron shackles and carried them off to the ship. One of the tribesmen captured was a very brave man. In fact, he was the tribe's rainmaker. It was said that he was a very spiritual man. Whenever there was drought and people were starving, the rainmaker would call upon the heavens to sprinkle their lives with precious rainwater—and the rain would fall."

"They made a man like that into a slave?" said Ryan, his tone underscoring the tragedy.

Hezekiah shook his head and said, "They tried, Ryan. But somehow, even after the slave hunters had bound his ankles with shackles, the rainmaker managed to escape. Vanished, is a better way to put it. The legend says that he simply disappeared, leaving behind only his iron shackle. This slave's shackle—this ring of metal—was the bracelet I was given by my tribal elders."

"Do you still have it?"

"I do. I keep it in a very special place."

"It would be a terrible thing if you were ever to lose it, I suppose."

"A terrible, terrible thing. I know this is going to be the really hard part for you to believe, but it's true. That bracelet—that shackle of my greatest ancestor—became the first leaphole. All leapholes derive their power from that very first one. Through the mystery of this brave rainmaker's escape and sudden disappearance, the leaphole was imbued with a magic that it has taken me over a century to understand and use."

"But how does it work?"

"I don't know, exactly. I've spoken to physicists, some very intelligent scientists. Time travel is possible, but you must create negative mass."

"You mean weightlessness, like when the astronauts float inside their space shuttle?"

"Below weightlessness. *Negative* mass, meaning less than zero."

"How is that possible?"

"That's beyond me, Ryan. But I'm told that sometimes when two pieces of metal are close together, negative mass can be achieved in the space between them."

Ryan thought for a moment, considering the implications for leapholes. "So the two shackles, the two rings of metal around the ankle of your ancestor, that created negative mass?"

Hezekiah shrugged. "Perhaps. But that still doesn't account for the energy that is necessary to launch time travel. Scientists tell me that it would take every bit of energy our sun could produce, and then some, just to make one trip."

"Where could that much energy come from?"

"The human spirit, maybe. The desire to be free. I don't know of anything more powerful than that."

Ryan considered it. Coming from anyone but Hezekiah, it might have sounded corny. But how else could leapholes be explained?

Hezekiah was on his feet again. "See that," he said. "Just talking about it has me energized and feeling better."

Ryan was not entirely convinced by his sudden recovery, but he knew that it was pointless to argue.

"Come on," said Hezekiah. "Let's have a look at that campsite."

They continued up the final hill. As they neared the top, Ryan heard something that sounded like static from a television set. He knew that was impossible. Even if television had existed in 1857, what would it be doing in the middle of nowhere? Still, the higher they climbed, the louder the static hiss. Finally, they reached the hill crest, and immediately they saw the source of the strange noise.

"Look," said Hezckiah, pointing.

Ryan looked straight west, toward the wide body of noisy, rushing water, glistening in the moonlight. "That's quite a river," said Ryan.

"That's not just *a* river. That's *the* river, as in the Mississippi. Do you know what that means?"

"We're east of the Mississippi."

"Yes, exactly. And that road we crossed on the way over here had to be the St. Louis-Vincennes Trace."

"The what?"

"The St. Louis-Vincennes Trace was a major transportation route in the nineteenth century. It ran from Vincennes, Indiana to St. Louis Missouri. Do you understand what I'm saying, Ryan? It cut across southern *Illinois.*"

A smile came to his lips. "Kaylee's leaphole whirled us east of St. Louis. We landed in a free state."

"You got it, buddy."

"That's . . . that's awesome. Hannah's baby was born in a free state. L'new was born free!"

"Never underestimate the power of leapholes," said Hezekiah

Ryan was about to shout with excitement, but Hezekiah quickly covered the boy's mouth with his hand. The old man's eyes filled with concern as he whispered, "Look down."

Ryan's gaze shifted from the river in the middle distance to the base of the hill directly below them. They had found the campsite on the bank of the river. Through the tree branches, Ryan counted eight men seated around the glowing campfire.

"It's the posse," Hezekiah whispered. "Come on. Follow me."

Slowly and very quietly they descended the hill for a closer look. A twig or two snapped beneath Ryan's step, but steady noise from the flowing river water was more than enough to drown out the sound. They hid behind a stack of gray boulders at the bottom of the hill.

Hezekiah whispered, "Look at the man third from the right. The one with the beard."

Ryan peered out over the top of the boulder. He and Hezekiah were hidden in darkness, but the men were plainly visible in the light of the campfire. Ryan's gaze locked onto that third man from the right, and shivers went down his spine. He recognized that long, gnarled beard and that broad felt hat. But the eyes were the clincher. Ryan had seen those eyes before, when that slave owner in Missouri had let his slaves in the cotton field drink from the mule's water bucket. Ryan would never forget those black, shark-like eyes.

"That's old man Barrow."

"You bet it is," said Hezekiah. "He's come to get me."

"But how could he find us? We spun clear out of Missouri with Kaylee's leaphole."

"I told you before. He's evil—with a capital E."

This time, there was no misunderstanding Hezekiah's implication. "Legal Evil," said Ryan. "Is this the place you told me about, where the brood follows the dam?"

"No," said Hezekiah, "but we're getting close. Let's go. We have to get back and warn Hannah."

"Are you going to be okay walking all that way?"

Hezekiah chuckled lightly, then pointed with a nod toward the team of horses hitched to a tree by the river. "Who said anything about walking?"

The old man had a sudden burst of energy, and Ryan hurried to catch up. They kept low to the ground and approached the horses slowly, careful not to startle them. A big weeping willow tree stood between the horses and the campsite, which only made their job easier.

"Should we turn them all loose?" whispered Ryan.

"No, no. The men will come after us with guns blazing. We'll just take one."

Hezekiah quickly untied the reins from the tree. He chose one, then reconsidered. He took the biggest, fastest-looking horse in the pack. Standing a good fifteen hands in height, its gorgeous black coat shone in the moonlight. Hezekiah stroked its powerful neck, and the horse let out a soft, throaty neigh.

"I think he likes me," said Hezekiah. He retied the other horses to the tree and led the big one away from the camp, along the riverbank. When they were a safe distance away from the posse, Hezekiah stopped.

"Isn't this stealing?" said Ryan.

"If Old Man Barrow can whip me like an animal and think nothing of it, God will surely forgive me for taking one of his horses. Now help me up."

The horse had no saddle, but riding bare back was preferable to the long walk home. Ryan gave the old man a shove, and Hezekiah was up quickly. He offered Ryan a hand and pulled the boy up behind him. With a gentle kick, Hezekiah brought the horse to a light trot. Ryan held on to him, but after a few minutes of riding, it felt more like he was holding up Hezekiah. Back at the river he had momentarily seemed like his old self. Clearly, that had been nothing but adrenalin. The sudden surge of strength had since passed, and Hezekiah was again slipping into his weakened state.

Ryan retreated into thought as they started back across the prairie toward the sod house. All he could think about was the posse, old man Barrow, and the determination of Legal Evil. It genuinely scared him.

He wondered if Hezekiah was up for the fight.

# 32

On the back of a lively thoroughbred, the ride back to the sod house took hardly any time at all. Ryan and Hezekiah dismounted and came through the front door to find Hannah's baby asleep in the young mother's arms. Ryan spoke softly, so as not to wake the infant, but the news was too good for Hannah to remain quiet.

"Illinois! We're in Illinois!" That was all she could say for about thirty seconds, grinning east to west. Miraculously, Baby L'new slept right through the excitement.

"Are you sure?" asked Abigail.

"No doubt in my mind," said Hezekiah. "We're east of the Mississippi River and just a couple miles south of the St. Louis-Vincennes Trace."

"Praise be," said Abigail. "Now that I know where we are, I can line up my contacts on the underground railroad. I can get you, Hannah, and her baby as far as Chicago, if need be."

"That might well be necessary," said Hezekiah.

Hannah looked confused. "Why do we have to go anywhere? Illinois is a free state. We's free, right?"

Hezekiah spoke gently, trying not to scare her. "Ryan and I spotted a posse on the Illinois side of the river. Slave catchers don't stop at borders, Hannah. It's best if we get as far away from Old Man Barrow's farm as we can."

"Is he coming for us?" she said, her eyes widening with fear. She held her sleeping baby close and added, "He can't come for my baby, can he?"

Hezekiah didn't answer directly. "Like I said, it's best to keep moving. If they catch us, they can take us back to slavery. That's the law."

"But not my baby, right? Little L'new was born right here in Illinois. He's born into freedom, right? He's no one's slave. No one can take him. Nu-uh, no way. Not this precious little boy." She rocked him in her arms, filling his tiny ear with a mother's loving whispers.

Hezekiah watched her, saying nothing. From the look on the old man's face, Ryan knew there was something Hezekiah couldn't bring himself to tell her.

"Where's Jarvis?" asked Hezekiah.

Abigail said, "He's been gone quite awhile now. Left right after you did. Said he was gonna try and find us some water."

Suddenly, they heard shouting outside. Ryan opened the door and saw Jarvis running toward the sod house, shouting, "Hezekiah! Hezekiah!"

Jarvis hurried inside and slammed the door shut. He was breathing heavily, on the verge of hyperventilation. He was trying to say something but couldn't.

"What is it?" demanded Abigail.

"The . . . posse." It was all he could manage to say.

"What about the posse?" said Ryan.

He struggled to catch his breath, then finally blurted out the rest. "They're coming!"

Hezekiah opened the door, and Ryan was right behind him. It was impossible to see across the prairie in the darkness, so

Hezekiah dropped to his knees and put his ear to the ground. Ryan did likewise, and the sound terrified him. It was very faint, more like a vibration than a noise. But it confirmed their fears: Horses were coming.

"How far away are they?" asked Hezekiah.

"Three, four minutes, tops," said Jarvis. His breathing was finally under control. "I spotted them when I was up by the stream. Ran here as fast as I could."

"Good thing you did," said Abigial. "What do we do now?"

Tears were streaming down Hannah's face. "We can't let them have my baby."

A pained expression came over Hezekiah's face. "There may be no way around that."

"No, don't you say that. Don't you dare say that. My baby is free." Hannah rose from her bedroll on the floor and handed Abigail her child. "You take him to Chicago. This posse, it can take me and Hezekiah, but I won't let them have my child."

"I can't take your baby," said Abigail.

"Yes, you take him. I don't want him growing up to be no slave. He's free."

Abigail tried to back away, but Hannah pushed her baby into the abolitionist's arms. "Go on, take him, please!"

Reluctantly, Abigail took the child. The moment she did, Hannah fell to her knees and sobbed uncontrollably, as if a part of her had just died. It was almost too agonizing for Ryan to watch. It wasn't easy to comprehend a mother's decision to give up a child she loved more than anything in the world. But Ryan had seen those recaptured slaves paraded down Main Street. He'd seen them drink from the mule's water bucket. He'd run from the plantation with Hannah and Hezekiah. He'd seen the marks of a bullwhip across Hezekiah's back. Because of all that, he understood how unselfish Hannah was being.

Hezekiah took the infant from Abigail and placed him back in his mother's arms. "Giving your baby away won't solve anything, Hannah."

"'Course it will," she said. "It's all I can do for my son."

"You just don't fully understand the situation," said Hezekiah.

Ryan stepped into the doorway and listened to the night. The horses were still in the distance, but he no longer needed to put his ear to the ground to discern their thundering hooves. The rumble was in the air.

Ryan asked, "If there's something you need to say, Hezekiah, go on and say it. I think Hannah has a right to know."

The old lawyer closed his eyes. Clearly, he was about to utter something unspeakable. It seemed to take every ounce of his strength, but finally the words came. "We've found the place. This is where the brood follows the dam."

Ryan felt chills down his spine.

Abigail said, "Now what on God's green earth are you talking about?"

Hezekiah said, "It's the law of the land as laid down by the United States Supreme Court. The brood follows the dam. It means that if the mother is a slave, it doesn't matter if her child is born in a free state. The 'brood' is the child. It follows the 'dam,' which is the mother. If the mother is a slave, the child is born a slave. It doesn't matter where the child is born."

"So, even if my baby was born in Illinois, he's still . . ."

"A slave," said Hezekiah. He shook his head in disgust, then glanced at Ryan. "This is where Legal Evil lives."

Hannah was stunned into silence, no tears left to cry. But there was no time to console her. Everyone in the room could hear the unmistakable pounding in the distance, the drum of galloping horses on the prairie. The posse was closing in. All eyes turned to Hezekiah, their last hope.

Unfortunately, Hezekiah appeared to be on the verge of collapse. As Old Man Barrow and his slave catchers drew closer, Hezekiah fell weaker. Ryan had seen the gashes on Hezekiah's back. Mere flesh wounds, however, could not account for his loss of strength. Perhaps he had suffered some kind of internal injury. Or maybe Legal Evil was sucking the very life out of him.

Abigail said, "Don't y'all have any more of those leapholes, or whatever you call them?"

"No," said Ryan. "None."

Hezekiah was looking even older than his years. He hobbled toward Ryan and said, "You have to find another leaphole."

"How do I do that?"

"Find another Legal Eagle, one who was alive in 1857."

"I don't even know where to look."

Hezekiah closed his eyes. His expression tightened as he retreated into thought. This close to Legal Evil, he was a mere shell of the Legal Eagle he once was. He was losing his powers of concentration, and he could give Ryan only bits of information.

"Go to Springfield, Illinois," he told Ryan. "Look for a stovepipe."

"What does that mean?"

Hezekiah shook his head, as if trying to focus. But his mind simply couldn't conjure up anything more helpful. "That's all the information I can get for you, Ryan."

The ground was beginning to vibrate beneath their feet. The posse was at full speed, bearing down on the sod house, probably less than a minute away. Hezekiah was struggling. Even so, it was clear from the determination in his eyes that a renewed sense of purpose had come over him. He gave Hannah a quick hug and told her that her baby deserved to be free.

"Promise me you'll raise him well," he said.

She nodded, confused by his words.

Then he looked at Ryan and said, "You find that leaphole. That's your only way home."

Before Ryan could ask what he was talking about, Hezekiah was out the door. Somehow the old man found the strength to run from the sod house and hop on the stolen horse.

"Hezekiah, stop!" shouted Ryan.

He glanced back and said, "It's me they want, Ryan. So it's me they'll get. You take Hannah, her baby, the others. You take them far away from here."

"But—"

"Yee-ha!" he shouted to the horse.

"Stop, you'll be caught!" cried Ryan.

The old man only waved and smiled. In seconds the thoroughbred was speeding away at full speed. Out of leapholes and with no way to get home, Hezekiah was headed straight for the posse.

Ryan watched in despair as the old man disappeared into the darkness. Hezekiah's voice rang through the night as he called out to the slave catchers. He was taunting them, daring them to come and get him. And then Ryan realized exactly what he was doing. Hezekiah wanted them to follow him. He was drawing the posse toward him, away from the young mother and her new baby. It was working. The posse was turning away. The slave catchers were chasing Hezekiah.

Ryan understood the plan, but that didn't make him feel any better.

"He's gone," said Ryan, not wanting to believe it. "Hezekiah is gone."

Abigail came to him. The two of them stood quietly in the darkness. They were unable to tear their eyes from that fading blur in the night. It would be their last memory of an old lawyer named Hezekiah.

"That man sure lives up to his name," said Abigail.

"What do you mean?"

"'Hezekiah.' It's Hebrew. It means 'God gives strength.'"

A flood of images suddenly ran through Ryan's mind—the first time he'd met Hezekiah, their amazing trips down the leapholes, and Ryan's argument to the Court of International Justice with Hezekiah at his side. But no single memory stood out. It was as if his mind were shutting down and his feelings were taking over. He felt sad, to be sure, but he was stronger than ever.

Above all else, he felt proud to have known Hezekiah.

"Come on," he told Abigail. "Hezekiah left us a job to do. Let's get Hannah and her boy back on the railroad." He started toward the sod house, then stopped. Jarvis was on horseback, ready to ride.

Ryan said, "Where'd you find the horse?"

"It was a gift. From the posse."

For a moment, Ryan couldn't speak. "What did you say?"

"You heard me," said Jarvis. "Don't worry, I got nothing against Hannah and her baby. I didn't even tell Old Man Barrow that she's here. Hezekiah was right. He's the one Barrow really wants. So Hezekiah's the only one I gave him."

"You snake. You turned in Hezekiah?"

Jarvis smiled thinly. "You didn't really think I was out fetching water in the middle of the night, did you?"

Ryan's blood was ready to boil. "You followed me and Hezekiah to the camp, didn't you? You told the posse where Hezekiah was. That's how you knew they were on their way."

"Such a clever boy. You know, you should be a Legal Eagle."

"I should have known not to trust you. Ever since I saw you on the slave owners's side of the street in St. Louis, stuffing your mouth with ribs and chicken. How much did Old Man Barrow pay you? What was the price on Hezekiah's head?"

Jarvis patted the bulging pouch of silver on his belt loop. "Quite a handsome price, I'd say. Anyway, good luck to you, Hannah, and her baby. Sure hope you keep your promise to Hezekiah and bring her to safety up north. Meanwhile, I'll be speeding on horseback to Springfield. I aim to find that stovepipe Hezekiah told you about. I'd bet every ounce of this silver that I get my hands on that leaphole before you do."

"Is that your plan? Leave me here?"

Again, he just smiled. "Have fun in the nineteenth century, Ryan. It's where you and Hezekiah belong."

With a deep, sinister laugh, he turned on his horse and galloped into the night.

# 33

**R**yan and his troop traveled all night. Hannah couldn't walk so soon after giving birth, but Abigail's underground railroad connections were already paying dividends. They borrowed a horse and wagon from an abolitionist who ran a tavern along the St. Louis-Vincennes Trace. Then they headed north. Hannah and her baby rode in comfort (nineteenth-century comfort, that is) all the way to Litchfield. Ryan, of course, hadn't forgotten what Hezekiah had told him about finding another leaphole.

They were halfway to Springfield. Just before sunrise, they found the house with the oil lamp burning in the window.

"That lights the way," she said. For many years, lamps were used all along the secret routes of the underground railroad to tell runaway slaves where it was safe to stop.

The Litchfield abolitionist was an old woman named Whitmore who baked the most delicious walnut bread Ryan had ever tasted. They ate their fill and then spent the daylight hours sleeping in the cellar. At nightfall, they were back in the wagon headed north again. Around midnight, Hannah's baby started to cry. And cry. And cry.

"What's wrong with him?" asked Hannah. She was riding in the back, trying to console her child.

"Ain't nothin' wrong with him," said Abigail. "He's two days old. That's what babies do when they got something to complain about."

"I don't know what he's fussin' about," said Hannah. "He ain't wet, and he ain't interested in eatin' none."

Ryan recalled how car trips seemed to put his little sister Ainsley right to sleep, but a wooden-wheeled wagon on a rutted dirt road was an entirely different ride. "Maybe it's all this bouncing around in the wagon that has him so upset," said Ryan. Let's stop a minute and see if he'll fall asleep."

Ryan steered them off the road. The wagon stopped behind a cluster of elm trees. Traveling with a runaway slave was risky any time of day, so it made no sense to be out on the open road if they weren't moving. They had to be on constant lookout for slave catchers.

"I'll take the south watch," said Ryan as he climbed down from the wagon.

"I'll take the north," said Abigail.

The two of them walked back to the road and then split. They positioned themselves about twenty yards apart, Ryan looking south for slave catchers, Abigail looking north. The wagon was completely hidden from view in the forest, but Ryan could hear Hannah's voice in the wind. She was singing her baby to sleep. Every time she stopped singing, however, the newborn started to cry again. Putting little L'new to sleep was going to take longer than expected.

Alone in the moonlight, Ryan's thoughts turned toward Hezekiah. He missed him, and it turned his stomach to think that he was back in the unmerciful hands of Old Man Barrow and his slave catchers. Hezekiah didn't deserve to be a slave. No one deserved that. Even criminals were protected from "cruel and unusual punishment," and Hezekiah was hardly a criminal. He was a hero who had sacrificed himself for his friends. For that, he would live the rest of his days in slavery. Ryan didn't know whether to feel sad or angry. He felt both.

His emotions, however, were more complicated than that. They stemmed from something deeper than the fact that Hezekiah was gone. Ryan wished he could feel the same sense of pride about his own father.

That hurt more than anything.

Ryan scanned the forest around him. The wagon was surrounded by tall, straight trees. In the darkness, they reminded him of iron bars. Prison bars. If he squinted, he could almost see his father standing behind those bars in the orange jump suit, his eyes filled with sadness, as he looked Ryan in the eye and said, "I didn't do it, son."

Ryan shook his head, trying to free his mind of the image. But he couldn't fight it. He hadn't slept well since losing Hezekiah. He was mentally and physically exhausted. His thoughts kept bouncing back and forth from Hezekiah's being hauled away by slave hunters to his father sitting alone in some prison cell. Slowly, against his own will, his thoughts took an even deeper turn toward his father. Ryan didn't want to go there, not even in his memories, but in his mind's eye he was reliving that awful day when the police had come to take his father away.

A swirl of blue lights swept the yard outside Ryan's bedroom window. He peered out from behind the curtain and saw two squad cars pulling into the Coolidge driveway. The car doors flew open, and men in dark blue police uniforms raced up the walkway.

Next came the pounding at the front door, the firm knock of authority.

Ryan hurried from his room and stopped at the top of the stairs. His father was already at the door. "What's going on, Dad?" said Ryan.

"Just go back to your room, son."

Ryan started down the hall, but he didn't return to his room. He ducked around the corner and kept watching and listening as his father opened the door.

Two police officers flashed their badges, along with an older man who was wearing a white shirt and red tie with the knot loosened at the throat. He looked like one of those detectives on television. "Is Dr. Coolidge at home?" he asked.

"No, she's at work."

"Are you Mr. Coolidge?"

"Yes, I am."

"We're with Metro-Police. We have a search warrant for these premises," he said as he presented the document.

"What's this about, officer?"

"We're here to execute the warrant, not answer questions. May we pass, please? Or are you resisting?"

"I'm not resisting. I just want to know what this—"

"Where's the master bedroom?"

"Upstairs to the right."

"Thank you." The detective and two officers blew past him and started upstairs. Two other officers suddenly appeared in the doorway, as if standing guard.

Ryan pinned his back to the wall and allowed the police to pass. They said nothing as they hurried by him and disappeared into his parents' bedroom. Ryan's father climbed halfway up the stairs, his eyes meeting Ryan's.

"Dad, what are they looking for?"

"Just don't worry, Ryan. It's going to be okay."

He spoke in that too-calm tone of voice that parents used to reassure themselves as much as their children. With a detective and two police officers rummaging through their house, Ryan had no reason to believe that everything was going to be okay.

Ryan stood behind his father outside the bedroom door. It took only a few minutes for the police to emerge. The detective was wearing latex gloves, and he was carrying something under his arm. It was Mr. Coolidge's camera bag.

"What do you want with that?" asked Ryan's father.

"Follow me, sir."

The detective led the way downstairs to the foyer. Ryan's father went with them. Ryan was watching from the top of the stairs as the detective laid the camera bag on the floor. One of the police officers was recording with a hand-held video camera.

The detective said, "Mr. Coolidge, would you please open the camera bag."

Ryan's father looked puzzled, but he did not object. The bag was about the size of a standard backpack, and it had a number of different zipper pockets on the front and sides. Mr. Coolidge unzipped the main compartment, which revealed nothing but a camera.

The detective said, "Open the side pocket, please. The one on the left."

Ryan's father obliged. This time, however, as he peeled back the open flap, his face turned ash white.

"Would you remove the contents, please?" the detective said flatly.

Mr. Coolidge had clearly heard him, but he suddenly couldn't move. "I—I don't know how this got here."

"Sir, please remove it."

His hand shook as he reached into the side pocket. He pulled out something that, from Ryan's distance, looked like a bright green piece of glass or a rock. A moment later, however, Ryan recognized it. His father was holding the precious stone that had choked that little girl on the beach. It was the same huge emerald that she had sucked off her grandmother's ring. Two weeks had passed since Ryan's mother saved the child's life, but Ryan would never forget a jewel like that one.

"Does this emerald belong to you?" the detective demanded.

"No, of course not."

The detective opened a small plastic bag and said, "Place it in the bag, please."

Ryan's father dropped the emerald into the bag, and the detective sealed it shut.

"Mr. Coolidge, do you have any idea how much this stone is worth?"

"I'm sure it's quite valuable."

"It's been appraised at thirty-one-thousand dollars, sir. You want to tell us how it ended up in your camera bag?"

"I don't know how."

"This *is* your camera bag, isn't it?"

"Yes, but I don't have any idea how that emerald ended up there. I really don't."

The officers exchanged glances, obviously skeptical. The detective said, "Would you mind coming downtown with us, sir? We'd like to ask you a few more questions."

"My wife is still at her mommy-and-me class with our daughter. I can't leave my son here by himself."

"Officer Tenet will be happy to walk your son over to a neighbor's house."

"Can't this wait until my wife comes home?"

The detective sneered. "I'm trying to be nice, sir. Don't force me to arrest you in front of your own child."

"Arrest me? For what?"

"For the last time, sir. Let's talk about it downtown. For your boy's sake."

Mr. Coolidge glanced toward Ryan, then swallowed the lump in his throat. "All right. Take my son to the Alvarez house. They live right next door."

The officer went to Ryan and led him downstairs. As they crossed the foyer, Ryan saw real fear in his father's eyes, which gave him even greater concern. "Dad, what's going on?"

"We'll talk more about this later, Ryan."

"But that's the emerald that flew out of that baby's mouth at the beach. What's it doing in your camera bag?"

"Ryan, be quiet."

"Are they saying you stole it?"

"I said we'll talk about this later," he said sternly. "This is obviously a mistake."

The police officer whisked Ryan out the door, as if he couldn't get the boy out of the house fast enough. Ryan was confused and angry at the same time. He had been so proud of his mother for saving that little girl's life. Dr. Coolidge had been the talk of the town. She'd been on the television news, her picture in the newspaper. She was a local hero. And now *this*? How could his father have spoiled everything? How could he have stooped so low as to steal the emerald that had popped from a choking baby's mouth?

As Ryan entered the neighbor's yard, he gave a quick glance over his shoulder. What he saw nearly knocked him off his feet—his father disappearing into the back seat of a police car, his head lowered in shame.

Ryan had seen plenty of cop shows on television. He'd seen criminals stuffed into squad cars on the nightly news. And he'd watched dozens of them look into the cameras and say exactly what his father had just told him: It was all "a mistake."

*Yeah, right.* They *always* said it was "a mistake."

He wanted to believe in his father's innocence, but he was already having doubts. How could a thirty-one-thousand-dollar emerald end up in his camera bag by "mistake"?

That was all Ryan wanted to know.

# 34

pringfield was the state capital of Illinois.
Ryan was convinced that it was also the stovepipe capital of the world.

Their borrowed wagon had crossed the city limits around five a.m. Abigail linked up with a fellow abolitionist who was willing to hide Hannah and her baby. Ryan was dead tired, but he couldn't afford to waste time sleeping. Jarvis already had a serious head start on finding the leaphole back to the twenty-first century. They'd both heard Hezekiah say that the key to finding it was to go to Springfield and look for a stovepipe.

He might as well have said go the beach and look for a grain of sand. Ryan had never seen so many stovepipes. Of course, never before had he searched for one in the middle of the nineteenth century.

"What exactly do you want me to look for?" asked Abigail.

"I'm not sure. Any stovepipe that looks out of the ordinary to you, point it out to me."

Abigail was not entirely comfortable with the whole concept of leapholes. However, she couldn't deny their inexplicable trip from Missouri to Illinois with Kaylee's help. Suffice it to say that she'd seen enough to help Ryan in any way she could.

From Ryan's standpoint, a pair of nineteenth-century eyes couldn't hurt his search through old Springfield.

They continued down Main Street. Black stovepipes protruded from every rooftop. In 1857, pot-bellied stoves were in practically every home, every store, every office. Coal or wood burned in the stove, heat filled the room, and smoke went up the pipe. Ryan looked around, confused and overwhelmed. He was determined to honor the promise he'd made to Hezekiah: He would bring Hannah and her baby north to safety. But he couldn't let Jarvis find that leaphole before he did. The race was on, and he had no idea where the finish line was.

Hopefully, neither did Jarvis.

They were about to cross the street when Ryan suddenly shoved Abigail into a narrow alley.

"What is it?" asked Abigail.

"I just saw Jarvis."

"Where?" she asked.

"Just ahead, at that restaurant on this same side of the street. He's having breakfast with a man outside on the terrace."

"You sure it's him?"

"Have you ever seen another human being with a face as flat as his?"

"Good point. Who's he talking to?"

"I don't know. But I'd sure like to find out."

"We can't let him see us. If he does, he'll know Hannah's in town. He might try to turn her in."

Ryan thought for a moment. "Let's see if there's a rear entrance to the restaurant. Maybe we can sneak up from the backside and get a closer look at him and his friend on the terrace."

They continued down a back alley. It was so narrow that their shoulders practically rubbed against the red brick walls on either side. The back end smelled like most alleys. Funny, but garbage always seemed to smell the same, whether it was yours or your neighbor's, whether it was from the nineteenth century or the twenty-first.

They rounded the back corner and found a rear entrance to the restaurant. Ryan entered first. Abigail followed. As it turned out, the restaurant was only on the front terrace, outdoors. The inside of the building was a general store.

"Can I help you find something?" asked the store owner. He was a kindly old man wearing a white apron and pince-nez eyeglasses that clipped to his considerable nose.

"No, thank you," Abigail said softly. "Just looking around."

"Take your time," he said. Then he grabbed his broom and started sweeping the floor.

Pretending to browse, Ryan and Abigail worked their way toward the front of the store. It was a mild spring day, and the front windows facing the terrace were open. The store was packed with merchandise. The aisles were not the perfectly straight, tidy aisles of modern-day supermarkets. Ryan and Abigail moved in almost zig-zag fashion to the front. They went from shelves of canned goods, to stacks of cornmeal, to a variety of things that were part of life before the Civil War. Ryan saw drip candles, bottled ink, and whale oil for lamps.

They stopped near a display of new chimney sweepers, then stopped. Standing just ten feet away from the open window, they couldn't see Jarvis, but they could hear his voice. It was coming from the outside terrace.

"What's he saying?" whispered Abigail.

"Can't hear."

"You think he found that leaphole you two are looking for?"

"Don't know." Ryan strained to listen, but Jarvis's voice was just noise. "I need to get closer."

Ryan checked over his shoulder. The store owner was still busy sweeping the floor. Quickly but quietly, Ryan stepped toward the window. Jarvis and his guest were seated at a small table on the terrace, just on the other side of the open window. Ryan hid behind a tall stack of jarred preserves, so they couldn't spot him. He could see *them*, however—and he could hear every word they were saying.

Abigail came to his side and whispered, "That man he's talking to is a federal marshal."

Ryan noted the badge on his vest. He was gnawing on a fatty slice of bacon. "I just don't think I can do it," the man said.

"Sure you can," said Jarvis. "All I'm asking you to do is arrest him, that's all."

"But on what charge?"

"I did some research over at the courthouse," said Jarvis. "The Fugitive Slave Law of 1850 makes it illegal to interfere with a slave owner's right to recover a runaway slave. Every chance he gets, this boy is interfering with Old Man Barrow's lawful right to recover his property."

Ryan went cold. The boy he was talking about was *him*.

Abigail whispered, "He's trying to get you arrested for aiding runaways."

Outside, the federal marshal took a long drink from his coffee mug. It was either too hot or too bitter, judging from the sour expression on his face. Then he looked at Jarvis and said, "Won't work."

"Why not?"

"Technically, you're right. The Fugitive Slave Law does spell out some pretty severe penalties for people who help slaves escape. But the fact is, that part of the law just isn't enforced all that much in this part of Illinois. Not anymore, anyway. People around here just don't support it."

"But the law is still on the books, right? You could enforce it."

"I could. But why would I?"

Jarvis was silent for a moment. Then he removed a little bag from his belt loop and placed it on the table. It was the bag of silver that Old Man Barrow had given him for turning in Hezekiah.

"Why *wouldn't* you?" said Jarvis as he pushed the bag toward the marshal's side of the table.

The marshal looked at the bag, saying nothing. It was as if the men came to a silent understanding. He took the bag of silver and tucked it into his pocket. "Well, maybe just this once I could enforce it."

"Good man," said Jarvis.

"Just so you understand," said the marshal. "Ain't no judge or jury who's gonna convict this boy for helping runaway slaves."

"All I want you to do is keep him behind bars for a few days. Just long enough to keep him out of my hair awhile."

Abigail leaned toward Ryan and whispered, "Just long enough to keep you from finding the leaphole before he does, is what he means."

"Let's go," whispered Ryan. "I heard enough."

"What are you two sneaking around about?" said the store owner.

The old man's accusatory tone startled both of them. As they backed away from the stack of preserves, Abigail tripped. She fell in the direction of an even bigger stack of jars behind them. Ryan tried to catch her, but the disaster was unavoidable. Abigail went down. Eight-dozen jars of sweet preserves came crashing to the floor with her. Many of them shattered, leaving gobs of sticky jam everywhere.

"You'll pay for those!" shouted the store owner.

The front door flew open, and the marshal rushed inside to check on all the racket. Jarvis was right behind him.

"That's him, that's the boy!" shouted Jarvis. But as the words left his lips, both he and the marshal stepped right into the slippery mess of spilled preserves. Their feet went out from under them, and they landed hard on the messy floor.

"Run for it!" shouted Abigail. She and Ryan raced out the front door.

"After him!" said Jarvis. But the marshal was too groggy to stand, having banged his head on the floor in the fall. Jarvis shook him, and the man groaned. He sat up and rubbed his head, still unable to climb to his feet. Jarvis grumbled and gave chase alone, his shirt and pants dripping of strawberry jam.

Ryan and Abigail rounded the corner. They continued at full speed down a side street. Jarvis was about twenty yards back, right on their trail. They cut behind a carriage and then around a team of horses. The alley beside the hotel looked like a good place to hide. They ducked behind a wagon and waited in silence.

A minute later, they saw Jarvis hurry past on the street. He didn't even look in their direction.

"He missed us," Ryan said with relief.

Abigail said, "We need to get Hannah out of town. This is getting too dangerous."

"But I can't leave Springfield until I find that leaphole."

"That's impossible. The minute you show your face on the streets, that federal marshal is going to arrest you for aiding a runaway slave."

Ryan knew she was right. Jarvis had totally fixed the race in his favor. Then something occurred to him. "I need a lawyer," he said.

"I don't see what good that'll do you. That marshal took a bribe. The best lawyer in the country couldn't keep him from arresting you."

"That's not why I need to find a lawyer. I was thinking about Hezekiah's clue. He said go to Springfield and look for a stovepipe. Then we'll find a leaphole. But maybe we've got it backwards."

"What do you mean?"

"The only person who would have a leaphole is a Legal Eagle. We should find the best lawyer in town, and *then* look for the stovepipe."

"How do find the best lawyer?" said Abigail.

"Reputation, I guess."

Abigail considered it. "There's only one lawyer I've ever heard of from Springfield. He's pretty well known. Three years ago he ran for U.S. Senate."

"Did he win?"

"No. But he bounced right back and sought his party's nomination for vice president at last year's national convention."

"Did he get it?"

"Actually, he got clobbered."

"Doesn't sound like much of a Legal Eagle to me."

"Oh, but he's real well liked, especially by folks who are against slavery. I believe his office is right above the federal courthouse. His name is—"

"Ryan Coolidge, you're under arrest," said the federal marshal at the end of the alley. Jarvis was standing right beside him. The marshal's uniform was still covered with jam, but he also had a gun. It was aimed right at Ryan.

"I thought your name was L'new," Abigail whispered through her teeth.

"That's a whole 'nother story," Ryan replied.

The marshal jerked his gun forward. "Quiet! Put your hands up over your head."

Ryan and Abigail raised their hands, but Ryan didn't keep quiet. "Is this your idea of justice, Marshal? Arresting people on bogus charges for a bagful of silver?"

The marshal's face was suddenly as red as his jam-smeared shirt. "What—uh. What are you talking about?"

"Don't play stupid with us," said Abigail. "We saw you take that bribe from Jarvis."

"That's right," said Ryan. "And the whole world is going to know about it, too. Unless you're prepared to gun us both down, right now."

Abigail cast a sideways glance, then whispered, "Not sure I would have put it quite that way, Ryan."

"Shoot them," said Jarvis.

"Now wait just a minute," said the marshal.

"You gotta shoot 'em. You just heard that little weasel say he was going to tell everyone about the bribe. Shoot him!"

"I can't just shoot a boy and a woman in cold blood."

"Then give me the gun. I'll do it."

Ryan said, "Have you gone crazy, Jarvis? Why do you hate me so much? I never did anything to you."

"Never *did* anything?" said Jarvis, groaning. "You are so clueless. For seventeen years I was a loyal apprentice. I did everything Hezekiah ever asked me to do. I studied, I worked overtime. I was just counting the days until Hezekiah would retire and name me his replacement. And then what does that ingrate do in the end? He says I'm not Legal Eagle material. He decides he's going to pass the baton to some school kid named Ryan."

"That wasn't my fault," said Ryan.

"I don't care whose fault it was." Jarvis turned to the marshal and said, "Now, give me that gun."

"No," said the marshal.

"Give it to me, or I'll take it from you."

The marshal pulled back. "I'm not getting involved in your jealous game of revenge."

Jarvis was suddenly on top of the Marshal like a T-Rex on lunch. Abigail screamed as the two men wrestled to the ground. They were punching and kicking, each trying to control the gun. Ryan started left and then right, but no matter which direction he moved, the gun seemed to be pointing right at him.

"Ryan, run for it!" shouted Abigail.

"I can't just leave you!" said Ryan.

"Go! You've already kept your promise to Hezekiah. I can take Hannah and her baby from here. It only gets easier as we go north."

Jarvis and the marshal were still locked in a wresting match. Ryan caught Abigail's eye, and he wished there were time for a proper goodbye. But there wasn't.

"Just git!" shouted Abigail.

Without another word, Ryan sprinted past Jarvis and the marshal. He burst from the tight alley as if it were the last day of school, and he hit the street at full speed. He wasn't sure where he was headed. Abigail had never said the name of that well-known lawyer from Springfield. But she did mention where his office was.

At the corner, Ryan stopped a well-to-do gentleman who was dressed smartly in a business suit. "Sir, can you tell me where the federal courthouse is?"

"Yes, of course. It's in the Tinsley Building. That redbrick building on the next corner."

Ryan could see it from where they were standing. He smiled a little, but then he glanced back toward the alley, and his excitement faded.

Jarvis emerged from the alley, the apparent victor in the battle with the marshal.

A half-second later, the marshal stumbled into the street and took aim with his revolver. "Stop, or I'll shoot!"

Jarvis kept running. The marshal was ready to squeeze off a shot, but a stagecoach rolled past, followed by a wagon. "He's got a gun!" shouted someone, which sent screaming pedestrians scurrying in every direction. There was too much traffic to let bullets fly, too high a risk of hitting innocent bystanders. The marshal gave chase on foot.

Ryan dashed off toward the Tinsley Building. This was his only chance to escape. He was betting everything on the hope that the best lawyer in town was a Legal Eagle. All he had to do then was find the stovepipe. His focus was on the building, totally on the redbrick building.

He didn't see the horse-drawn carriage coming from his right.

The horses neighed and the carriage twisted. It wasn't a direct hit, but Ryan took a hard tumble and landed face down in the street. He pushed himself up and shook off the dizziness. Jarvis was barreling down on him. Ryan turned and ran as fast as he could, but Jarvis was gaining ground. The gap closed to within two steps. He could hear Jarvis breathing heavily behind him. Ryan did a gut-check, reached inside for the afterburners, and started to pull away.

Just ahead, the sign on the door read *Law Office*. Ryan knew that he was in the right place. Courtesy dictated a knock, but he couldn't let Jarvis catch up. The door was unlocked, and Ryan burst inside. A man rose from his desk and said, "Can I help you, son?"

"I'm looking for a lawyer."

"This is the courthouse entrance. The law office is on the third floor."

Before Ryan could thank him, the door floor open. Jarvis entered with a flurry. Ryan scurried up the tight wooden stairwell. He whipped around the turn at the second floor. He was halfway up the stairs to the third when he felt the firm grasp of a huge hand around his ankle. Jarvis had him.

Ryan kicked like a mule, which sent Jarvis tumbling back down the stairs. He landed with a crash at the bottom step. At the top of the staircase, a door opened. Standing in the doorway was a very tall, thin-faced man.

"What's all the noise out here?" he said.

Ryan climbed to the top of the steps, and salvation came into view. Resting on a chair in the foyer next to the man's coat was a black hat. It was a tall, thin hat. A *stovepipe* hat.

Ryan took a good look at the man. He was clean shaven, which confused Ryan for a moment. But then he remembered that the beard had come only after the presidential inauguration. "You're Abraham Lincoln," said Ryan.

"Yes, I am. And who are you?"

Ryan grinned and said, "I'm the happiest person on earth."

Jarvis was charging back up the stairs. "Stop that kid! He's a lawbreaker."

Ryan had no time to explain, almost no time to think. Lincoln's hat was resting on the chair. Its opening was round and black and seemingly bottomless—just like the open end of the leapholes in Hezekiah's jar back at his office. Ryan dug into his pocket for the spent leaphole—the one that had brought him from Hezekiah's office to St. Louis. He wasn't exactly sure what he was doing, but he remembered that Kaylee had used her spent leaphole when activating a return leaphole. It was the only way back to the starting point.

Jarvis was just three steps away when he dove for Ryan's ankles. On impulse, Ryan lunged toward the hat. As he soared across the threshold, a seed of doubt sprouted in his mind. *What if this doesn't work?* But his thoughts turned to Hezekiah and the old legend of the rainmaker's shackle, and all doubt evaporated. He buried his hand in the hat's opening. The power pulsated in his hand. Like lightening, it surged up his arm and throughout his entire body. Perhaps it was the power of Lincoln's leaphole. Or perhaps it was just the urgency of the situation. In a single flash of orange light, Ryan was sucked into the opening without delay.

The futile cries from Jarvis were just an echo in the distance. *"Ryan Coolidge, don't you dare leave me here!"*

Right away, Ryan realized that this was no ordinary leaphole. This had to be some kind of supercharged, highspeed *reverse* legal leaphole. It was only befitting of one of the most courageous lawyers the world had ever known. At first, he experienced only the intense vibration of forward motion, as if he were being launched into another universe. Wind and heat caressed his cheeks, a surge of pure energy. The blinding light ahead was like staring straight into a spotlight. The noise was as deafening as a freight train. In fact, he could hear the clacking of iron wheels on rails. The noise grew louder and louder. The oncoming spotlight became more and more intense. Around him, outside the beam of light, there was only darkness. It was as if he were speeding through a tunnel. Suddenly, he heard the familiar steam whistle of a locomotive. He was on a train. This was indeed a railroad, and then Ryan realized what was happening.

The leaphole had found a *real* underground railroad.

The steam whistle blew again. The locomotive sped off even faster. Ryan was hanging on by his fingertips for a spectacular journey. In a flash, the train whipped through the nineteenth century. Snippets of history flashed in the darkness. It was all happening so quickly that Ryan could barely process the images, but he recognized some things. He saw soldiers falling as men in blue and gray uniforms clashed at Gettysburg. Teddy Roosevelt and the Rough Riders were charging up San Juan Hill. With another flash, he was suddenly into the twentieth century, passing the Wright Brothers and their first airplane.

Then, in an even bigger flash, the sounds of the old steam locomotive gave way to the rumble of an even greater force. It hardly seemed possible, but the speed intensified. Ryan was aboard a roaring diesel engine. He could barely hold on as he zipped past the horrors of war in Europe and the Pacific. He sailed over a sea of civil-rights marchers on the Washington Mall, and then past the space shuttle on its journey to outer space. Ryan was both frightened and exhilarated. In some ways, he didn't want the trip to end. But he could feel the train gathering momentum. He braced himself for something even faster than diesel.

Finally, he was hanging on for dear life on a speeding bullet train, barreling toward home in the twenty-first century.

# 35

**R**yan landed in Hezekiah's law office. Hard.

"Man, I need to work on those landings," he said to himself as he massaged the pain out of his tail bone.

Hezekiah's office was even more of a shambles than Ryan had remembered. The beginnings were such a blur to him. He remembered the SWAT team invasion, but it had happened so fast. There had been no time to assess the damage before he and Jarvis took the leaphole to the nineteenth century. As he looked around the room, he was seeing for the first time the mess they had left behind. Nearly every bookshelf was down. Several lamps were broken. Chairs were overturned. Countless case books lay scattered across the room.

Ryan picked himself up from the carpet and walked slowly to Hezekiah's study area. He sorted through the jumble of books atop the table. The old one from 1857—the one that contained the Dred Scott decision—was missing, which was no surprise. Kaylee had brought the book with her to nineteenth-century Missouri. But if she was now back in the twenty-first century, why hadn't she returned it?

*If* she was back. That was the question.

Hezekiah had seemed confident that Kaylee would return safely to the twenty-first century. Only Ryan and the others had been thrown off course into Illinois when Jarvis broke the human chain. But what if she, too, had been thrown off course? Was it possible that she'd landed somewhere between 1857 and the twenty-first century? It was a disturbing thought. If she had fallen short on her return, that meant she was still out there, somewhere, God only knew where—without a leaphole.

She would have no way home.

Ryan was getting worried. To be sure, it felt plenty good to be back. He wanted to tell his mother to stop worrying, that he was safe. He wanted to hug his sister Ainsley and tackle his dog Sam. He was glad to be away from that double-crossing Jarvis. But the loss of Hezekiah was beginning to feel like a death in his family, and his new concerns about Kaylee weren't making it any easier to cope.

Ryan glanced under the table, then did a double take. He noticed Hezekiah's jar. The last time Ryan had laid eyes on it, the jar had been filled with leapholes. Now, it was completely empty.

Something very strange was going on here.

Suddenly, there was a curious vibration beneath his feet. It was almost unnoticeable. It reminded Ryan of being in that sod house in southern Illinois, the way the ground seemed to shake right before the posse arrived. Ryan put his ear to the floor and listened. Maybe he was crazy, but he was almost certain that he detected the faint clatter of horse hooves.

Soon, it was no longer just a vibration in the floor. He could hear the sound of a galloping horse on the roof, in the walls, all around him. The noise grew louder until he could have sworn that a thoroughbred was racing through the room.

Then he heard the unmistakable neigh of a horse and a man crying *Whooooaaaaa!*

A rush of wind whipped through the library, followed by a bright blast of light. Ryan dove beneath the table just in time to avoid being trampled by a speeding thoroughbred.

"I said *Whoooooaaa!*" shouted Hezekiah. The excited horse stopped short. Another two feet and it would have slammed into the wall.

"Hezekiah!" Ryan shouted.

"In the flesh," he said as he turned his horse to face Ryan. Only then did Ryan notice that Kaylee was hanging off the other side of the horse.

She righted herself and said, "Where the heck did you learn to ride, Hezekiah? Next time *I* take the reins."

Ryan was so happy he was about to burst. "How did you two get here?" he said, his voice racing.

"Kaylee came back for me," said Hezekiah.

"So, you didn't get thrown off course when the rest of us broke away?" said Ryan.

"No way," said Kaylee. "There was no malfunction. You guys broke away only because Jarvis let go."

"He *let go*?" said Ryan.

"Yes," said Hezekiah. "It took us a while to see his true colors. But Jarvis was apparently planning all along to leave you and me trapped in the nineteenth century."

"I know. He told me everything after you rode off on horseback toward the posse. He was angry at you for not picking him as your replacement, and he was jealous of me for getting selected. He sold you out to Old Man Barrow."

"Well, Old Man Barrow sure didn't get his money's worth. The posse never caught me."

"How is that possible?" said Ryan.

Hezekiah gave his thoroughbred an affectionate pat on the neck. "You're looking at the great, great, great, great, great-grandfather of a Triple-Crown-winning racehorse by the name of *Seattle Slew*. There was absolutely no way those other horses in the posse were going to catch this stallion."

"That's awesome," said Ryan. Then his excitement turned to concern. "But, what will happen to Jarvis now? I had to leave him in the nineteenth century."

"You made the right choice," said Hezekiah. "That's where Jarvis belongs: Where the brood follows the dam."

"So, that's where Legal Evil lives?" said Ryan. "In the nineteenth century?"

"Yes, but don't be misled, Ryan. It's not the *only* place it lives. Where the brood follows the dam is where Legal Evil is most obvious. The fact is, it lives in every city, in every country, in every century. Sometimes it's just not so easy to see it."

Ryan considered those words for a moment. Suddenly, it was as if the proverbial lightbulb had blinked on over his head. If it lived in every city, in every country, in every century, and if it wasn't always easy to see, maybe he'd actually seen Legal Evil before. Maybe he just hadn't recognized it.

Maybe his father *was* innocent.

Hezekiah climbed down from his horse. "Ryan, you have shown great courage over the past few days. Over and over again, you have proven yourself worthy of distinction, honor, and respect. It's time now for your reward."

"My reward?"

He stepped closer, placed his hands on Ryan's shoulders, and looked him squarely in the eye. "Congratulations. You are ready to become a Legal Eagle."

Ryan didn't know what to say. "Thank you," were the only words he could muster.

Kaylee smiled and said, "Congratulations, Ryan. You'll love the swearing-in ceremony. It's the most amazing party you've ever seen."

"Can I get my leaphole first?"

"What?" said Hezekiah.

"My leaphole. Kaylee said you get a leaphole and a return leaphole when you become a Legal Eagle. I'd like to get mine before the swearing-in ceremony, if I can."

"What's the rush?" said Hezekiah.

"There's something very important I need to check out."

"I'm sure there is," Hezekiah said proudly. "What would you like to do first? Go back to Philadelphia in 1776 and witness the signing of the Declaration of Independence? Or perhaps you'd like to see Clarence Darrow do battle with William Jennings Bryan in the Scopes monkey trial."

Ryan shook his head. As interesting as it would be to meet the greatest lawyers of all time, he didn't want to go back that far. Not nearly. He had already resolved to use his first leaphole to travel back just a matter of months.

"I want to go back to the case of *State versus Coolidge*," said Ryan. "I want to know if my father is really innocent."

# 36

yan shot like a comet through his first leaphole. The distance was short, so the trip was a mere blink of an eye. One moment, Ryan was standing in Hezekiah's office, his leaphole in hand. A split second later, he was crouched behind a bushy potted plant, hidden from view in the corner of a strange room. A woman wearing a gray business suit was seated behind an antique mahogany desk. Her law school diploma hung on the wall beside her. In the chairs facing the lawyer's desk sat a man and a woman. Ryan recognized them both immediately. The man was his father. The woman was his mother. They both looked distraught.

The lawyer said, "As I've told you from the beginning, the value of this emerald makes this a very serious crime. We're talking grand larceny, a first-degree felony."

"We know that," said Dr. Sharon Coolidge. "But where's the proof?"

"I just met with the prosecutor this morning. He laid out the evidence for me. The case against you is very strong, I'm afraid."

"That's not possible," said Mr. Coolidge. "They must be making things up."

"They have videotape," the lawyer said gravely. "When Dr. Coolidge was on the beach saving that little girl, the excitement apparently drew a crowd."

"Yes," said Ryan's mother. "Lots of people gathered round."

"One of them had a video camera," said the lawyer. "Some tourists were celebrating their son's birthday at the beach. When they saw all the commotion, they turned their camera toward the emergency."

"I don't understand," said Dr. Coolidge. "The only thing that could be on that tape is me saving that little girl. That's hardly a crime."

The lawyer sighed and said, "Let's watch the tape, shall we? Then we can talk." She rose and walked toward a television set in the corner. She inserted the tape into the player. The screen turned bright blue, then snow followed. She pushed another button, and the image came into focus.

Ryan watched the screen. For a moment, he was reliving that day. The child was choking and turning blue. The lifeguard was trying desperately but unsuccessfully to dislodge the emerald in her throat. Ryan's mother stepped forward and took the child in her arms. On her third attempt, the stone shot from the child's mouth and landed in the sand. The child was revived, and the crowd cheered with delight.

The videotape kept running.

"Watch carefully now," said the lawyer.

The crowd scattered as a team of paramedics rushed in. The little girl's mother and grandmother were half-crying and half-celebrating, not sure whether the ordeal was over yet. Dr. Coolidge was doing her best to assist the paramedics. She offered medical suggestions and gave them details about the child's status. Amidst all the chaos and confusion, Ryan's mother stooped down, raked her hand through the sand and found the big precious stone. Quickly—it happened in just a few quick frames of videotape—she tucked the green stone into the side pocket of the camera bag. The bag belonged to Ryan's father. She had been carrying it with her all day, taking photographs.

The lawyer stopped the videotape.

"Oh my gosh," said Ryan's mother.

Ryan's father looked at her. "Honey, you didn't tell me that you put it in the bag."

Dr. Coolidge buried her face in her hands.

The lawyer said, "Now you see the problem. This is why you've been charged, Sharon."

*Sharon*? thought Ryan. That was his mother's name. *She* was the one they had charged?

Dr. Coolidge caught her breath. "I swear, I had no recollection of putting that stone in the bag until you showed me this videotape. I was just acting on impulse. I saw it on the ground, and instinctively I picked it up and put it away for safekeeping. But honest, I forgot. Everything was so crazy then. I was worried about saving the girl's life. I just had no recollection of ever touching the stone."

"That's the problem," said the lawyer. "If you had returned the stone a day or even a week later, no one would have made a stink about it. But that grandmother called you several times and asked if you had the stone. Each time, you said you didn't."

"I didn't think I did. I had no memory of picking up that stone. I'm a doctor. There was a medical emergency, and I was in my emergency mind-set. You focus on the patient, not on all the other distractions that are going on around you."

The lawyer said, "Unfortunately, the prosecutor isn't convinced that it was an honest mistake. He says you stole it."

"But I didn't steal anything. All I did was save that girl."

"In his opinion, that's how you rationalized keeping the stone. His argument is that your mind worked this way: 'I saved that girl, I deserve a reward. I'll keep the emerald, and no one will ever know who took it.'"

Ryan was unaware, but his mouth was hanging open in shock. His mother had indeed been the one accused of stealing. Not his father.

Dr. Coolidge rose from her chair and started to pace. "We simply have to go to trial. We'll show the jury that I'm innocent."

The lawyer shook her head. "I don't recommend it. If you're convicted by a jury, that could mean serious prison time."

"Prison?" she said, her voice cracking. "This is unbelievable."

Mr. Coolidge asked, "What do you recommend, then?"

"The prosecutor is offering a plea bargain," said the lawyer. "If Sharon admits to the crime, he'll reduce the charges to petty larceny. That's a misdemeanor. He's agreed to recommend no jail time."

"But I'm completely innocent," said Dr. Coolidge.

The lawyer said, "You may be innocent, but the videotape shows you stuffing the stone into your bag. And then each time the rightful owner called to retrieve it, you denied that you had it. I may be able to get you off, but I'm not guaranteeing anything."

Ryan's mother was on the verge of tears. It was painful to watch her in this state, but Ryan was unable to tear his eyes away. He wished that his mother had never fired Hezekiah and hired this new lawyer. Hezekiah would have convinced the jury that she was innocent. As he watched the new attorney more closely, however, he realized the true nature of the problem. This attorney wasn't evil or incompetent.

She simply didn't believe in her own client's innocence.

Dr. Coolidge said, "Are you sure that if I take the plea bargain, this will all be over? No jail time. That's it?"

"Well, there is one other condition to the offer," said the lawyer. "This ties in with the prosecutor's theory that you tried to keep the emerald as a fee for your emergency service. You can no longer practice medicine in this state. You must agree to forfeit your license."

Her eyes widened with panic. "But I've worked all my life to be a doctor."

"It beats going to jail," said the lawyer. "I'll give you a minute to talk it over with your husband, but you really don't have a choice. Either plead guilty now and take probation, or go to trial and take a serious risk of lengthy jail time. The fact that you're innocent isn't going to change that. I'm sorry. I wish I had better news."

The lawyer left the room, and Ryan's parents immediately embraced. Dr. Coolidge's voice shook as she looked at her husband and said, "I can't lose my medical license. I can't stop being a doctor. I didn't do anything wrong."

They held each other tight, sitting in silence, just the two of them in the room—with Ryan watching through his leaphole.

She sniffled and said, "You believe me, don't you? I didn't do anything wrong."

Mr. Coolidge fell silent, seeming to mull over his thoughts. Finally he said, "I know you didn't do anything wrong. I did."

"You did?"

He broke the embrace, then looked his wife in the eye. "Don't you remember, sweetheart? The day after you saved that little girl, you told me that you'd put the emerald in my camera bag for safekeeping. You asked me to be sure to return the stone to the owners. I told you that I had already returned it. But I lied to you. I never returned it. I kept it."

Dr. Coolidge looked at her husband, confused. "That's not true at all. I never told you about the emerald. I never asked you to return it to the owners. I couldn't have. I didn't even remember putting it in your bag in the first place."

"Listen to me," he said, his voice filled with urgency. "You heard what that lawyer said. You may be innocent, but your best bet is to plead guilty and put it behind you. But I'm giving us another choice."

"What are you saying?"

"*I'm* pleading guilty," he said.

"What?"

"I told you that I had returned the emerald. But I never returned it. I kept it."

"That's not true!"

"Stop arguing with me, Sharon. From the minute we open that door and the lawyer comes back in here, that is going to be our story. Do you understand me? You can't stop being a doctor over this. And Ryan needs his mother."

"He needs a father, too."

"He needs you more." Ryan's father swallowed hard, as if building his resolve. Then he drew a deep breath and said, "So it's settled. I'm pleading guilty."

Ryan wanted to leap from his hiding spot and yell, *Dad, don't do it! Get rid of that lousy lawyer and go back with Hezekiah! Let Mom go to trial!*

But the minute he tried to say a word—the instant he consciously tried to alter history and change what had happened on that day—he felt himself being sucked from the room. He struggled to stay. But the force of the return leaphole was completely overpowering. He saw his mother crying and his father holding her tightly in his arms.

Then he saw that familiar bright light, and time was flying past him.

# 37

yan's landing was much better this time, but he hardly noticed the improvement.

He didn't feel like talking when he returned. Hezekiah and Kaylee gave him some time to himself. He could hardly believe what he'd just seen. His father was innocent. So was his mother. In fact, no one had stolen anything. That stupid emerald had simply been misplaced. Yet the Coolidge family had been disgraced. Ryan's father was sitting in jail, and everyone in town assumed that Ryan was headed there someday himself. The apple doesn't fall far from the tree, right?

What more proof did he need that Legal Evil was alive and well?

"Now you know," said Hezekiah.

"Yes," said Ryan. "Now I know. But why didn't my parents just tell me?"

"It's a tough situation, Ryan. The prosecutor suspected that your father was protecting your mother. He warned them: 'If I get a hint from anyone that Mr. Coolidge is taking the fall for his wife, I'll come after Dr. Coolidge with a vengeance. No deals, no mercy. I'll do everything in my power to put her away for the maximum sentence."

"So they couldn't tell anyone. Not even me."

"Not even you, Ryan."

"Then how do you know all this?" said Ryan.

"I was their first attorney, remember? Then your mother fired me. You think I wasn't curious to know what happened? I was shooting down a leaphole to *State versus Coolidge* as soon as your father went to jail."

"That's something else I don't understand. The prosecutor recommended no jail time. Why was my father sentenced to prison?"

"Just because a prosecutor promises to recommend no jail time doesn't mean that the judge will honor the agreement. Usually, if a prosecutor strikes a deal, the judge goes along with it. But the judge in your father's case didn't."

"Why not?"

"Ah, Legal Evil strikes again, Ryan. Your father's a journalist, right?"

"Yes. He writes for the *Tribune*."

"Three years ago, your father wrote an article that exposed some very questionable conduct by a certain judge. As luck would have it, he turned out to be the judge in your father's case. That grumpy old codger was all too happy to disregard the prosecutor's recommendation of no jail time and put your father behind bars."

"That stinks," said Ryan.

"That's what I'm up against every day," said Hezekiah. "Why do you think I need more people like you on my side?"

Ryan nodded, glad to be on the team.

"You should get home now," said Hezekiah.

"Yeah, you're right. I'm pretty eager to see my mom." Then a wry smile came to his lips. "And my dad."

Hezekiah returned the smile. "Tell your father hello for me, will you?"

Little more needed to be said. They both realized that Ryan had a lot to talk out with his father. Ryan would be seeing a lot more of his father, even if he was in prison. "I sure will," said Ryan.

"You want me to give you a ride home?" asked Hezekiah.

"Aren't you a little old to be driving a car?"

"I didn't mean by car. I'll take you on my horse."

Kaylee groaned. "No way, Hezekiah! You nearly killed me *and* you on the ride here. Ryan, you can borrow the horse and bring it back later. Come on. Let's get our four-legged friend outside where he belongs."

Ryan reached out to shake Hezekiah's hand, but the old man pulled him close and hugged him. Ryan smiled and whispered, "See you soon." Then he and Kaylee led the horse toward the door. It behaved like a skittish thoroughbred at the gate as they lowered its head and led it through the doorway. Finally, it settled down when they were outdoors.

As Ryan climbed up on the horse's back, Kaylee asked, "Do you remember your way home from here?"

"I'm pretty sure I do."

"Good. Now, remember. If you need any tips or have any questions about being a junior Legal Eagle, call me. I mean, if you want."

"I'd like that. I think I will."

She smiled. "Good. I'll see you around, then. Right, L'new?"

"Yeah, definitely. And by the way."

"What?"

"The name's Coolidge. From now on, I'm Ryan Coolidge."

"That's a good name, too."

"Yeah. I didn't always think so. But now I do." He gave her a little mock salute, and she fired one back.

"Oh, one more thing," she said. "This horse is very—"

Ryan barely laid a heel on the horse's ribs, and he was off like a rocket.

"Sensitive," she added, chuckling under her breath as Ryan raced toward home on the back of Hezekiah's one-hundred-and-forty-seven-year-old thoroughbred.

# Discussion Questions for *Leapholes*

1. What is "legal precedent?" Should something that happened to real people a long time ago have any impact on how we decide what is right or wrong in today's society? Why or why not?

2. In *Leapholes*, Legal Evil lives "where the brood follows the dam." That doctrine was created in ancient times to determine ownership rights over animals, such as horses or cattle. If someone owned the mother (the "dam"), they also owned her offspring (the "brood"). In 1842, the U.S. Supreme Court extended that doctrine to human beings. The Court decided that any child born to a slave was also a slave, even if the child was born in a state where slavery was illegal. Was this a proper use of legal precedent? Why or why not?

3. Hezekiah warns that Legal Evil is alive and well today. Can you think of any modern-day examples of Legal Evil at work? Does everyone in today's society have equal rights under the law?

4. Helping others through personal sacrifice is a recurring theme throughout *Leapholes*. When six people are infected with a deadly virus, Ryan refuses to cast lots and insists that the five vaccines be stretched into six. Hezekiah rides straight into the slave catchers so that they will not capture Hannah and her baby. Ryan's father pleads guilty to stealing

the emerald so that Ryan's mother will not be charged with a crime. Who made the bravest sacrifice? Please explain your answer.

5. Ryan's father is in prison because he pleaded guilty to a crime. He tells Ryan, however, that he is innocent. Can you think of any reasons why a person might plead guilty to a crime that he did not commit? Have you ever confessed to something you did not do in order to protect someone else? Can people be forced into a confession? What makes a confession reliable? How can we decide if a confession is reliable?

6. In the real life case about the sinking of a ship called *The William Brown*, a badly overloaded lifeboat was taking on seawater. Several crewmen began throwing passengers overboard so that the lifeboat would not sink. When the survivors made it to shore, one of the crewmen was put on trial for manslaughter. The judge condemned the crewman's actions. In his opinion, the passengers should have cast lots to determine who should live and who should die. Was the judge right? What would you have done if you had been on that sinking lifeboat?

7. Hezekiah, the greatest Legal Eagle of all, chose Ryan over Jarvis to become the next Legal Eagle. What character traits did Ryan possess that made it possible for him to become a Legal Eagle? What character traits did Jarvis possess that made it impossible for him to become a Legal Eagle?

# A Note From the Author

# Historical Accuracy of *Leapholes*

On April 19, 1841, the American ship *William Brown* hit an iceberg in the North Atlantic while en route from Liverpool to Philadelphia. It was loaded with Irish emigrants. Roughly half the passengers went down with the ship, and the rest piled into two lifeboats. The boat commanded by the first mate was so badly overloaded that it began to sink. In the face of crashing waves and a driving rainstorm, the first mate in utter desperation ordered his crew to lighten the load. Twelve men and two women were thrown overboard and drowned at sea.

When the survivors finally reached land, one of the crewmen who had thrown passengers overboard faced criminal charges. It was undisputed that the lifeboat would have sunk and all would have perished if it had remained in its overloaded state. However, the American judge who decided the prisoner's fate wrote that the passengers should have cast lots to determine who should live and who should die. This opinion sparked sharp debate among jurists and legal scholars. Some believed that casting lots was fair, almost an appeal to God. Others believed that casting lots was effectively "playing God," a practice that dehumanized all of us.

The case of the *William Brown* has fascinated me since law school. It presents the ultimate survival dilemma—to save ourselves or to save others. That dilemma is a theme that runs throughout *Leapholes*. Ryan Coolidge is forced to confront that issue head on. But he does it in a way he had never imagined he would. Ryan encounters a magical lawyer who puts a new spin on time travel—a lawyer with the power of legal "leapholes," the power to bring to life the people behind famous legal decisions like the *William Brown*.

All of the cases woven into the *Leapholes* storyline are actual cases from American legal history. The case of the *William Brown* is reported at *United States v. Holmes* (1842). The Supreme Court's decision that slaves are property, not people, appears at *Dred Scott v. Sandford* (1857). The slave doctrine that "the brood follows the dam" was embraced by the U.S. Supreme Court in *Prigg v. Pennsylvania* (1842). I've tried to present these and other snippets of legal history in a way that makes for exciting reading. Hopefully, it will provoke thoughtful discussion, not only about the law, but also about the people whose lives were affected by the thousands of reported decisions in our law libraries. It's a fun way to discover that legal precedents are not just words on paper. They are about real people with real problems. And for many, the law was a matter of life and death.

# Afterword

Have you ever thought about becoming a lawyer? Or, maybe you've wondered how real-life lawyers decided to become lawyers in the first place. The American Bar Association asked some of the best lawyers and lawyer/authors in the country that very question: What person or event from your childhood sparked your interest in the legal profession? Here are some of the responses we received. They may surprise you!

# David Baldacci

I was seven years old when I was dubbed the "Austin Avenue Lawyer" denoting both the street I lived on and my ability to think on my feet. Regrettably though, my skills were usually needed to extricate myself from some trouble connected to parents, school principals or other persons in authority.

Even with that title I had no burning desire to become a lawyer. However, as a political science major, I had two choices for my future: I could do postgraduate work in my field and teach, or I could go to law school. Well, I loved to write, enjoyed research, and, as my mother liked to remind me, I *was* the Austin Avenue Lawyer.

As a trial lawyer one case I remember was helping an elderly woman whose family member had embezzled all of her money. I spent a year of my life, mostly unpaid, getting it back, including chasing the guilty party through bankruptcy. Another case involved representing an individual against a goliath corporation whose only intent was to squash him even though they were in the wrong. Memories of those cases never fail to bring a smile.

People tend to dislike lawyers until they need one. Yet many of the significant rights we enjoy today started in the fertile mind of a lawyer who had the courage and ability to bring such freedoms to the people. A profession that spawns such champions is not a pariah, but the foundation of our democracy.

David Baldacci is the author of numerous # 1 best-selling suspense novels. He has also written *The Christmas Train,* a warmhearted contemporary classic; *Wish You Well*, which is currently taught in schools across the country; and the *"Freddie and the French Fries"* young adult series. Mr. Baldacci is published in more than 80 countries and in 37 languages, with nearly 45 million books in print worldwide. He earned his law degree from the University of Virginia and practiced law for nine years in Washington, D.C., as both a trial and corporate attorney.

# Roy Black

Where do we learn what justice really is? In our places of worship? Sure. From the Bible and other holy books? Certainly. But I think we learn a lot about justice in school.

Before we start school, our parents, of course, are our first teachers. But parents can be terribly unjust at times. They're human. They lose patience with us. They shout at us and may even spank us sometimes when we're not really to blame. If you are the oldest child in your family, you often get punished more than your younger brother or sister, because your parents are still learning how to be parents. They practice on you! You're the guinea pig! All you oldest children, boys and girls, know what I'm talking about.

In my long career as a defense attorney, I've seen astonishing things: Parents who were monsters, children who were devils, parents who never stopped loving their children, no matter what, and children who were sad innocents. I once had to defend a boy who killed an old woman because she complained he was playing his boom-box too loud. But his parents still loved him, and I did my best to stand up for him in court. I lost. He went to jail, probably for the rest of his life.

My parents moved me to Jamaica when I was still in high school. If you've read the James Bond books you may think Jamaica is paradise. It is a very beautiful island, but for me it was a living nightmare. The move came as a shock. One day I was the typical American high-school student in suburban Stamford, Connecticut. The next, I was on a slow-moving boat sailing across the Caribbean Sea, headed for a home on a mountaintop perched above exotic and foreign Kingston, Jamaica. I remember the black newsboys in the streets of

Kingston, selling the *Daily Gleaner* newspaper with their musical cries: "Gleanah! Gleanah!"

My life up until then had been like vanilla ice cream. I grew up in Stamford in the 1950s when Dwight D. Eisenhower was president. America was a very safe, plain, cheerful place in those years. We had just won World War II. The country was rich and at peace. Television was a new invention. We had only three TV channels showing only westerns and herky-jerky cartoons and soap operas. I was growing up as a typical American teenager in a white middle-class suburb, blissfully unaware of how the rest of the world lived.

I was living in a dream world. Once in Jamaica, I woke up fast. For one thing, there was no TV. My new school was grandly named Jamaica College. It was a British "public school" that was not public at all. It was for spoiled rich children who couldn't go to the really classy schools like Eton and Rugby back in England. The staff included a lot of colonial British numbskulls who had failed back in their mother country and had washed up in Jamaica, where they could still pretend to be somebody.

We had to salute the British flag every morning and sing "God Save the Queen" on festive occasions. There were very cruel beatings, which were called "canings," and which were administered all the time. British author P.G. Wodehouse has written about canings he himself suffered back in England, and the cane that, in the words of the Bible, "biteth like a serpent and stingeth like an adder." But until you have felt the cane across your legs and bottom, you don't know what injustice is. To feel physical pain, and to be utterly powerless to make it stop, or to reason it away—that is true injustice.

Even worse was the prejudice. To this day I can't understand what those British teachers had against me, unless it was that we Americans had declared our independence from Britain in 1776. I wasn't Mel Gibson in "The Patriot." I was just a middle-class kid from the Connecticut suburbs! But somehow, for some reason, I was singled out for special mistreatment.

There was one teacher in particular who seemed to hate me—my math teacher. He detested me, I guess, just because I was an American. Nothing I could do could please him. I recall him deliberately making a fool out of me, forcing me to stand in front of the classroom, trying to explain the intricate arithmetic of British money: Pounds, shillings, guineas, and even pence. My fellow students smirked and giggled.

For your information, one pound was worth about $2.40 in those days. That meant it had 240 pennies or "pence" in it. But it also had 20 shillings in it, each shilling worth 12 pence. Half a shilling was sixpence. A guinea was a pound plus a shilling. A pound coin was called a "sovereign." A paper pound banknote was called a "quid." Something worthless was "not worth tuppence," or two pence. It was the craziest money system I've ever had to deal with in my life!

Yet I owe that hateful teacher something, and I am going to pay the debt now. By showing me injustice, he taught me to love justice. By teaching me what pain and humiliation were all about, he awakened my heart to mercy. Through these hardships, I learned hard lessons. Fight against prejudice, battle the oppressors, support the underdog. Question authority, shake up the system, never be discouraged by hard times and hard people. Embrace those who are placed last, to whom even the bottom looks like up.

It took me some time to find my mission in life—that of a criminal defense lawyer. But that school, and that teacher, put me on my true path. So do not be discouraged. Even thorns and thistles can teach you something, and lead to success.

A Miami criminal defense attorney, highly sought after by the national media for his views on high-profile criminal justice issues facing America, Roy Black became an NBC News legal analyst in 2003, appearing regularly on *The Today Show (NBC)* and other NBC and MSNBC news programs. In 2005, Roy played the managing partner in NBC's alternative drama reality TV show *The Law Firm*. He is regarded as a favorite among journalists and viewers alike for his poignant expert analysis, warm demeanor, and quick wit.

# David Boies

Because I have dyslexia (a learning disability that makes it difficult to recognize words), reading has never been easy for me. I did not learn to read until I was in third grade, and throughout elementary and high school reading was hard and slow. I tried to make up for what I missed in reading assignments by paying close attention in class and by asking a lot of questions. Participating in class discussions, answering teachers' questions, and arguing points of view also gave me an opportunity to show that I could learn and express myself well even if I was a poor reader. Over the years I became comfortable, confident, and experienced in thinking and speaking on my feet; I also became good at learning and listening.

When, in high school, I became a member of the debate team, I found that my dyslexia prevented me from being able to use scripts and note cards when I spoke—so I learned to speak without them. I would prepare an outline of major points, learn the outline, and then use the outline to organize my presentation. Speaking only from an outline in my head required me to know the subject I was talking about thoroughly. In addition, because I did not have a fixed script my speaking tended to be more informal, flexible, and conversational—all of which ended up making me more interesting and persuasive.

I suspect I would have become a lawyer whether or not reading was easy—being a trial lawyer is exciting and challenging, and the cause of justice is an important one. However, the traits and techniques I learned coping with my dyslexia—being comfortable thinking and speaking on my feet, the discipline of thorough preparation, the ability to speak without notes, an informal and conversational speaking style, the patience and ability to listen carefully, skill in asking and answering questions orally—all have contributed to my success in the courtroom.

Dubbed by the *New York Times* as "the lawyer everyone wants," David Boies has handled many famous cases, including *New York Yankees v. Major League Baseball*, in which he represented the most famous team in sports history, and *United States v. Microsoft,* where his cross examination of Bill Gates became legendary. He also argued before the U.S. Supreme Court in *Bush v. Gore,* a case that decided the 2000 presidential election. Mr. Boies is chairman of the law firm of Boies, Schiller & Flexner, LLP, and he is the author of *Courting Justice* (Miramax 2004), a memoir that recounts his life as one of the most respected lawyers in America.

# Nick Buoniconti

I have always been on the smallish side. When I decided to play football I was nine years old. I couldn't wait for my first practice and when that day arrived I grabbed my helmet, my cleats and the rest of my equipment and off I went.

I was running across the street to the practice field when I tripped over my own feet and fell flat on my face. I looked at my arm and a bone was out of line. My mom took me to the doctor and I left there with a cast on my broken arm and a broken heart as my football season was over before it started.

Football has always paved the way for me. In high school I was 13 years old and was the starting middle linebacker for our team. It was through football that I received a scholarship to the University of Notre Dame. When I went to Notre Dame, I was told that they gave me the last scholarship for that year and that they really didn't think I would last there because of my small size and my lack of academic preparation. Well, I was an All-American and captain of my team and finished in the top third of my class with an Economics degree.

I have always relished the role of the underdog and have welcomed the challenges as they presented themselves.

I wasn't drafted by the N.F.L. because they thought I was too small. The then Boston Patriots of the AFL gave me a chance and, in a fifteen-year career that included seven with Boston and eight with the Miami Dolphins, I was All Pro nine times, won two Super Bowls, and was on the only undefeated team in N.F.L. history in 1972. I was inducted into the N.F.L. Hall of Fame in 2001.

What I have learned over the years is that old adage about, "it's not the size of the dog in the fight that counts. It's the size of the fight in the dog that counts." It may sound corny and not cool, but it has gotten me through some difficult times and has made me a real competitor.

I went to Suffolk Law School in Boston, Massachusetts, when I was playing with the Boston Patriots. I decided to plan for my life after football as a 23-year-old law student. I went to Suffolk for four years in their night school. I would practice football during the day and three days a week would go from the practice field to the Law Library to prepare for class. I was very fortunate to have great classmates and understanding professors, as my football schedule on occasion took me away from school for two weeks at a time. While all my teammates went out to dinner and played golf, I was studying my law books just trying to keep up with the class. I graduated in 1968 and passed the Massachusetts Bar in 1969 and the Florida Bar in 1970.

My law school education helped me follow a path that took me from representing athletes to becoming president of a *Fortune* 500 company. It taught me that no one is above the law and that in the end you have to protect your reputation by doing what is right.

I believe that the practice of law can be an honorable profession but only so if you put yourself in your client's shoes and do what's right for them, for the right reason, and not solely for the money. I wish all of you the best and hope that if Law is your future, you will be an honorable attorney.

Hall of Fame football player Nick Buoniconti juggled the rigors of a sports career and law school to become a successful attorney. He is a graduate of Suffolk University Law School and a member of the bar in both Florida and in Massachusetts. For twenty-three seasons Mr. Buoniconti was co-host of the longest-running, critically acclaimed, weekly television sports show "Inside the NFL." Since his son Marc suffered a devastating spinal cord injury in 1985, he helped found and serves as a national spokesman and fundraiser for the Miami Project to Cure Paralysis, which has grown to become internationally recognized as the leading research center for spinal cord injuries in the world.

# Benjamin R. Civiletti

As a child, during the Second World War, my family moved a lot. Between 1940 and 1946, by the fifth grade, I attended more than six grade schools in as many different states. I was always the "new" kid. Naturally, my friends were those left out of the regular circles of classmates. The minority students, immigrant children, and "different" kids accepted me as a pal. I developed affection for those in need of one kind of help or another. This desire to help others in need led me later in college to decide to be a lawyer.

Added to this desire to help were two other influences on me. One was that I loved to argue and my mother, with whom I argued most, often would say, "You should be a lawyer." Two, I was an athlete in high school and college, and I loved to compete and win at sports, although I was not a "good" loser. The will to compete led me to be a trial lawyer who competes in court to win the case for his client. I thought it would be exciting and worthwhile.

I have enjoyed the practice of law very much, and I have loved trying cases in all levels of courts from traffic court to the United States Supreme Court and even to the World Court at The Hague in The Netherlands.

I treasure the help I have been able to give.

Mr. Civiletti, while U.S. Attorney General, has represented the United States before both the Supreme Court and the International Court of Justice. He has also served as Chair of the Litigation Section of the ABA and is its representative to the United Nations. He is a Fellow of the American College of Trial Lawyers. He is now Chair of the law firm of Venable.

# Linda Fairstein

On my eleventh birthday, my parents took me into New York City to go to a Broadway show. I had been to many musicals as a kid, but this time we were going to a serious drama, a brilliant play called *Inherit the Wind*. The reason for the gift was that my childhood dream was to become a writer, and this work had been acclaimed for the power of its language. It told the story of the 1925 trial of John Scopes—the debate about the teaching of evolutionism versus creationism—and featured the eloquent arguments of two of America's greatest lawyers, William Jennings Bryan and Clarence Darrow. The experience was pretty overwhelming at my age, but I came away with great admiration for Darrow's defense of Scopes and the courage of his position.

A few years later—and still, as an aspiring writer—I took a book off my father's shelf because I seemed to have inherited his love for mystery fiction. The novel I devoured was called *Compulsion,* and, like the play that had so affected me, I learned it was also based on a real event. The chilling story was a retelling of the murder of a boy just about my age—fourteen—in Chicago, exactly a year before the famous Scopes trial. The killing of Bobby Franks by two men who came from good families and were college-educated—Nathan Leopold and Richard Loeb—was heartbreaking. They had planned the senseless act simply in order to commit the perfect crime—a completely arrogant and selfish taking of human life for no more than sport. The lead defense attorney was the same man who had emerged as my legal hero on the Broadway stage—Clarence Darrow.

Too young to fully understand the importance of the rights of the accused, my spirit was broken by the fictionalized Darrow's defense of the thrill-killers. I wanted his power to represent the voice of the victim, I wanted him to fight on behalf of the child who was picked at random for this brutal crime. A decade later, when I found myself studying criminal law and making my own career choice, it was easy for me to decide that I wanted to join the office of a great prosecutor. I wanted a career in which I could work on behalf of victims without voices, representing them in their efforts to seek justice before the court, helping them to triumph over some of the senseless evil in our world and restore to them the dignity we all deserve.

Linda Fairstein is the author of the Alexandra Cooper series of crime novels, including the eighth book, entitled *Death Dance,* published in January, 2006. For thirty years, Linda was a prosecutor in the office of the New York County District Attorney specializing in crimes of violence against women and children.

# Willie Gary

I was the sixth of my parents' eleven children, and I grew up in a three-room shack in one of this country's poorest communities. I often walked to school in my bare feet, and at the age of ten I was picking corn to help support our family. Needless to say, there were not many lawyers around. Even so, the idea of being a leader, if not a lawyer, came to me when I was just five years old. Back in the early 1950s, we didn't have a church in our community, at least not a church in the sense of a building with four walls and roof overhead. We conducted Sunday school outdoors. I thought it was the best church in the world. Two towering Australian pine trees reached up to the heavens like twin steeples. Our pews were tomato crates turned upside down. My aunt recited bible verses to us, and she would ask for volunteers to recite them back to the whole class. My hand was always the first one in the air. I *loved* public speaking.

When I was a little older, I learned about a very famous black lawyer named Thurgood Marshall. He argued the winning side of *Brown v. Board of Education*, one of the most important cases in American history. Mr. Marshall later became Justice Marshall, the first black man ever appointed to the United States Supreme Court. Closer to home, however, were two brothers from West Palm Beach, each of whom had earned the name "Lawyer Cunningham" in our community. Malcolm and TJ Cunningham went to law school at a time when no Florida school would admit black applicants, but the state would pay for blacks to attend law school out of state. The Cunningham brothers were not in the same league as Thurgood Marshall, but the perseverance of these two trailblazers made them an inspiration to boys like me. If they could do it, why couldn't I do it, too?

When I was thirteen years old, a tragedy in our family made me more determined than ever to reach my goal. My older brother—my hero—was shot and killed. My brother was unarmed. The man who shot him was put on trial, but the jury acquitted him. The guy got away with it. I knew there was only one thing I could do to keep injustices like that from happening. From that point on, I knew that I was going to become "Lawyer Gary."

With over a hundred verdicts and settlements of a million dollars or more—including a record-setting $500 million award from a Mississippi jury—Willie Gary is one of the most successful civil trial lawyers in history. His clients range from civil rights icon Rosa Parks and the legendary Don King to the descendant of slave owners. Through the Gary Foundation, he has donated millions of dollars to improve education for young people. He has been especially supportive of his alma mater, Shaw University, and other historically black colleges. Mr. Gary is the founding partner of Gary, Williams, Parenti, Finney, Lewis, McManus, Watson & Sperando, P.L. in Stuart, Florida.

# Jamie S. Gorelick

"It's not fair!"

Like most children, I complained—"It's not fair!"—when I thought that my parents were favoring my brother, or when they told me I couldn't do what I wanted.

But my parents also taught me the importance of fairness. They were children of poor immigrants, Jews in a mostly Christian society, so they were acutely aware of protections that our form of government provides to minorities and to the less powerful. Their parents had sacrificed to get to this country because of those protections.

Fairness was not just an abstract idea to me. When I was in grade school, I watched on television as federal marshals escorted black children my own age into schools so they wouldn't be hurt by those who wanted them kept out. I cried at the cruelty and the unfairness and cheered those who stood up to bullies filled with hate. One of those I cheered was Martin Luther King, Jr., who led the historic March on Washington to protest segregation at lunch counters and in schools and to demand the right to vote.

And then, in the spring of my senior year in high school, first Dr. King and then Bobby Kennedy—President Kennedy's brother, the former Attorney General and then Senator who was fighting for civil rights—were gunned down. My world was rocked by the unfairness both to their own young children and to the country, whose better nature was being seriously challenged.

I went to college and then retreated into academia, deciding to become a historian. But, in the end, the law beckoned. It presented a tool for achieving fairness. I practiced law for nearly two decades, representing those facing the power of the government or powerful foes. When I left private law practice to work in government, I took with me a sense of obligation to use that power carefully and fairly.

Jamie Gorelick has had several careers—as a litigator representing clients in court; as Deputy Attorney General (the number two position) in the U.S. Department of Justice; as general counsel of the Department of Defense; and as member of the 9/11 Commission that investigated why the country was unprepared for the attacks of September 11, 2001. She is a partner at Wilmer Cutler Pickering Hale & Dorr LLP in Washington, D.C.

# James Grippando

My favorite subject in middle school was American history. I wasn't so much into memorizing dates, names, and places. I was more interested in what it must have been like to live in those times. What was it like to go to school each day on horseback? What did kids do after school for fun? The time period that fascinated me most was right around the Civil War.

I grew up in Illinois, the "Land of Lincoln." Abraham Lincoln was a great president, and he was also a lawyer. I became especially interested in learning about Lincoln after my parents told me that we were related to him. As it turns out, my step-grandmother's grandmother was Abe Lincoln's mother's cousin. Okay, that's a stretch. But Abe and I are related. That's my story, and I'm sticking to it.

In the early 1970s, my parents took me to Springfield, the state capital. We visited Lincoln's old law office. Imagining him at work there made me want to become a lawyer. Later that year, a little trouble at school convinced me to follow that path.

I was on my way to the boys' restroom during study break. Another boy nearly knocked me over as he was running out the door. He stopped, grabbed me by the collar, and said, "If you say a word, you're dead meat." I had no idea what he was talking about. When I went inside the bathroom, I found black paint smeared all over the walls. The boy had stolen tubes of acrylic paint from the art room and vandalized the place.

The boy was older and bigger than me. I believed him when he said I'd be dead meat—maybe not literally, but at least missing a few teeth. I didn't know what to do. I agonized about it through the rest of the study hour. Should I tell, or should I keep my mouth shut? Before I could decide, I was called into the principal's office. The boy was there. He admitted to having smeared paint on the walls, but he swore that he did it only because I had dared him to. The principal believed his lie. I was suspended from school for three days right on the spot. I thought it was completely unfair, but I didn't know what to do about it. Those three days I spent at home, I decided that I never wanted to be in that position again. I always wanted to know my rights. I decided to become a lawyer.

# Jeremiah Healy

I grew up in the 1950s and early 1960s, when the *Perry Mason* television series was *the* "legal thriller" show. It was broadcast (we had no "cable TV" back then) from September 1957, through September 1966, and starred Raymond Burr playing a criminal defense attorney who never seemed to lose a case. Never? In ten *years*?

Young as I was, and even with no lawyers in my own family to confirm it, I found his record hard to believe. But I do remember when I decided to become an attorney myself. It was the first time I saw another television show, *The Defenders*, which was broadcast from September, 1961 to September, 1965, when I was thirteen to seventeen. Starring E.G. Marshall as a middle-aged lawyer and Robert Reed (yes, later of *The Brady Bunch*) as his young lawyer son, the series dealt with their efforts to "defend" people, but not always on criminal charges. Many of the stories dealt with subjects that simply were never mentioned on television in those sensitive, up-tight years, such as civil rights for racial minorities. Because many of the shows were predominantly trials, I had the chance to see how attorneys could help judges and juries deciding both criminal and civil cases understand the different points of view that litigants might hold fanatically, only to appreciate themselves—through something an attorney said or made *them* say from the witness stand—that they were not quite so "right" as they'd earlier believed. Those episodes featured future famous stars like Robert Redford, Dustin Hoffman, Gene Hackman, and Martin Sheen, but were also showcases for marvelous African-American actors like James Earl Jones and Ossie Davis, when blacks in general were never seen on television (not even in commercials, if you can believe that).

And, the father-and-son legal team often lost in court, a valuable lesson for me in those days as well as later in life. Back then, though, I thought that if lawyers could do that— help people see other, different people's points of view, and resolve their problems without violence—that's what I wanted to do, too. And I've never regretted it.

Jeremiah Healy, a graduate of Harvard Law School, practiced and taught law in Boston, Massachusetts for twenty-two years. He's written eighteen novels, including three legal thrillers under his pen-name of "Terry Devane." For more information, visit www.jeremiahhealy.com.

# Judge Phyllis Kravitch

As a young girl growing up in Georgia in the 1920s and 1930s I never considered a legal career. Rather I envisioned myself pursuing dance and becoming a ballerina. However, when I was eleven years old, my father, a trial attorney, was appointed by the court to represent an African-American man who had been accused of murder. The case was highly publicized and—because of the defendant's race—made my father very unpopular. As a result I was shunned by some of my schoolmates, and was the only girl in my scout troop not invited to another girl's birthday party. This upset me very much. In his attempt to console me, my father explained the importance of our Constitution, and especially the Sixth Amendment, which guarantees everyone accused of a crime the right to a jury trial and to be represented by an attorney which, he explained, meant regardless of a defendant's race, wealth or social status. At the time this seemed somewhat abstract, and certainly didn't make me feel any better about being excluded. He finally said "when you are a little older you will understand that there are more important things in life than birthday parties."

Over the next few years I began to understand what he meant as he taught me more about the Constitution, our judicial system and the role of lawyers in helping others and protecting the rights and liberties of us all. The more I learned the more interested I became.

Although few women were in the legal profession at that time, especially in the South, my father encouraged me to go to law school and practice law. I followed his advice and his example and it is a decision I have never regretted.

Since 1979 Judge Phyllis Kravitch has served as a judge on the United States Court of Appeals for the Eleventh Circuit. When she was appointed by President Jimmy Carter, she was only the third woman in the United States to become a United States Circuit Judge and the first female federal judge in the Southeast. Prior to that appointment, she practiced law in Savannah, Georgia, and was the first female Superior Court Judge in the state.

# Lance Liebman

Many lawyers go to court and argue cases for their clients. The client believes she is innocent of a crime or was injured by another driver's bad driving or seeks custody of a child after an unhappy divorce.

But other lawyers make laws, and that has been my focus since I was 13 years old. In that year, my parents moved to Frankfort, the very small capital city of the Commonwealth of Kentucky.

Every other year, the Kentucky legislature would come to Frankfort. These were elected senators and representatives from all 120 of Kentucky's counties. Some were from cities like Louisville. Others were from coal mining areas, tobacco farming areas, and horse breeding areas. The legislature, with participation by the Governor, can change the laws. They can give more rights to women and members of minority groups. They can improve health insurance. They can decide how much money will go to the public schools or to build new roads or for a new state office building or to reduce taxes.

I could walk from our house or from my high school to the state capitol building where the legislature met. I often watched meetings. When I went to college, I wrote my major paper on how the Kentucky Legislature did its work. Two summers during college, I worked at the Legislative Research Bureau, which collected information to help the legislature make decisions. Now, 40 years after I finished college, I am head of the American Law Institute, which recommends new laws and new legal rules to state legislatures, to the Congress of the United States, and to state and federal judges who must decide new and difficult legal questions.

If you think this country should do some things differently, then you should help your state or the entire country get new laws. You can persuade people to vote for you and then you will be a member of the legislature and can vote for and against new laws. That is democracy, and it is the most important thing that the American Revolution created to guarantee the liberty of the American people.

Lance Liebman is the director of the American Law Institute, the nation's leading organization for the promotion of legal reform. He is only the fifth lawyer to receive the high honor of serving as director since the Institute's formation in 1923. The Institute's founders and earliest supporters included such famous jurists as Chief Justice and former President William Howard Taft, Chief Justice Charles Evans Hughes, and Judges Benjamin Cardozo and Learned Hand. Mr. Liebman is a William S. Beinecke Professor of Law at Columbia University, where he also served as Dean. For 21 years he taught law at his alma mater, Harvard University, where he was associate dean.

# Phillip Margolin

I hated elementary school—I was always in trouble for bad behavior and my grades were awful—but I loved to read. My favorite murder mysteries starred criminal defense attorney Perry Mason, who always won the cases that no one thought he could win.

When I started the seventh grade, I was doing so badly in school that my parents sent me to a private school for children who were messing up big time. At the private school, when you were accused of causing trouble, you were tried in student court and a student jury decided your fate. The student judge, student prosecutor and student defense attorney were elected by the student body. You can guess what position I ran for.

I loved being the school defense attorney, and the incident that cemented my desire to be a lawyer came in the trial of a tough guy named Gary, who was accused of cursing out a teacher. The teacher didn't come to Gary's trial, so the prosecutor called another teacher who wasn't there when the incident occurred. When she tried to tell the jury what the other teacher had told her I remembered that Perry Mason always objected if a witness tried to testify about something they hadn't heard. "Objection, hearsay," I said, leaping to my feet. None of the students knew what to do, but the school lawyer was in the audience. I remember the look on her face when she had to tell the judge that I was right. In a real courtroom, I would have won because the prosecutor had no other witness to what happened, but the school lawyer ordered us to put the trial over to the next week. Gary was convicted when the teacher he'd cursed at testified, but having that objection upheld was such a thrill that I decided right then and there that I would definitely become a criminal defense lawyer when I grew up. And that's what I did for twenty-five years.

Phillip Margolin is the author of nine *New York Times* best-selling novels. He grew up in New York City, served as a Peace Corps volunteer in West Africa, and then worked his way through New York University School of Law by teaching junior high school in the South Bronx. As a trial lawyer, he specialized in criminal defense in Portland, Oregon, where he handled all sorts of cases—including a case that went all the way to the United States Supreme Court. He stopped practicing law in 1996 and since then has been a fulltime writer and the president and chairman of the board of Chess for Success, a nonprofit charity that uses chess to teach study skills to elementary and middle school children in Title I schools. His wife, Doreen, is also a successful lawyer, and they have two children, Ami and Daniel. *Lost Lake*, his most recent novel, was published in 2005.

# Senator Mel Martinez

I came to America from Cuba when I was fifteen years old to escape the oppression of communist government. I came without my family and with nothing more than a suitcase and the clothes on my back, but was soon greeted with an unexpected amount of love, freedom and compassion. A family volunteered to take me into their home and their hearts even though they knew nothing about me and didn't even speak the same language as me!

Just as this family gave me so much, I too wanted to give to my community. Therefore my decision to go to law school and practice law was not a hard decision for me to make. Soon after I came to the United States, I realized that the key to my success was through education. Education was the tool that I could use to achieve a better life and a better future, but more importantly practicing law was a way to give back and serve the community in ways that other professions might not.

When I finished law school and first began practicing law, I was one of the first bilingual lawyers in the Orlando area. So I became the person that poor, Hispanic families would turn to for legal advice and representation. I helped them however I could and learned a lot about the law standing at their side.

By helping these people and the many others that I represented during my time as a lawyer, I learned that if you allow yourself to be guided by compassion for others, you will have many opportunities, both inside and outside of your work, to change someone else's life at the same time you enrich your own.

Officially sworn in on January 4, 2005, as the thirty-third senator of the State of Florida, Senator Mel Martinez made history when he assumed his role as the first Cuban-American U.S. senator. Prior to the Senate, Martinez served President Bush in his Cabinet as the nation's twelfth Housing and Urban Development Secretary and was the first popularly elected Republican to serve as Orange County Chairman in Orlando, Florida. He met his wife Kitty while attending Florida State University, where he studied for his undergraduate and law degrees. Senator Martinez and Kitty have three children, Lauren Shea, John and Andrew.

# Marilyn Milian

From a very young age, all my teachers would tell my parents, "*This* one will make a good lawyer!" They meant it not as a compliment, but as a complaint that I was just too argumentative for a child. If someone laid down a rule, I always wanted to know the rationale behind it. If it didn't make sense, I wanted to debate it and expose its unfairness. When I saw a student treat another student unfairly, I wanted to fix it; and when they told me it was none of my business, it only made me want to fix it more.

Lawyers have lately become a magnet for criticism and blame for all manner of problems confronting our society. Some think we fight too much, or bring too many cases to court. They make jokes about lawyers. They quote Shakespeare's famous line that "First thing we do, is kill all the lawyers." Of course, that line in fact paid lawyers the greatest compliment. He wrote that line for a character commenting on how to best plot the overthrow of the government, a scheme that would not be possible unless the lawyers were gone.

That's because a lawyer's job is to see to it that wrongs are righted. When someone suffers a great harm and there is no one else to turn to . . . we seek out a lawyer. Before becoming a judge I spent ten years fighting for victims' rights at the prosecutor's office. Day after day people came to me with awful stories about the wrongs that others had done to them. Sadly, many of these victims were children. My job was to go into court and try to make things better for them by stopping the person who did the crime from doing it again, whether by putting them in jail or by forcing them to get counseling. I could not erase what had happened; but I could help to make things better, and prevent others from being victimized.

That's why I love being a judge. People come to me with their problems when they are at wit's end . . . they can't solve it on their own. They are upset, they think they have been wronged, and they want me to force someone to do what they think is the right thing. Sometimes these people are right, sometimes they are wrong. But always, I do my best to listen to both sides and try to come up with a solution to the problem that is fair and just. Now, fixing unfairness *is* my business, all day long!

Judge Marilyn Milian serves as the judge of the hit television series "The People's Court". Before that she served as a judge in Miami-Dade County in the civil, criminal and domestic violence courts. Prior to her appointment to the bench she was a prosecutor under Janet Reno for ten years, handling narcotics, robbery, and homicide cases.

# Justice Alan C. Page

Long before my career in football, I had an interest in the law. Growing up as a black child in Ohio during the 1950s, I had noticed that judges could play a significant role in people's lives.

I remember as a nine-year-old child reading newspaper articles about the *Brown vs. Board of Education* school desegregation case in which the United States Supreme Court ruled against states operating "separate but equal" schools for black children. It was the beginning of the end of state-sponsored segregation in the United States.

From that case I developed a sense of the real power that judges have and the importance of what they do. For me, that power was *hope*. Hope that fairness could prevail and that issues related to race might one day be resolved. Hope that the judicial system and its judges could be trusted.

As I continued to learn about the courts, I came to believe even more deeply in the principle of "equal justice under the law." These weren't just words to me. They had meaning; they still do.

As I saw it, judges were the only ones who had the power to ensure that fairness "happens." Even before I was old enough to understand what it was all about, I had the impression that fairness was dependent upon impartiality and that this, in turn, was why we could trust judges.

As I continued down my educational and career paths, I thought a lot about the intertwined concepts of trust and fairness. Eventually, my interest in "equal justice" led me to law school, and then to run for and win a seat on the Minnesota Supreme

Court. It all started with a nine-year-old child reading news stories about a court case in faraway Kansas.

Minnesota's first African-American Supreme Court Justice, Alan C. Page, was elected to the court in 1992. He was reelected in 1998 and 2004. Previously he served as an assistant attorney general, a special assistant attorney general, and was an associate with the Minnesota law firm of Lindquist and Vennum. Page is widely renowned for his career as a professional football player. Elected to the Pro Football Hall of Fame in 1988, he is best known for his defensive efforts with the Minnesota Vikings in the 1970s. Page, who attended law school at the University of Minnesota during the height of his football career, is an ardent defender of equal education for children. He is the founder of the Page Education Foundation, which assists minority and other disadvantaged youth with post-secondary education.

# John Safer

Why did I become a lawyer? It was 1946, World War II had just ended. I had spent over four years in the Air Force. I was delighted and surprised to find that I was still alive. So I decided to do something worthwhile with the rest of my life I had not expected to see.

My father was a lawyer and very much wanted me to follow in his footsteps. The government was willing to pay the tuition for any school to which I could gain admission. So I sent off applications to Harvard, Yale, and Columbia Law Schools. Yale and Columbia sent back forms saying that I could apply for admission if I would write a long (and to me, pointless) essay on why I wanted to become a lawyer. Harvard wrote back to say that I was admitted and classes would start in four weeks. The choice was not difficult to make, and, as a result, I enrolled in Harvard Law School.

After I graduated, I did become a member of the bar, but went off into other fields of endeavor—television, electronics, and real estate development. I then spent the last thirty years of my business career as chairman of the board of various banks. At the same time I embarked on a parallel career as a sculptor. My principal contribution to the law probably is "Judgment," a seven-ton bronze sculpture on the campus of Harvard Law School, which was the gift of my class at our thirtieth reunion.

However, the law has made a major contribution to my life. Throughout my business career, particularly in real estate and banking, my legal training was very helpful, and at times, invaluable. My knowledge of the purpose and philosophy of our legal system enabled me, over and over, to solve problems and handle difficult situations in ways that would have been impossible without my law school background.

Now an internationally renowned sculptor, John Safer first used his training as a lawyer to become a successful entrepreneur. *The New York Times* has compared Safer's position as a sculptor to that of Georgia O'Keeffe as a painter and Ansel Adams as a photographer. The United States Department of State has sent Safer sculptures abroad to represent the finest in American art. His work today stands in over one thousand private collections and public sites and has been exhibited in museums, embassies and universities throughout the world. *Ascent*, a seventy-foot high, polished-steel sculpture, stands before the entrance to the Smithsonian Institution's new Air and Space Museum at Dulles Airport and has been described as one of the great sculptures of this era.

# Lisa Scottoline

When I was in middle school, adults used to ask me, "What do you want to be when you grow up?"

"I don't know," I would answer. This was true, but elicited a frown. Clearly, I needed a better answer. Even my little brother knew what he wanted to be, so the next time someone asked me, I tried *his* answer:

"A fireman?"

But that only made them laugh. I wracked my brain, trying to come up with the right answer. My father was an architect, but I didn't like math, so I didn't want to be that. My mother was a secretary, but I didn't like typing. What I liked was tennis, and played all the time with my best friend, Miriam. Her father, Mr. Silver, was the nicest and smartest man, and he gave me tennis lessons for free. In the summertime, the three of us would practice until so late at night that it would be hard to see. One evening, I remember Mr. Silver was watching Miriam and me play. I hit the ball, and Miriam called it out of bounds. I said it was in, but I couldn't tell in the twilight. So Miriam asked her father, "Dad, was it in or out?"

Mr. Silver answered, "It was in. Sorry, kiddo, but what's right is right, no matter what."

Miriam got angry, but I felt the warmth of admiration rush over me. Much later, I learned what Mr. Silver did for a living. He was a lawyer. So the next time someone asked me what I wanted to be when I grew up, I finally knew. I answered that I wanted to be a lawyer, and they nodded with approval. And when I grew up, I became a lawyer. But deep inside, what I really wanted to be was Mr. Silver.

And, some day, I will be.

Lisa Scottoline graduated from the University of Pennsylvania and its law school, where she served on the *Law Review*. She was a law clerk, then practiced law at the Dechert firm, until she left to raise her daughter. She is now a *New York Times* best-selling author of suspense fiction.

# Dick Thornburgh

Most of my family members were engineers. Almost by default, I studied engineering while in college. I did not do well. Late in my senior year I took a required course entitled "Business Law for Engineers," designed to give engineering graduates a nodding acquaintance with elementary legal principles. Its effect upon me was electric. After struggling with math and science courses for four years, I had finally found a field where I could combine my longtime interests in reading and writing and in history and politics. I immediately applied to law school.

In my law practice, I quickly discovered that the law could be used for public good as well as to resolve private differences. During the 1960s I took part in the civil rights movement, which had swept the nation. My particular cause was providing free legal advice to people who could not afford a lawyer, through publicly funded organizations such as Neighborhood Legal Services. We all need legal advice to help us through the maze of laws, regulations, and rules of procedure that affect our daily lives. Providing lawyers for low-income people charged with crimes or who had claims to assert or defend seemed to me an absolute necessity in a nation that subscribes to the rule of law.

Years later, as attorney general in the administrations of Presidents Ronald Reagan and George H.W. Bush, I had the opportunity to participate in the effort to secure the civil rights of 54 million Americans with disabilities. Passage of the Americans with Disabilities Act was especially important to my family as we have a son with mental retardation. Since this law was signed by President Bush in 1990, it has advanced the cause of disability rights in our country and around the world.

My inspiration for these aspects of my experience in the law? It comes from the simple admonition of one of America's greatest judges, Learned Hand, "Thou shalt not ration justice."

During his twenty-five years in public life, Dick Thornburgh served as governor of Pennsylvania, attorney general of the United States, and under-secretary-general of the United Nations. He is currently counsel to the international law firm of Kirkpatrick & Lockhart Nicholson Graham LLP in Washington, D.C. His autobiography, *Where the Evidence Leads,* was published in 2003 by the University of Pittsburgh Press.

# Acknowledgments

When my first novel, *The Pardon*, was published in 1994, I wrote an article for the ABA Journal in which I took issue with the gratuitous lawyer bashing in today's fiction. Eleven novels later, I still believe the law can be a noble profession. Corny, I know. But that's the reason I'm so grateful to the American Bar Association's Criminal Justice Section for making *Leapholes* the first novel for young readers that the ABA has ever published.

As with all books, *Leaphholes* was a team effort. First and foremost, I want to thank all of the great lawyers who have shared their personal stories in the special *Leapholes* Afterword: David Baldacci, Roy Black, David Boies, Nick Buoniconti, General Benjamin Civiletti, Linda Fairstein, Willie Gary, Jamie Gorelick, Jeremiah Healy, Judge Phyllis Kravitch, Lance Liebman, Phillip Margolin, Senator Mel Martinez, Judge Marilyn Milian, Justice Alan C. Page, John Safer, Lisa Scottoline, and General Richard Thornburgh. In appreciation of their contributions, a portion of the profits from *Leapholes* will be donated to charity to promote children's literacy. I'm also indebted to the folks who worked behind the scenes to bring the Afterword together, including Linda Carson, Agatha Ellis, James Fox Miller, Wanda Lamar, Carolyn Marino, John O'Sullivan, Benjamine Reid, John Schlessinger, Stuart Singer, and Carlos Sires.

My young readers were a tremendous help in gearing this story toward a middle school and YA audience. Thanks to Allison Freedman, Reid McWilliams, John Joseph O'Sullivan, and Andrew Roberts. My young-at-heart readers were also a big help: Gayle DeJulio, Dr. Gloria Grippando, Susan Katz, Amy Kovner, Eleanor Raynor, and Gloria Villa.

I also want to thank Richard Pine, for staying with the project through its many iterations and finding the perfect home for it with the ABA, and Tim Brandhorst, Associate Director of ABA Book Publishing, for his vision and enthusiasm for the book from our very first exchange.

I would be remiss if I did not acknowledge the influence of the late Thomas A Clark, who gave me my first job out of law school and who served on the U.S. Court of Appeals for the Eleventh Circuit until his retirement in 1999. Upon Judge Clark's passing in 2005, the circuit's chief judge J.L. Edmondson remarked, "Never have I known a judge who was more humane than Tom Clark. Never did he lose sight of the fact that these cases with which we deal actually involve individual human beings." Judge Clark's vision captures the spirit of this novel, and in my mind's eye I can see him speeding through leapholes, traveling through time, and teaching young people that each of the countless cases reported in those dusty law books up on the shelves is about a real person who had a very real problem—and that for some, it was literally a matter of life or death.

Finally, my deepest thank you goes to my wife, Tiffany, for her enduring love and support, and to our children, Kaylee, Ryan, and Ainsley, for inspiring me to write this book for them.

# *About the Author . . .*

James Grippando is the nationally best-selling author of eleven previous novels of suspense, including the critically acclaimed series featuring Miami criminal defense lawyer Jack Swyteck. His novels are enjoyed worldwide in over twenty languages, and he was the 2005 recipient of the Distinguished Author Award from the University of Scranton. *Leapholes*, his twelfth novel in as many years, is his first novel for younger readers.

James' first job out of law school plunged him headlong into death penalty cases. That experience was an inspiration for his debut novel, *The Pardon*, a legal thriller that critics heralded as a "bona fide blockbuster." Before *The Pardon*, James was a successful trial lawyer at Steel Hector & Davis in Miami, and he is now Counsel to the law firm of Boies, Schiller & Flexner, LLP. James has published extensively in some of the nation's top law reviews, and his scholarly writings are frequently cited with approval by state and federal courts. He was a faculty member with the National Institute of Trial Advocacy, and he has served as an adjunct professor of law. James attended college and law school at the University of Florida. He graduated second in his class and was elected to Phi Beta Kappa in 1980. In 1982 he received his J.D. with honors and was elected to the Order of the Coif after serving as an editor on the Florida Law Review. He served as law clerk to the Honorable Thomas A. Clark on the U.S. Court of Appeals for the Eleventh Circuit, and he was named by *Florida Trend Magazine* as one of Florida's emerging leaders.

James has always enjoyed children, and he understands them well. As a lawyer, he was a frequent volunteer in the Miami-Dade County guardian ad litem program, where he represented neglected children in custody proceedings. As a writer, James lectures frequently to schoolchildren about his craft, and he is an active participant in the "Kids Love a Mystery Program" sponsored by the Mystery Writers of America. He serves on the Board of Trustees at St. Thomas Episcopal Parish elementary school, where he takes aspiring young writers with him on research trips to fun places like crime labs. He also coaches the soccer team.

James lives and writes in Coral Gables, Florida, and he is married to Tiffany, who has been his unofficial editor since book one. They have three children: Kaylee, Ryan, and Ainsley. For more information about James and his books, please visit www.jamesgrippando.com.